PICKING UP THE PIECES

Misha M. Herwin has written short stories, plays and novels, for both children and adults. She has two grown-up children and lives in Staffordshire with her ever patient husband and a very demanding cat. When not writing she likes to bake. Muffins are a speciality.

www.http//mishaherwin.wordpress.com/

Also by Misha M Herwin

House of Shadows

Writing as Misha Herwin

Dragonfire

Juggler of Shapes

Master of Trades

Clear Gold

PICKING UP THE PIECES

Misha M. Herwin

For Tracy,
who showed what
truly supportive
friends can do

PENKHULL PRESS

Book design by Peter Coleborn

Published by arrangement with the author

First edition

ISBN 978-0-9930008-5-0

Published by Penkhull Press
Staffordshire

PENKHULL PRESS

ACKNOWLEDGEMENTS

There are many people who have helped with the making of this book:

My excellent editor Jan Edwards

Nadine Feldman and Brenda Lawton, trusty beta-readers; Julia Hudson for her skill in proof reading and asking awkward questions; and Heather Steele for her insightful comments.

Peter Coleborn for his design and endless patience

My sister Anuk Naumann for allowing me to use her image for the cover

Room in the Roof writing group for their comments

Mike Herwin for being there

DEDICATION

For Karen

PICKING UP THE PIECES

ONE

"YOU WILL BE there, Liz, won't you?" Elsa's voice on the other end of the phone was high and strained.

"Of course, I said I would."

"And Bernie's going to be there. It will be the three of us, just like in the old days at St. Cecilia's," Elsa continued brightly as if high tea at The Grand was something they did every day.

"Elsa, what's wrong? What are you trying to tell me?" It was no use: Elsa had ended the call.

TYPICAL, LIZ THOUGHT, *after all these years Elsa still made a drama out of every situation.* There was no need for all this mystery, unless whatever she had to say was so bad that it could only be said face to face. But why choose the most expensive hotel in Bristol? Surely their usual café would do. Liz smiled wryly at the memory of long ago afternoons in coffee bars, earnestly sorting out first their homework, then their clothes and their love lives. And worse.

Suppressing her growing unease she opened the wardrobe door, surveyed the bulging rails, and swore. What did one wear to The Grand? Did it matter? Deciding that she would not compromise her style she took out a red gold skirt and brown silk T-shirt. She twisted her hair, dark and streaked with silver, onto the top of her head and secured it with a pair of tortoiseshell combs, ignoring tendrils that wisped around her face and trailed down the back of her neck.

"Not bad for an old bag in her fifties," she told the cat curled up on the bed. "I should chase you off," she continued, "but who would keep my feet warm at night?" The cat put its paws over its nose. "Right, here we go." She blew a kiss to the black and white photograph of Poppy hanging on the wall. "Hope I look as good as you do, kid," she told her far away grown-up daughter, and picking up her bag hurried down the stairs.

LIZ SAW ELSA as soon as she stepped through the etched-glass doors of the Palm Court. She was sitting at a table by one of the curved windows that looked out over the rugged cliffs and wild tumble of the trees of the Avon Gorge.

Even in an emergency Elsa manages to have the best seats in the place, Liz thought as she followed the slim-hipped waiter past the retired couples taking tea, the wealthy young mothers gossiping with their friends while nannies took care of their babies, the tourists taking in another of the city's sights.

"Liz, darling, you're here!" Elsa rose to her feet. Immaculately dressed as always, blonde hair swept into a perfect chignon, pale-gold shift and jacket toning, she flung out her arms as if they were long lost sisters meeting on some desolate station platform.

"Bernie's not here yet." Elsa gave a little pout.

"She's probably had a morning shift at the supermarket." Liz sat down. "It's only just gone three and she'll have had to go home and change."

"Of course." Elsa waved her hands and her rings sparkled in the April sunlight.

You've no idea, Liz thought and hastily suppressed the scratch of irritation at Elsa's perverse ignorance of working life.

On the small stage the trio broke in to a muted version of the "Arrival of the Queen of Sheba" and

Bernie walked through the door. For a moment she appeared confused as if she wasn't quite sure she was in the right place. Liz was pushing back her chair ready to rescue her when the maître d' swooped. Bernie nodded, flushing in embarrassment in her too tight navy dress. She kept her eyes on Liz and Elsa as she followed the waiter to their table where she wasn't quite fast enough to stop Elsa leaping to her feet and kissing her extravagantly. As soon as she could Bernie stepped out of her friend's embrace, stowed her over-large handbag carefully under the table, and settled herself in a spindly chair.

"Now are you going to tell us what this is all about?" Liz came straight to the point.

"How are your boys?" Ignoring Liz's question, Elsa cocked her head to one side, innocent blue eyes focussed on Bernie.

"No. You're not getting away with it like that," Liz said. "You can't expect us to sit here worrying while you burble on about nothing."

"Children aren't *nothing.*" Elsa turned her gaze reproachfully on Liz.

Has something's happened to James? Liz thought.

"Your champagne, madam," the waiter announced and she realised that she'd been wrong. There was no crisis. They'd been summoned to celebrate another of the golden boy's achievements. She glanced at Bernie who shook her head to say she too had no idea about what was going on.

The waiter uncorked the bottle and poured three glasses of the finest Krug. The bubbles fizzed and caught the pale spring sunlight as Elsa lifted her glass.

"To us. Me and my oldest and best of friends."

Liz took a sip, savouring the tingle of alcohol in her mouth. "This is wonderful but why today? What exactly are we celebrating?"

"It's not a celebration." Elsa paused. "It's a farewell.

My life…" She gestured to the waiter to top up their glasses.

She's got cancer and it's advanced. Liz's heart thumped. This was not about Elsa's beloved only son. They'd been called because Elsa was sick and she needed her friends.

"Oh my God, Elsa, whatever is it? Are you ill?" Bernie put their fears into words. "Is it…" Her fingers crept to the cross she wore around her neck as she looked helplessly at Liz.

She doesn't want to say it. Neither of us do. Liz fought to suppress the shudder that crawled up her back.

Elsa stared at them blankly for a moment. Her face trembled and she took another sip.

"I'm not ill. It's worse than that. I'm broke. Absolutely utterly and completely broke. There's no more money, nothing." Her eyes swam with tears then she curved her glossy lips into a bright, false smile. "The alimony's dried up. It's the bloody Sahara desert."

"Elsa!" Relief made Liz furious. What was it with the woman's sense of perspective? Didn't Elsa realise that there were far worse things in life than not being rich?

"Thank God for that." Bernie's fingers tightened around her cross. "That you're okay, I mean," she added hastily.

"I'm not," Elsa wailed.

"Okay," Liz said carefully, fighting to keep her anger under control. "Is there really any need to make such a fuss? Lionel's been so good to you all these years surely you can work something out between you? I can't see him leaving you with nothing."

"He wouldn't, if he could help it." Elsa heaved a sigh. "The poor darling. It's not his fault. He's lost all his money. He's gone bankrupt, taken his beloved Adrian and fled the country. I think they've gone to some deserted island in the Caribbean to grow peanuts or pineapples, or something."

"Peanuts don't grow in the Caribbean," Liz snapped.

"Liz." Bernie stared at her in reproach.

"Sorry. It must be the shock driving me into teacher mode. I can't imagine Lionel of all people with no money. What about his house in Clifton, the Porsche, the wine cellar and, well, everything?"

"I know," Elsa sighed again. "It doesn't feel real. But it is, I promise you. Darling Lionel has lost it all. You know what it's been like with this banking thing. He's awfully sorry but there's nothing left, not even the tiniest bit for his ex-wife." She waved her hand at the opulence of the Palm Court. "All this is my last fling and I want to share it with my oldest friends. Champagne at The Grand, that's the way to go. Then bring on the bag lady and the cardboard box under the arches."

"Don't be silly," Liz said sharply.

"I'm not. Believe me, I've lain awake at night trying to think what I can do but I've got no marketable skills. I couldn't even finish that flower arranging course Mother wanted me to do. I've never had a job. The apartment's not paid for. Lionel did something about re-mortgaging it, or something, a while back. So you see Liz, Bernie, your useless friend Elsa is about to slide down into the gutter." She stopped and for a moment Liz thought she was going to burst into tears, then the old Elsa reasserted herself. She straightened her shoulders and lifted her chin. "In the meantime let's enjoy. If I'm going under, I'm doing it in style."

TWO

"THIS IS RIDICULOUS," Liz said, draining the last of her champagne. "Elsa, there has to be something that can be done."

"I don't know what." Elsa licked a crumb of chocolate cake from her lip. "Lionel's solicitor tried to explain it to me, but as far as I can make out it's hopeless."

"You can't give up. We won't let you."

"No." Bernie shook her head, which due to the unaccustomed alcohol, spun alarmingly. Giving up was wrong, they all knew that. Sister Mary Catherine would never allow it.

"What would you suggest?" Elsa held out her hands.

"You could, well you could – get a job, or retrain, or something. You know what they say."

"That life begins at fifty."

"Forty," Liz corrected. "And people do start careers at that age. It might not be as easy as it would have been when you were younger. You have to face it, we all do, if we're going to be honest that employers tend to want younger people because in general they are less expensive and given the unstable economic climate that's not unreasonable. Having said that, it doesn't mean you have to give up. Let me think about it. How about we all meet up at my house tomorrow night and we'll sort you out?"

"Yes," Bernie said, keeping her head as still as she could. Liz would put them right. You could always rely on Liz in a crisis. And now she had a definite feeling that it was time to go home. Bernie stole a glance at her watch, squinting as she tried to pin down the figures. They seemed to be moving around, or was it that she needed her glasses? She bent down and rummaged in her bag. The light slanted in under the glass topped table. Liz had scarlet nail varnish on her toes, and there was a flake of pastry on the tip of Elsa's designer shoes.

Woody would have that like a shot. Bernie felt a terrible urge to giggle at the image of the curly haired Water Spaniel licking Elsa's feet. Slapping a hand over her mouth she eased herself up into a sitting position. Her control pants were digging in something cruel, but without them she'd never have squeezed into her best dress. Keeping one hand on the table she got herself to her feet. "It's been..." As usual words failed her.

"Oh Bernie," Elsa cried. "Thank you so, so much for being here for me." She jumped up and before Bernie could stop her she kissed her on both cheeks.

"Yes, um, no," Bernie stuttered in an agony of embarrassment as the heat rose from somewhere in her middle and swept over her face and arms. Elsa's mother might have been a Hungarian refugee but that didn't mean her daughter had to behave like this in public. Or was it only Bernie that found it so uncomfortable? Liz shot her an understanding glance and she felt a little better.

"I'm sorry, but it's past five. I'll be late for the boys. They've both been out today but, well, it's the school holidays and I haven't seen much of them and I want to be in when they get back." Bernie hauled her bag on to her shoulder and waited, hoping that Liz would offer her a lift but Liz said nothing and somewhere deep in the fuzz that was taking over her brain, Bernie remembered her saying that she'd left the car at home and walked across the Downs.

The bus it was then.

I'm drunk, she thought as the number forty-one drew

up at the stop. *I can't remember the last time I felt like this. It feels really wicked and I'll have a terrible head tomorrow.* The bubbles rose in her throat and she burped loudly as she stepped on board.

"Sorry," she mouthed and sinking down into the nearest seat she eased the shoes from her feet. She really shouldn't have had so much champagne but it was only once and it was to help out an old friend, because Elsa so needed her friends around her at this dreadful time.

"Poor Elsa," Bernie sighed, but whatever pity she felt was swept away by a warm glow of satisfaction. She shouldn't gloat, she knew it was wrong, she'd been taught all her life to be charitable, but she simply couldn't help it. After all their advantages she'd done better in life than either Elsa or Liz.

Sister Mary Catherine had called them "the clever one, the good one, the glamorous one", and as predicted Liz had gone to Oxford and got a first while Elsa had led a life of utter luxury and indulgence. She meanwhile had done what all good Catholic girls of her age were expected to do. She had married Trevor Driscoll, her first boyfriend, and had been rewarded with a happy marriage and four sons.

As the bus neared Napier Road, Bernie felt for her pumps. Her toes scrabbled on the floor, she stretched her legs under the seat in front, bent them behind her, but the shoes were nowhere to be found. What was she going to do? She couldn't walk down the street in her tights. Everyone would laugh. They'd think she was losing her mind, turning into the sort of mad old woman her mother always warned her about.

"Holy Mary Mother of God," she prayed frantically and just as the bus lurched to a stop her toes made contact with patent leather. One shoe, but where-o-where was the other? "Thank you," she breathed as she located its pair and pushed her feet into pumps that seemed to have shrunk since she put them on only a few hours ago. She hobbled down the aisle, thanked the driver and got out onto the pavement.

Like her shoes, the concrete had changed. It was no longer firm but spongey and bouncy. If there had been a good old fashioned fence to grab Bernie would have clung on to it but the rows of new houses were bounded by low walls, or struggling hedges, so she had to walk very slowly to stop herself from tipping over onto her face.

"Never again," she vowed as the road curved into their cul-de-sac. Only a little further and she'd be home. She'd get out of her good clothes, make herself a strong cup of tea and share a biscuit or two with the dog. Drinking in the middle of the day had never suited her, not even on special occasions.

In spite of herself, her mouth curved upwards. It all went to show that you couldn't rely on your luck for ever. Or your looks. The nuns were right when they drilled it into you that plodding away at the boring day-to-day things brought its own reward. The Driscolls might not be rich but Trev was in a good job and the house was just what she'd always wanted. Or rather had become what she wanted because it was the best they could afford.

"Cut your cloth and count your blessings," her mum always said. But what happened when your blessings ran out? Bernie stopped and stared at the car parked in the drive. Fingers scrabbling for the cross round her neck, she shuddered under the waves of icy chill rippling down her back.

Trev never came home this early. Something terrible must have happened. Something so bad he had to tell her himself and it was all her fault for not squashing that small spark of pleasure at the news of Elsa's disaster.

"Please, please don't let it be one of the boys," she

prayed as with trembling hands she tried to fit the key in the lock. When she finally managed to open the door she was greeted by a deathly silence. There was no thump of music from Joe's room; no blare of a sports commentary coming from the TV in the lounge; no brown furry dog bounding out of the laundry barking a greeting; no grunt of acknowledgment from her weary husband.

He's taken Woody for a walk, that's where he is, she told herself in an effort to still the frantic beating of her heart. *It's got to be that. The boys are still out. Trev happened to come home early and thought he'd take the dog out. After all, it is his dog. He was the one that wanted him.*

Then she remembered that Trev never, ever walked Woody on a work day. And he shouldn't be back; the office hadn't shut yet, so it had to be one of the boys. Something had happened to Joe or Pat while he'd been out with Tom and his dad, and Trev had been called to the hospital. No doubt Trev had been trying to get hold of her but just for once, because she'd wanted that little bit of time for herself, she'd kept her mobile switched off.

"Holy Mother of God, I swear to you I won't ever miss Mass again; I'll go on a diet; I'll give up chocolate; I'll do anything, if only they're all okay," Bernie prayed, her mouth dry, her knees weak. She'd gloried in her good fortune and now because God, as she'd been brought up to believe, was nothing if not fair and just, she'd have to face whatever tragedy lay before her.

Which of the boys would it be? For a terrible, shameful moment she found herself wondering who would she miss least; whose death would cause her the least pain. Aidan as the eldest had already lived some of his life, got some of the things he wanted, so had Chris; but the younger two, they were still babies. It would be so wrong, so unfair, if they were taken because of something she had done.

Bernie gulped back a sob and tried to blink away the vision of their faces, blissfully innocent and at peace as the rest of the family filed past the open casket. She'd be in black, a lace mantilla hiding her face, clinging to Trev's arm to stop herself from swooning.

Unless, of course, it was Trev in the coffin. Hastily, Bernie changed the scenario. He was lying unconscious on their bed. He'd come home early feeling ill. She wasn't in the house and he had collapsed. She could see him now lying on the bed, the man she had been married to all her adult life. The only man she had ever loved. Was she too late or was there still time to dial 999? She had to go and see. Her hand on the bannister was slippery with sweat, her stomach churned and contracted.

"Trev," she called tentatively. "Trev are you all right?"

He came out of the kitchen with an odd expression on his face. He was still wearing his work suit but without the jacket, and his tie was loose.

"Bernie?" He looked at her as if she had no right to be there, then recovering himself he kissed her on the cheek. "I wasn't expecting you." Her heart rate slowed; she gulped down her tears and a stupid urge to giggle. She thought she could smell drink on his breath, then realised it was the champagne on hers.

"Oh Trev..." Her voice shook with a crazy mix of relief and irritation. "...I told you I'd changed my shifts."

"You've been at work?"

"No." Bernie stared at her husband. Why couldn't he see that she was wearing her good dress and shoes? "I've been out. I've been to The Grand with Elsa and Liz. We had tea there, or rather we had champagne and then tea and cakes. Elsa wanted to talk to us. You see, Lionel has lost all his money and..."

The kitchen door opened and a woman came into the hall. She was about thirty, slim and beautifully made up. Dressed in a smart suit, her blonde hair pinned up on the top of her head, she was like a Business Woman of the Year or "how I made a fortune from control pants without really trying" from one of Bernie's mum's magazines. No one this elegant had ever been seen in Bernie's house, let alone her kitchen. Her mouth opened and she knew she had to say something, but all that she could think of was what had they done with the dog.

"Where's Woody?" she blurted.

"I shut him in the shed. Amanda doesn't like dogs."

"Oh." Somehow Bernie remembered to shut her mouth but she continued to stare at the stranger in her house.

"Amanda, this is my wife Bernie." Amanda held out her hand. Her perfume was sharp and cool, her nails painted a pale pink. She smiled but her eyes didn't meet Bernie's.

She's probably embarrassed meeting the boss's wife like this, Bernie thought hopefully. The champagne was still fizzing in her head and in her throat. She put her hand over her mouth but she couldn't stop the burst of wind.

"Sorry. Tea at The Grand."

"Lucky you. I've always wanted to do that. One day I will."

Did she slip a glance at Trev or am I imagining things? God but I need to lie down.

"I'm sure you're always so busy working and that. I know Trev never has a minute. Even when he's home he's got paper work to do."

Why am I going on like this? Bernie thought desperately. *I've got to shut up. Now. Before I say anything really stupid.*

"Amanda was just passing so she stopped to drop off some information I need."

"And Trevor invited me in for a coffee," Amanda finished smoothly.

Bernie felt a flush rise from her toes to the top of her head. The sweat broke out under her arms at the thought of this immaculately dressed woman sitting in her disaster of a kitchen drinking coffee out of a stained mug. "I'm sorry about the mess. It's not usually like this, only I've been out all day and the boys, well you know boys: they've no idea." Aware that Amanda's attention was wandering she faltered to a halt. The other woman smiled thinly.

"I must be going." She turned to Trev. "Thanks for the coffee. I'll do what you suggested on that case."

"I'll see you out," he said and Amanda slipped past Bernie who was all too conscious of the smell of sweat and drink that hung around her like a miasma. Now she'd really blown it. Amanda would go back to the office and tell them all the boss's wife was a drunken hag. Trev held open the door and they stepped out into the drive. Bernie was too flustered to hear their murmured conversation before the door closed and Trev was back inside.

"Oh my God, what must she think?" Bernie cried.

"Amanda won't think anything. She's not that sort," Trev said coldly.

"Why did you have to take her into the kitchen of all places?"

"Would the lounge be any better?"

"I don't know," Bernie wailed. Flinging open the door she recoiled in horror at the smell of dog, the apple core on the sofa, the dirty plates and CD covers strewn all over the floor.

"That's not how I left it."

"It doesn't matter," Trev said. "Don't let it bother you."

"But it does. I wouldn't want her to think we live like this."

"I told you, it doesn't matter."

"No, I suppose in the greater scheme of things it

doesn't." Bernie tried to comfort herself as she shut the door on the mess. "You know, when I saw your car I thought something terrible had happened. I was so scared." She put out her arms and fell against him. "I couldn't bear it if anything had happened to you," she murmured.

Very gently, as if unknotting string, he loosened her grip and propped her against the wall.

"I've got to be getting back. There's things I've got to check."

"But," Bernie cried.

"I'm okay. All in one piece. No car crash or broken bones. As far as I know the boys are, too. If you'd looked properly and not panicked like you do, you'd have seen Amanda's car. Right. I've got a lot of paper work to catch up on. See you." He shrugged on his jacket, kissed her briskly, and before she could say anything more was gone.

The clunk of the front door echoed through the empty house. Bernie subsided onto the bottom step. Her hands dangled between her thighs. She was fat and flabby and unattractive. Amanda was young and slim and clever. She was a professional woman. Her house, or flat, or riverside apartment, would be white and clean and minimalist, like in the colour supplements. There would be no dirty dishes or scruffy furniture covered in dog hairs.

A car drew up outside the house.

"Mum," Pat shouted before she had even opened the front door. "It was great. Can we go, all of us? Will you take me? Next weekend?" His face was flushed making the freckles on his nose stand out. He was little and excited and he wanted to share his day with her. Flooded by a wave of love, Bernie slipped her arm around his shoulders and pressed him close.

"We'll see," she murmured, breathing in his warm little boy scent and promising herself that somehow she'd manage to persuade Trev to spend a day at the amusement park with their sons.

"I went on that new ride. The one that makes you go upside down. It's all dark and someone was sick. That was yuk."

"Did you say thank you to Tom's dad for taking you?"

"Oh no, I forgot." Pat's face dropped. He was a naturally polite child who hated to think that he might have hurt or upset anyone. Breaking free he darted back down the drive.

"Thank you," he yelled after the departing car.

"Do you want some tea?" Bernie made her way to the kitchen.

"I'm not hungry. I had burger and chips then an ice cream and a coke."

"Sure?"

"Is there any pizza?"

"I'll heat you up a slice."

"Can I have it in front of the TV?"

"Where else?" Bernie laughed. She put on the kettle and waited for the microwave to ping. As if summoned by the sound, Joe sloped in through the back door. Head down, hands in the pockets of his jeans, he was dressed entirely in black. His face was pale and he looked and smelled as if he hadn't washed for days.

"Have you had a good time?" Bernie asked, though experience had taught her that it was better to say nothing. As expected Joe growled some incomprehensible reply. Undaunted she went on, "Where's your bag?"

"Didn't take it."

"You mean you've not changed since yesterday." He didn't answer but wandered towards the microwave. "Pizza?" Bernie asked. Her son growled again. She took another slice out of the freezer. A frantic scrabbling and whining echoed from the garden shed.

"Joe, if you could just let Woody out for me?" She

turned around but Joe had taken Pat's pizza and gone. The door to his room slammed shut; then came a blast of music.

"Turn it down and take a shower when you've got a minute," Bernie yelled.

She let the dog out of shed. Desperate to pee Woody cocked his leg against the nearest available surface. Bernie jumped to one side to avoid the evil smelling puddle as it spread slowly out from the corner of the garage wall. Later she would pour disinfectant over it, but for now she had had enough. All she wanted was to sit down in peace and quiet and have a cuppa.

She cleared a chair and put on the kettle. The thud of some obscure group was still pounding through the house and she shut the door on it, slipped off her shoes and heaped three spoons full of sugar into her mug. She mashed the tea bags with a spoon and let them brew. The tea was thick and brown, like her mum made it, strong enough to take the enamel from your teeth.

Not like the posh stuff they serve at The Grand. I'm glad Elsa went for the champagne, but then she would. That's the sort of life she's been used to. That uppity waiter talked about Mrs Houghton's usual table. Well not any more.

Bernie shook her head in disbelief. Two hours ago she was in the Palm Court sipping champagne and being waited on hand and foot, listening to a desperate tale of a lost fortune. There was something wildly romantic about Elsa's situation. There she was, kept by her ex-husband in an expensive apartment overlooking the Downs; given everything she could possibly want; never having to lift a finger and now suddenly like some Russian princess deposed by the Revolution, she was destitute.

Bernie sighed and took a sip of the hot sweet tea. This was her life, this house and these children.

The shadows lengthened in the garden. Pat went

upstairs; water gurgling through the pipes told her Joe was finally in the shower. There was no sign of Trev. Another late night in the office. He could at least have rung to tell her what time he would be back but he rarely did these days.

Woody whickered softly and settled himself at her feet. The oily scent of Irish Water Spaniel filled the room. Beneath it lurked the smell of unwashed dishes. Bernie shifted her weight from one buttock to the other. The top of her control knickers dug into her side. When she peeled them off there would be a great red welt around her waist. It would take all night to fade. She should think seriously about going on a diet. There was a good one in that magazine she'd seen at her mum's. She'll ask if she could borrow it next time she went round. In the meantime, however...

Bernie stretched across to the packet of biscuits she had not put away from the day's shopping and suddenly her mood changed. As if a light had gone out, leaving her in greyness, all the excitement of the day ebbed away and without knowing quite why she began to cry.

THREE

"DARLING, YOU ARE not going to walk." Elsa put her soft warm hand on Liz's arm.

"I'm certainly not driving. After all that champagne I don't think I could have got the car out of the car park."

"Then I'll give you a lift. My taxi will be here in a minute and you only live around the corner from me."

"You can drop me off at yours and then I'll walk."

Elsa gave a pretty little pout.

"Are you in a fit state to walk?" Before Liz could answer the waiter materialised at their side.

"Your taxi is here, Madam."

"You see, no problem." Elsa was triumphant. Liz pushed back her chair but as she got to her feet, green, gold and rose – the colours of the Palm Court – swirled around her head.

"I told you," Elsa's voice held echoes of long ago playgrounds. "I said you'd need a lift."

"Tell me Elsa," Liz said as she flopped gratefully into the cab. "Why did you never learn to drive?"

Elsa's forehead contracted, then instantly she smoothed out the frown lines and smiled brightly. "There never seemed any point. Lionel always took me everywhere and then there were taxis. I never needed to bother with a car. Now I suppose it will have to be the bus." She shuddered, her mouth turned down, and for a moment her face registered despair before she automatically curved her lips into a smile.

The wind had dropped when they reached the

apartment block. In spite of Liz's protests Elsa insisted on paying, pulling out the money with a flourish and adding a large tip. Then they had to go through the ritual kissing of cheeks until Liz was finally free to go. She didn't look back. Under that defiant air of bravado her friend was scared and vulnerable, but at that moment there was nothing she could do about it.

Solving problems and making decisions were a daily part of her job as Head of English. She'd sort Elsa, or if she couldn't she'd find someone who could. Wrapped in thought she hardly noticed where she was going and only by stepping off the pavement at the last moment did she avoid colliding with the figure lumbering towards her. Filthy coat flapping, hair matted, eyes blank, Iris mumbled and muttered, lost in a bizarre conversation only she understood. The plastic carrier bags that contained all she owned swung terrifyingly near as Liz, caught between pity and fear, rummaged in her handbag for the coins she always found for the bag lady.

How did she come to this? Where was her family? Was there no one that cared for her? At the very least there were hostels and social services, yet somehow Iris had slipped through their safety net.

Or was it possible that she preferred to live like that? There were people that would rather have the freedom of the streets than the confines of a house. If she did it was something Liz could not even begin to understand.

Everyone should have a home of their own, Liz thought as she opened her front door. In the late afternoon light the hall was full of shadows. Switching on the light she was filled, as always, with a heady sense of achievement.

Through the open door of the dining room she saw the lilies on the mantelpiece, their white flowers reflected in the gold-framed mirror, their scent filling the house. Liz sighed a pleasurable and contented sigh. Elsa might have had the money and the penthouse, but this small Edwardian terraced house was hers. She had worked hard for it, which was as it should be because having things handed to you on a plate was not good for you. It was all a question of control and Elsa had no control of either her life or her destiny.

The black and white tiled hall was quiet. If Poppy were at home there would be music and her daughter's voice calling down to ask how Elsa's tea party had gone. Poppy, however, was in a play touring in the Far East.

"I'll text her later, Timbo," Liz told the black cat that sauntered down the stairs and began to twine around her calves. "But I'll feed you first since you insist."

Running water into the sink, she filled a glass and took a sip before spooning Timbo's supper into his dish. Then she wandered over to the fridge. She was not hungry but it would be sensible to eat something to sop up all that alcohol. Opening the door she scanned the contents and was overtaken by a desire for scrambled eggs on toast. This was her comfort food. Why did she need it now?

Something stirred at the edge of her mind and she blanked it rigorously. She was not going to give in. She was not one of those teachers who had nightmares at the start of a new term. She was capable and competent and tomorrow she would turn her thoughts to preparing for Monday. Tonight, however, she was going to bask in the remembered glory of tea in the Palm Court. Two, or was it three, bottles of the best bubbly and plate after plate of cakes. At The Grand they all came in miniature, tiny éclairs, chocolate brownies, iced lemon sponges trimmed with crystal violets. Delicious at first, but ultimately too sweet.

Liz tore up salad leaves, chopped tomatoes and apples and celery. She grated a carrot, added nuts and plunging her hand into the bowl mixed the ingredients together. Dusting the salad with grated parmesan, she sprinkled in an olive oil and vinegar dressing. She lay a blue cloth over the kitchen table, put a hunk of cheddar onto a willow-patterned plate and buttered a crusty brown roll. Should she have a glass of wine? Why not? She would stick to water tomorrow.

The light leached from the garden. Liz switched on the lamp and ate. The cat flap flipped and Timbo slid out into the dusk. It had been an odd afternoon. She was struck by the contrast between the opulence of The Grand and her own rather eccentric home. And then there was Elsa, who had always seemed so lucky. The three of them had met at St. Cecilia's when she and Bernie had passed their eleven plus. Had Elsa? Or had she been one of the few private pupils whose parents paid for them to have a convent education? She certainly wasn't as clever as they were but she'd done all right for herself. Until now.

"If I were her..." Liz's voice echoed around the room and she was aware that she had spoken out loud.

My God, she thought, *I'm going mad. Or getting old, or lonely.*

"Bollocks." She was never lonely. She enjoyed her own company, revelled in it. Liz glanced over to the console table in the hall where she had left her bag and mobile. If only it wasn't too late to ring Poppy. If she weren't at the other side of the world they could have an enjoyable hour dissecting and analysing every particle of the conversation at The Grand. All the same, she would check her messages. There was one from Dermot, her ex-husband and Poppy's father, asking if she wanted to go out for a drink.

Thnks, but no thnks, she texted back.

She was proud of the way they had kept in touch, were almost friends, but the relationship was rather one-sided. Months would pass without Dermot getting in touch and when he did want her company it usually meant he was between women and feeling lonely.

One last scroll down but there was nothing from Poppy. If only she wasn't so far away... Liz blinked fiercely. She was being stupid: there were times when she missed her daughter so badly. Tomorrow she'd send an e-mail, or text. If Poppy was somewhere with wireless connection she'd pick up her messages.

What she had to do now was to turn her thoughts to Elsa's problem. They'd all been too drunk to think sensibly that afternoon but it would be different at their brainstorming session on Saturday night. They were three intelligent, well-educated and experienced women; they'd think of something.

That was what your women friends were for. When push came to shove they stood by you whatever happened. Elsa had turned to her and Bernie. Her beloved James didn't even get a mention. Which was very odd as Elsa was always boasting about who he had seen and which clubs he had been to. She liked to make out that her son was something and was going places though it was obvious to the careful listener that he was only hanging around the edges of the celebrity crowd.

He wouldn't make it, even on one of those TV programmes where people you've never heard of make fools of themselves, Liz thought caustically. *He clings on to the coat tails of others hoping to be pulled up to some sort of success.*

Elsa's son had always lacked determination, in her opinion. Not like Poppy. Liz poured herself another slurp of wine and allowed herself a self-congratulatory smile. From the moment her daughter could speak she had wanted to be an actress, and as soon as she could she was out there. First a degree in Theatre Studies, then audition after audition, never letting rejections get her down.

"It's their loss," she always said when yet another job fell through. "I'll get the next one." And she did.

That's the attitude you need to succeed, Liz thought.

Poppy and me, we're like that. We keep going until we get what we want. We don't give up. Ever.

She set down her glass a little too forcefully and the wine sloshed over the edge onto the table leaving a ragged stain on the blue and white cloth.

FOUR

THE THUMP OF Heavy Metal, a shutter banging in the wind, an iron band wound tight around her temples. Grappling with the pain, Liz opened her eyes. If she moved her head would fall off; but her mouth was dry as sand, her eyes itched, and if she didn't get a drink of water she'd die.

She stretched gingerly testing the extent of her tolerance. There was a glass by the side of the bed but when she tried to raise her head the ceiling swam alarmingly. Liz groaned. She shouldn't have had that second glass of red wine, not after all that champagne. In fact she shouldn't have had any red wine. But it was still the Easter holidays and such indulgences were allowed. She winced and forced herself upright. The throbbing between her eyes was not too bad and when she managed to reach the glass, the water, though it tasted flat, slid down easily.

Liz shut her eyes and tried to focus. She had to get up. She had too much to do to lie in bed all day however bad she felt. The house had to be cleaned and tidied in preparation for the working week and there was the marking that she had been putting off to be tackled.

Covered with a faint film of dust, the pile of papers was stacked on the dining room table. Liz made room for her cup of coffee and sneezed. Pain sliced through her head. Of all the pupils she taught, 10C were the most frustrating because they simply didn't care. Even when she gave them a writing frame, when all they had to do was fill in the spaces, they couldn't be bothered. She'd tried explaining that course work mattered, that it made up part of their exam results and it was vital to get an English qualification for any job they might want, but it made no difference. Letters home were ignored. Detentions never attended. In spite of everything she did to enthuse them the only skill the class had perfected was the art of doing nothing for a whole hour. The boys were especially good at it. Dean could take forty minutes to write one sentence. He was a bright boy and capable of doing well but it was not cool to be seen to work. The girls were not much better. There were a few conscientious ones, like Laura Harris, who tried their best, but mostly they too wasted her time.

Liz picked up the first script. A crudely drawn heart and one scrawled paragraph was Samantha Boyd's attempt at an essay on Romeo and Juliet. Holding the paper between finger and thumb, Liz was seized by a scarlet flash of fury. She had spent hours with this girl, explaining, cajoling, going over and over what must surely be one of the most moving love stories of all time, only to be met by a blank faced stare and this almost obscenely insulting effort.

How dare she? Liz thumped the table with her fist and was rewarded by a thunderbolt between the eyes. She sat back, breathed in deeply and then out. She had to let go. There was no point in taking it personally. This was no reflection on her professionalism. Times were changing, it was harder and harder to motivate pupils, added to which Samantha, like the rest of the Boyd family, was not very academic.

They used to call it thick. Before, you had to be politically correct; before, there had to be an excuse for any child that didn't want to work. Now it's: they came from a deprived background, their dad's left home, the dog's died and their grandma's been run over by a train.

Don't go there, Liz told herself. Even if Samantha

wanted to, she wasn't capable of doing better. She set Sam's work apart to be looked at when she was calmer and began flicking through the rest of the pile. Whatever the attitude of the class, she would not give up on them. In every child she had ever taught she had always found something she could work with. However difficult 10C might be, she would find a way through to them. Liz drained her coffee cup and went to make a more soothing pot of Earl Grey tea but before the kettle had boiled the phone rang.

"Liz? Liz Mckendrick." The headmaster's voice was oddly hesitant.

"Yes," she replied, wondering why Norman Johnson was ringing her at home on the last day of the school holidays when he would be seeing her at the planning day on Monday. Didn't he realise that she would be working? Didn't he know that was how his staff spent the last free days of their holiday? Timbo raised his head from the windowsill where he was bathing in the sunshine and mewed sharply. Liz tapped her pen on the table. "Is there anything wrong?" she said.

There was a pause, then on the other end of the line the Head cleared his throat. "In a manner of speaking there is. The governors have told me to inform you that from today onwards you are not to come in to or go anywhere near the school."

"What!" The word shrieked through her headache. Was the man crazy or was she still dreaming? "I'm sorry, I don't understand. What's happened?"

Norman's voice was cold. "I'm afraid I can't go into detail. All I can say is that it is a matter of child protection and I have been advised that until further notice, you are not to be allowed on the school premises. In view of the seriousness of the matter it is imperative that you do not communicate with any of your colleagues."

"But," Liz stammered. The blood was pounding in her

ears making it almost impossible to think clearly. "Look, there must be some mistake. I haven't done anything. I have no idea what this is all about. I..."

"You will be notified of our next move in due course. In the meantime I suggest you get in touch with your union representative." He cut the connection.

She reeled towards the table, swearing as she hit her hip on the side.

"You can't do this to me. I haven't done anything," she said out loud. "You know perfectly well I don't abuse kids. I teach them. Right, I'm getting this sorted." Determined to stay calm and in control, she rummaged in her handbag for her mobile, scrolled down and found the number. "Be there," she hissed as the phone rang and rang in what could be an empty house.

"Hullo, this is Andrew Martin speaking."

"Andy." Her throat was suddenly dry. "I need your help. It's a union matter. The Head's just rung me. He says I'm not to go back to work this term. I don't know why and he won't tell me. Apparently it's to do with child protection so I suppose they think I've done something to one of my pupils. This just isn't right. Surely he can't do this to me without some sort of evidence. At the very least he should be asking me about what did or didn't happen."

"Oh Liz." There was a long pause. Liz's heart began to race. Did her union rep know something more? Was it possible that she could have done something without realising? Liz screwed up her eyes, the pain in her head was growing fiercer. It was like a vice squeezing her brain. If Andy didn't say something soon she wouldn't be able to stop herself from groaning. There was a rustle of papers. He cleared his voice. Even over the phone she sensed his embarrassment.

"Look Liz. I can't help you on this one. It's beyond my competence. You'll have to go to the area rep. I've got her number. Have you got a pen?"

"There's one in my bag. Hang on a minute." Writing down the number steadied her. She and Andy had always been friends. They had known each other for years, weathered a number of crises at work. Surely for her he'd be willing to bend the rules.

"Andy, come on, tell me what's going on. I need to know. Can't you see that? This could be my whole life on the line." He said nothing. "Please," Liz said softly and when he still did not reply the fear slithered up from the pit of her stomach, the world darkened and she had to stick her nails into the palms of her hands to stop herself from losing consciousness.

"I'm sorry, Liz. It's not allowed and in any event it wouldn't help. What you've got to do now is ring Marion."

"Thanks Andy," she said bitterly, but he had already gone.

Marion Tolgarth's attitude was brisk. She listened carefully to Liz's garbled account of Norman's phone call.

"You do realise how serious this is?" she said at last.

"Of course I do. It could mean the end of my teaching career. The irony is, I can't think of anything I might have done."

"That is not necessarily relevant. What we have to deal with is the accusation. I'll get in touch with the union lawyers. Now remember you are to stay at home and not to discuss the matter with anyone at school. It won't do your case any good."

"What I don't understand is why Norman won't tell me what this is all about."

"He's following procedure. If the matter has been put in the hands of the police you will be notified. I will be in touch with the school to see where things stand. Then we will know how to proceed."

The police! They'd make her a criminal. She'd have a record. Liz's head whirled there were a million questions she needed to ask but Marion had rung off. Liz forced herself to think rationally. She had done nothing; therefore nothing was going to happen. The whole thing must have been a misunderstanding which would be cleared up as soon as the kids came back into school. That was the only reasonable explanation. It had to be. The alternative was too terrible. If she was convicted of a crime against a pupil she would never work again. With no job how would she pay the mortgage? Or the bills? She already had an overdraft. What would she do if the bank wouldn't give her any more credit? Her stomach cramped and she had a fleeting vision of herself in Iris's filthy matted coat, lurching across the Downs with hand outstretched, begging for loose change.

"Stop it. Stop it now." Liz forced the words from between her lips. She was in danger of giving up before she knew the facts of the case. Some kid had made it all up. It was not an uncommon situation and with the union's help it would soon be cleared up.

"We'll fight this." She raised her fist high towards the photo of Poppy that stood on the mantelpiece. "No one's going to drag us down."

The phone rang and for one insane moment she thought it would be the Head telling her it was all some ghastly mistake and apologising for worrying and upsetting her.

"Hi Liz," Jilly, her second in the department, breezed cheerily. "Have you had a good holiday?"

Liz swallowed and said, "Not too bad."

"Great. I had a wonderful time. The man and I had a cottage in the Lake District. Loads of books, log fires, bed and booze. Bliss! Still, reality calls. What I was ringing for is to ask if there's anything you want me to do for the department meeting on Monday."

Liz bit her lip. "I won't be there on Monday."

"Oh, I'm sorry. Are you sick?"

"Sick. I wish," she managed to say.

"What's up?"

"I am as of this moment persona non-grata. A child abuser, in fact, if I understand the Head correctly."

"You what?"

"I've been accused of doing something to a kid."

"You! That's bollocks."

"I shouldn't even have told you. Apparently I'm not to discuss this with anyone."

"That's crazy. Don't you worry, I'll do my best to find out who started this and believe me when I've finished dealing with them, I'll be the one on a charge. You take this as a lucky break. An extended holiday. Think about it. You're going to have time off and you're being paid. Do the garden or put your feet up. Whatever. And make the most of it. You'll be back by the end of the week."

"I should hope so. In the meantime, Year 10's marking."

"I could come and fetch it," Jilly said helpfully. "Though..." Her voice faltered. "If it isn't urgent and it's not coursework then it can wait until you get back."

It's beginning already, Liz thought. *She wants to stick to the rules, which means treating me as guilty until proved innocent.*

"Right. In that case let's leave it for the time being."

"Okay." Was there a note of relief in Jilly's voice? "Look after yourself and I'll see you soon."

"Yes, possibly." Liz sensed the negativity building up inside her.

"Definitely," Jilly said firmly.

For a moment Liz believed her. Then a wave of horror washed over. She thought of Elsa, no income, no job and soon no home. How long would it be before she was in the same situation?

FIVE

"THERE ARE OVEN chips in the freezer and some of yesterday's stew in the fridge," Bernie said as she whipped up egg whites and folded them into the chocolate mixture. "All you need to do is heat them up. There's plenty for you and the boys." She slid the pudding into the oven and set the timer. There was no way she was going to Liz's without bringing something for the meal, and they all loved chocolate. Sharing her gooey, flour-free dark chocolate cake would be like it used to be when they could demolish a box of Black Magic or Dairy Milk between them.

"I won't be eating," Trev said.

"Why not?"

"I'm going out."

"You can't be. I told you, I'm going to Liz's to help out with Elsa. We've got to come up with ideas for raising money."

"Tell her to sell that penthouse."

"It's not hers. It still belongs to Lionel. Goodness only knows what she's going to do. It's no fun suddenly being poor at our age. Anyway, I'm going and you said you'd be here for the boys."

"Something came up."

"But..." Bernie's voice rose to a wail.

"They're old enough for God's sake. Joe's thirteen. Pat's twelve."

"That's the problem," Bernie snapped, thinking of wild parties and drunken gate crashers trashing the house. “What if something happens? What if they need us?”

“You won’t be that far away,” Trev said reasonably.

“Where are you going, then?”

“Pub on the other side of the city. The one on the Bath Road. Darren’s getting married next week so a group of us are going out for a drink.”

“He’s getting married again?”

“The first time didn’t work out. They had that big wedding and then it was downhill all the way.”

“That’s a shame,” Bernie sighed, remembering the do in the church, the horse drawn carriage, the four matching bridesmaids and the lavish reception at the country house hotel. “So what went wrong?” she asked. Trev looked bored.

“Who knows? These things happen. People change.” His voice had a strange note to it that she couldn’t quite identify. He sounded cold and hard, not like her Trevor. For a crazy moment she wondered if he was trying to tell her something and breathed a silent prayer to St. Joseph the patron saint of marriage. “You baby those boys.” Trev picked up the evening paper and made for the stairs. “It’s time you gave them some space. Let them be more independent.”

“They are independent. They’re always going off on their own. It’s just I’m not happy leaving them in the house without anyone. I’ll worry.”

“If anything happens they can ring you.”

“And how am I supposed to do anything? You’ll have the car.”

“Yes. And you know what the traffic will be like on a Saturday night. For God’s sake, Bernie, get a taxi if you have to.” He searched in his pocket for his wallet and peeled off a wad of notes. “There. No worries.” Trev slapped the money down on the table and walked out of the kitchen.

Bernie eyed it warily. It was far more than she would

need and there was something tainted about the way it had been thrown at her.

I've been bought off, she thought. In the bedroom above the shower was running in the en-suite.

"Damn," Bernie swore as she loaded the dishwasher, if Trev was ensconced she would have to use the boys' bathroom. She took a clean towel from the airing cupboard and cleared a path through the fetid debris of dirty socks and discarded underpants. Was it only yesterday that she'd cleaned it all up? What was it about teenage boys that made them leave a trail of muck and chaos in their wake? Would it have been different if she'd had girls? Being the only woman in a house full of men was not easy. As she was about to get into the shower she realised she'd forgotten her shower gel, the special one she liked to use before she went out. She reached for her dressing gown, then stopped, oddly reluctant to go back into the bedroom where her husband would still be in the shower.

ELSA'S BATHROOM WAS lined with pink marble. A flattering colour that warmed the skin and made her look better however terrible she felt. Her moisturiser was the most expensive money could buy but cheaper than having a face lift. Elsa lifted her chin and squinted at her profile in the mirror. Not bad for a woman in her fifties. Not bad at all. She had contemplated Botox; she even had the number of the doctor who was highly recommended by various acquaintances but under the present circumstances she was not sure she could justify the expense. Money. It was such a pain. She simply wasn't going to think of the stack of brown envelopes piling up on the hall table. After all, most of them were addressed to Lionel. At the thought of her ex her breath caught in her throat and her eyes filled with tears.

Lovely Lionel, so handsome and sophisticated. If only

he were here to look after her. If only he hadn't lost all that money. He should have been more careful. He should have known she couldn't look after herself.

She was only seventeen when she met him. Straight out of school, in her first term at college. He was so glamorous, so rich. He'd treated her like a lady, introduced her to a way of living she had only ever dreamed about. Her parents were relatively well off but they did not have a huge house in Clifton, nor fly to the Caribbean for their holidays. She was dazzled, she had to admit, by this older man who said he adored her.

He showered her with diamonds and flowers. He always noticed what she wore and commented if she did something different to her hair or her make-up. He was very gentle. He liked to stroke her arm and they always kissed, but when it came to anything more he was not very interested and neither, to tell the truth, was she.

Lionel was happy to wait until she was twenty-one before they got married and their only child was the result of a quick honeymoon encounter. Of course she didn't realise Lionel was gay. In those days she didn't even know that homosexuality existed. She thought he was being considerate and when he saw that she didn't much like it, he held back. Ironically, in that respect they were well suited. Neither of them needed sex. Or at least that's how it had seemed. They could have gone on living together for the rest of their lives if only he hadn't fallen in love.

His coming out hadn't upset her. From being her husband he became her dearest friend and the person she could turn to whenever she needed anything. He was always there for her. Even after Adrian came into his life if she needed anything she had only to pick up the phone and ask. And now he was gone and she was on her own. Her credit cards were well over their limit. There was no money coming in and she knew, though she wasn't going to look at them, at least not yet, that there were bills to be paid.

Her lip trembled but she would not let herself cry. If she did her make-up would run and she'd have to start on her face all over again and that would make her late for Liz. Liz had always been the competent one, the one who knew exactly what to do. Elsa crossed her fingers. Together they would work out a plan and in a few months everything would be back the way it was before. What did they say in those magazine articles that told you how to run your life? If you believed hard enough, anything was possible.

"It's all going to be all right." Murmuring her new mantra, she was zipping up her dress when the phone rang.

"How you doing, Mum?"

"James," Elsa breathed.

"Are you all right? You sound a little far away."

"I'm fine." Elsa steadied herself against the dressing table. It was a good thing they weren't on Skype. She looked quite pale, and had she lost weight? Her hand plucked at her waist. What was she going to say? What could she tell her darling boy?

"Are you sure?"

"No," Elsa wailed and it all came pouring out. When she'd finished there was silence. Elsa's heart fluttered wildly. She'd upset her only child and there was nothing she could do about it. James had never had to do without anything and now she couldn't even send him a plane ticket home from Indonesia. Was he angry with her? Did he blame her? If he did she wouldn't be able to bear it. Her life would be ruined.

"That's bad, Mum," James said. His voice was calm and steady. Didn't he realise what a state she was in? He was usually so sensitive to her moods, so comforting, so like his father except for the string of girlfriends.

"If there's anything I can do, I will, but it's not possible right now."

"I know," Elsa murmured weakly, stunned that he wasn't going to ditch the job and come home to look after her.

"Mum, call your friends, have them over. Auntie Liz will be there for you."

"That's where I'm going."

"Great. She'll take care of you."

Elsa lifted her chin. James was right. He was being grown up and responsible. There was no need for him to give up everything. Not for her. She drew in her stomach and smiled at her reflection, because if you smiled the person on the other end of the line could hear it in your voice.

"I'm so glad you called, darling. I'm feeling better all ready."

"Give Liz my love and lots to you."

"And to you, too," Elsa whispered. The call was over but she held on to the mobile pressing it close to her heart. How she loved her tall dark-haired boy.

She should have had his portrait done, she thought as she moved through the drawing room. There was something so delicious about beautiful boys. Their skin, their hair, the way they moved. She could quite see why Lionel had turned out the way he did. She hooked her bag over her arm and was about to let herself out of the penthouse when she remembered that she had not bought any flowers.

The text on her mobile told her the taxi she'd ordered was at the door but to go without anything would be so rude. Elsa went back into the drawing room and lifted the roses out of the vase. The stems smelled stale and slimy but it was the best she could do in the circumstances. She hurried to the kitchen and snipped off the rancid stalk-ends, hastily wrapping the blooms in the tissue paper she used for packing her clothes, and holding it at arm's length carried the improvised bouquet down to the waiting taxi.

SIX

LIZ STIRRED TOGETHER a rich mix of meat, mushrooms and tomatoes, tipped in some red wine and poured the rest into her glass. The food smelled good, the salad was crisp and crunchy, but she wasn't sure she was going to be able to eat it. Not when her entire body was tensed against the fear that seemed to have taken up permanent residence inside her. There was a voice inside her head she couldn't switch off.

You can't trust anything, it told her. *Doesn't matter how hard you work, one false move, one mistake, and it's down the slippery slope. You're too old. You're past fifty. Lose this job and you will never get another one. No one will want you and there's no one you can turn to for help. Poppy has no money. Your parents are dead. You'll end up like Iris, dragging your life behind you in carrier bags.*

"No." Liz thumped her fist down on the kitchen worktop. This wasn't going to happen to her. It couldn't.

Oh yes it can, the insidious little voice murmured, bringing with it a racing heart and sweating palms, which she wiped on the kitchen towel as a car door slammed. Moments later the doorbell rang.

Only Elsa would arrive by taxi when she lives around the corner, Liz thought as she hurried into the hall. *On the other hand, perhaps it shows courage not to admit defeat until you have to. Better be like that than crumble into a quivering wreck. What is wrong with me? I am going to have to pull myself together and that's that.*

As soon as the door was opened Elsa thrust a bunch

of slightly overblown roses into her arms and kissed her on both cheeks.

"It's so good of you to do all this." Elsa waved a hand at the cooker and settled down at the table while Liz found a vase for the flowers.

"I'll finish arranging them." As the doorbell rang Elsa jumped to her feet and she was busy tweaking the blooms when Liz came back in with Bernie, who was carrying a large Tupperware container.

"Chocolate time," Bernie announced, lifting the lid on a cream and chocolate confection.

"Perfection," Elsa breathed, "just like the old days."

"Chocolate was always the drug of choice," Liz said dryly. They had worked their way through four packets of Maltesers when Derek Mason had dumped her in favour of that slag Julie Myers. They had stuffed themselves with Toffee Crisps and Mars Bars on the morning of the O Level results when Elsa had failed Latin, which meant that she would not be able to join them in the sixth form. Only Bernie's morning sickness was proof against the power of chocolate and even then Liz and Elsa had been so upset that they devoured a whole box of Milk Tray, then another of Belgian chocolates that Elsa had lifted from her parents, and they had all ended up feeling sick together. Liz poured three glasses of wine.

"Business first, then food. Okay with everyone?" She led them into the dining room where she had set out pens and paper. "We'll start with individual brain-storms. Jot down anything you think is relevant to Elsa's situation, even the negative points, then we'll collate what we have and by focusing on the positive we'll end up narrowing the options."

"That's Liz, always the teacher," Elsa remarked and without warning Liz's eyes filled with tears. She gulped, clenched her teeth, but however hard she tried to stop the tears poured down her cheeks.

"Liz, whatever's wrong?" Bernie put her arms around her. Liz wept, great hard sobs, which sent her whole body heaving and juddering.

"I'm sorry," she finally managed to gasp. "I didn't mean this to happen but I'm so on edge."

"What's happened? Is it Poppy? You should have called us," Bernie cried. Liz rummaged in her pocket for a tissue and blew her nose.

"I thought I was going to be okay, that I could deal with it rationally, until you said that about being a teacher. I don't know why but it really got to me. Sorry. This just isn't me." The tears welled up again.

"It's all right. We're here for you. You don't have to be the strong one all the time, you know," Bernie said.

"Drink this." Elsa topped up Liz's glass and Bernie eased her gently into a chair and kept her arm around her shoulders until she was calm enough to tell them about the phone call from the Head.

"He won't even tell you what you're supposed to have done?" Bernie asked.

"The bastard. He can't treat you like this. It's against your human rights. What you need is a good lawyer, sue the balls off him for slander, libel, everything," Elsa declared.

"He hasn't any balls," Liz said, "that's the problem. If he had, he could have sorted it out before it came to this."

"We'll get him then. As soon as they've proved you're innocent we're going to court. We'll have him for breakfast. We'll fry his balls."

Liz smiled weakly. She was beginning to feel better; looking at her friends, Elsa incandescent with anger on her behalf, Bernie quietly supportive, some of the fear faded. She felt warm and hopeful. Since there was nothing she could do at that moment the sensible thing was to get on with the matter in hand.

"Okay, that's me. Now let's concentrate on you, Elsa.

Come on, write down what she's good at."

They picked up their pens and began.

"I can arrange flowers," Elsa said. She wrote that down then sucked the end of her biro and gazed around the room. She sighed heavily, as if they were all in an exam and she was the one that hadn't done her revision.

Socialising, being outrageous. She's funny, intentionally and unintentionally. Good with people, Liz scribbled down her first thoughts, paused, then added a question mark to the last statement. There were times when Elsa could be remarkably unperceptive, dense even. To be honest she never seemed to see anything beyond her own experience.

Elsa is a good friend. She is kind and loyal and she always looks good. Liz sneaked a look at what Bernie had written and bit back a stab of irritation; this was what Elsa was, not what she could do. Elsa, in the meantime, was sitting there sipping wine and looking vacant.

"Look at what you've done over the years," Liz prompted.

"I've travelled, arranged dinner parties. I can't do this." Elsa flung down her pen. "I don't know what to put."

"You brought up a child. That goes well on a job application," Bernie said.

"So I could be a nanny," Elsa shrieked. "All that cack and puke and muck. I don't think so."

"Well, you've run a house."

"I have a woman who comes in and cleans."

"Okay. At least you're being honest," Liz admitted. "Going back to your first point, you did start a floristry course and you have great style."

"You could do makeovers like on the TV." Bernie clapped her hands.

"And deal with horrid little houses." Elsa wrinkled

her nose.

"Elsa we're only trying to help."

"I know, I'm sorry, but I don't think that's me. Anyway, to do interior design don't you have to have some sort of certificate or something?"

"You could go to university," Liz suggested.

"Me, a student?" Elsa gasped. Liz thought of Elsa in her designer clothes, her killer heels, weekly manicure and massages.

"Perhaps not," she conceded.

"See, it's hopeless," Elsa wailed, resting her head in her hands. Liz's stomach growled.

"No it's not. We've only scratched the surface. Let's eat and then we'll do some more."

They cleared away the papers, set the table and lit candles. Liz served deep plates of pasta and sumptuous meaty sauce and opened another bottle of wine.

"This is so good," Bernie sighed, leaning back in her chair.

"There may be doubts about my professional competence but I can still cook." Liz laughed.

"Then that's what you should do."

"What work in the school canteen? I doubt they'd even employ me as a dinner lady with my record of beating kids up."

"Catering. That's what we should do." Elsa's face lit up; she waved her hands and her rings sparkled in the candlelight.

"You don't cook," Bernie said.

"No, but you two do so it doesn't matter. I'll do the organising. You cater. That'll work out brilliantly because I've got lots of contacts. We'll be away in no time at all. Liz, you're off school at the moment so you've got the time and it will be a good way of earning some extra money."

"If I'm going to use the time for anything I'll use it for my photography, not for cooking," Liz protested but Elsa ignored her and turned instead to Bernie, the most amenable of the three of them, who was always eager to please and never liked saying no.

"You do shifts so you could fit it in with work."

"I suppose," Bernie said slowly then added eagerly, "and I get staff discount at the store."

"Great! Liz you have a car," Elsa continued. She and Bernie looked at Liz.

There was a moment of silence, then: "Well, why not?" Liz made up her mind. Even if Elsa managed to find them some clients, cooking a few dinners wouldn't take up much of her time.

"We're in business." Elsa clasped her hands and beamed at her friends.

The pasta was eaten; the chocolate pudding brought out. They sat and giggled and reminisced until the gilt clock on the mantelpiece struck eleven.

"Oh my God, the last bus," Bernie pushed back her chair and scrabbled for her bag. "If I go now I should just catch it."

"There's no need to rush off. You can stay the night. There's loads of room."

"I can't. I've left the boys on their own and Pat will be getting worried. He hates it if there is no one in when he's in bed."

"Then share my taxi," Elsa offered.

"But it's miles out of your way."

"Bernie," Liz said sternly, "stop being a martyr."

"Sorry." Bernie flushed. "You're right, I'll ring Trev. He can pick me up on his way home. Okay?" Liz nodded and began carrying the dirty dishes into the kitchen.

In the hall Bernie tried Trev's mobile. It rang but he did not pick up.

"Come on." Bernie chewed her lip. Why wasn't he answering? Sometimes she wished mobiles had never been invented. In the old days when you couldn't get in touch with people at any time of the day or night you didn't worry if they weren't instantly available. She waited then tried again. He might have been in the loo or at the bar getting in another round. Still no answer.

There was something wrong. While she was enjoying herself with her friends, drinking red wine and scoffing chocolate pudding, something terrible had happened to her husband. Something so awful that no one was answering his phone. It could be lying there ringing in the middle of a field while his burnt-out car was upside down in a ditch. She had to go home and face the worst. If the police came they wouldn't know where to find her.

"I can't get hold of him." Bernie did her best to keep her voice steady. "So I'm getting the bus."

"I'll walk you to the stop," Liz offered.

"No." Bernie knew she was being stupid but she needed to be alone with her fears. It was no good anyone telling her it might never happen. She knew that one day it would. It was the price she'd have to pay for going against everything the Church and her family believed in, for getting pregnant and having to get married, for having sex before marriage. Ever since that moment when Trev had told her he was going to stand by her, that they'd tell her parents together, that it would all work out, she'd been waiting for the retribution to catch up with her. You couldn't get away with breaking the rules, not if you were Bernadette Driscoll.

SEVEN

BERNIE'S HEELS CLATTERED alarmingly along the empty streets. It was almost midnight and most of the houses were dark, their blinds and curtains drawn against the night. Telling herself she was being stupid, that she would turn the corner and their car would be parked safely in the drive, and once again her legs would wobble and her eyes fill with tears of relief, she quickened her pace.

As she neared the house the security light came on. The drive stretched bleak and empty. Trev was not at home.

A sleepy Woody staggered out of his basket to greet her. Bernie ran her fingers through his curls as she checked the answerphone for messages. Nothing. Didn't someone once tell her that no news was good, that if there was an accident the police were quick to get in touch?

Bernie crept up the stairs to check on the boys. Joe slept in his usual position buried deep under his duvet. His room was heavy with the smell of unwashed adolescent, ripe sweat and musk. Pat lay on his back, his face flushed slightly, his breath sweet. Bernie stifled the urge to sweep her baby into her arms and hold him close. What would the boys do if they didn't have a dad? How would they cope? How would she cope? As it was her whole life seemed to lurch from crisis to crisis and without Trev she'd fall to pieces. She needed him, they all did. He was the glue that bound the family together.

The taste of Bolognese and chocolate rose queasily into her throat. Would a cup of tea settle her stomach? Settle her? Putting the kettle on, she could not imagine why it was taking so long to boil, but when the tea was made she could not keep still long enough to drink it.

Pacing up and down the kitchen, then into the hall, she listened for the sound of a key in the lock; when it did not come she went into the living room and peered through the slatted blinds. Like roosting birds, every other car in the cul-de-sac was parked in its drive and in the orange glow of the street lamps the road beyond shone black and empty. Bernie's ears strained for the sound of an engine. Nothing. Her heart felt as if it was bursting out of her chest. Her ears rang. She couldn't be like this. When the worst happened she would have to be in control. To quell her rising panic Bernie began to count, telling herself, willing it to be true, that by the time she reached two hundred Trev would be home.

"One hundred and ninety-nine." The words choked in her throat. *Dear Mother of God, please keep him safe,* she prayed silently, her hands knotting. The Blessed Virgin was good with miracles. She cared about Her children, so if she went back to the kitchen and started the whole ritual again this time it would be all right. As she stepped back from the window she heard the roar of an engine.

"Thank you," Bernie breathed, promising that she would say at least two Novenas in gratitude. She'd been so silly, getting herself in a state because Trev wasn't back when she thought he should be. She pulled aside the blind and saw not her husband but a dark figure in helmet and leathers. It was her neighbour's son wheeling his bike into his parents' garage.

Bernie slapped her forehead. She was losing the plot and she had to pull herself together. The tea had gone cold in the pot and she poured it down the sink. She brewed more and this time forced herself to drink.

The kitchen clock said one a.m. The pub would have shut hours ago. Logically there was only one explanation for why he was so late. There had been an accident.

Hand over her mouth Bernie muffled a sob. After all their years it was going to end like this and they'd spent so little time together. Trev was always busy at work and her shifts meant that she was never in when he was. What free time they had they spent with the boys so there was never any left over for them as a couple. Even household chores kept them apart: Trev did the garden, she cleaned and cooked and walked the dog.

Bernie looked up and saw her reflection in the kitchen window. Face puffy, hair all over the place; where had the milky-skinned curvy Bernadette O' Farrell gone to? Was this what she had become, one of those ravening hags in those Greek plays they'd had to read at St. Cecilia's?

Bernadette Driscoll pulled back her shoulders, drank more tea and vowed that if, no when, Trev came home everything was going to change.

At two o'clock she found herself thinking quite calmly about ringing the police. It was possible that in the accident all Trev's identification had been lost. He might have been taken to hospital and no one knew who he was. She reached for the phone then hand in mid-air stopped herself. It was too soon. She would be branded a stupid panicking woman. She would give herself another hour, wait until three. The dead time of night. The time when the human soul was most vulnerable, most likely to slip out of the body and make its journey into eternity.

"Our Father," Bernie murmured. The familiar words washed comfortingly over her. There was no more panic because as expected her sins had finally caught up with her. The nuns had been right, the best way was to accept her fate.

A car drew up in the drive. The front door opened. Woody bounded into the hall tail wagging frantically.

"There boy, quiet now, you don't want to wake the whole house."

"Trev?" Hauling herself to her feet, Bernie went out to greet her husband. Fear and panic turned to anger and she had to stop herself from flying at him, slapping and pinching his stupid face. How dare he put her through all this? Couldn't he have rung her, sent her a text, telling that he was going to be late?

"Where have you been?" she cried. His face closed. The smile with which he greeted Woody disappeared.

"I told you. I was at the pub."

"Till this time?"

"No," he said through clenched teeth. "We went on somewhere afterwards."

"And you couldn't be bothered to let me know."

"There wasn't the opportunity."

"The opportunity. What the hell do you mean? I tried your mobile and it rang and rang but you didn't answer. I thought, God help me, that something had happened to you." Trev patted the dog and started for the stairs. "I was worried." Bernie followed him.

"There was no need. I'm okay." He turned and faced her, talking to her as if she were a child. "I didn't ring because you were out and then I thought as you were on early shift tomorrow you'd be in bed, so I didn't want to wake you. Okay?"

"Yes," Bernie whispered. *No,* she screamed in her heart. *After all these years you should know that I'd be frantic.* He went up the stairs and into their bedroom. "I thought..." she began and stopped.

"You worry too much." He turned to her and his face was cold and remote. "It makes me feel trapped."

"Trapped!" It was as if all the air had been punched from her lungs.

"I need my space. I need you to treat me like an

adult. Not like one of the boys, always fussing over me, wanting to know what time I'm coming in, where I'm going."

"It's because I care." Bernie collapsed onto the bed. She waited for him to come and hold her, kiss her and tell her she was being stupid, that he still loved her. Trev walked into the en-suite. After a while she heard the shower running.

Bernie used the boys' bathroom. When she got back Trev was already asleep. Where had he been? She picked up his shirt and sniffed. Could she smell perfume? Beer, or fried food from the pub?

Trev lay with his back to her and she could not face getting in beside him. She thought of the immaculate Amanda in her business suit and her own flabby middle-aged body. She pulled on a dressing gown and went back to the kitchen. Trev had left his jacket hanging over the rail and for a moment she was tempted, oh so tempted, to look through the pockets.

Don't, she told herself. *You're getting paranoid. He's tired. He's working too hard. And the boys aren't easy. And there's Chris never being able to hold down a job. Always needing help with money. At our age we should be thinking of slowing down instead of worrying about how we're going to manage. We've got the mortgage and Joe and Pat to get through university. No wonder he's down. He needs a break. He needs a holiday.*

"He could even be depressed," she told the dog as the kettle clicked off and she made yet more tea. "It's hard for men to admit it but maybe he needs to go to the doctors. I'll see what I can do to get him there." She held the steaming mug in her hand while a puzzled Woody settled down at her feet. Her face reflected in the blackness of the window was white and strained.

EIGHT

FROM HER PENTHOUSE window Elsa looked down on a froth of white blossom. Her idea was going to solve all her problems and at the same time it would help Liz keep her mind off her troubles. Doodling ideas for place cards on her notepad, she wondered if she could ask James to design something for her. He was sure to come up with a fantastic logo. He'd be so proud of her new career and once the business got going she would be able to sub him the odd hundred, or even more, when he needed it. James was always short of money. He was an artist like her and while she had never pursued her talent, his time had not yet come. One day, however, he was going to win an Oscar for his directing and she'd be there, tissue in hand, when he walked up to that podium and said, "If it wasn't for my darling mother I wouldn't be here today."

Elsa sighed happily at the image and put down her pencil. She had an appointment to keep, one that she had been putting off for far too long.

"WE HAVEN'T SEEN you for a while, Mrs Haughton." The masseuse rubbed oil on Elsa's back with firm long strokes.

"Umm," Elsa moaned pleasurably.

"Too busy?"

"Something like that," she said vaguely. She wished the girl would stop talking and concentrate on the rhythmic pounding of her body. She'd come here to relax and forget all the horrors of the past weeks, and she had no intention of telling anyone why she had been restricting her visits to the spa. She'd even gone without her monthly facial but now that the business was up and running there was no longer any need to be careful.

Treatment over, feeling relaxed and confident, Elsa wandered into the coffee shop and ordered a large cappuccino with double chocolate and two spoons full of brown sugar. She found a table overlooking the pool and sipped contently as the swimmers ploughed up and down the lanes and the walkers sweated on their treadmills.

Why do they do it? she pondered. *It's so mucky and unattractive. And in public, too. How can they bear anyone to see them like that, with their flab bursting out of their Lycra? It's much more civilized to go on one of those tables that shake the extra weight off you. Besides, when you get to a certain age you need a little covering otherwise you look like a skeleton.*

"Mind if I join you?" Her musing was interrupted by her old friend Valerie. Now there was someone who did not need to exercise. Stick thin with hawk-like features, Val carried no spare flesh.

"Val, darling, of course not. It's been ages. Have you been working out?"

"Not really. Just doing the usual routine with my trainer. Darryl is so good. He keeps me up to scratch." She took a sip of fruit tea. "If it wasn't for him there would always be some excuse not to go and I have to admit that I always feel so much better after a visit to the gym." Elsa held back a shudder.

"Those machines scare me," she said with a little pout. "A bit of gentle swimming is all I can manage."

"I was like that at first." Val nodded. "But it's quite different once you know what you're doing. Having a tailor made routine helps too. To be honest, with all the stress of the job, I don't know how I'd manage without it. After a good work out the tension melts away and I can re-join the human race. If I didn't exercise I think Bob would divorce me. Especially after a week like this. I'm surprised I haven't gone completely crazy."

"Bad time at work?" Elsa feigned interest; other people's jobs and careers never failed to bore her.

"Work." Val shrugged expressively. "Work is a doddle compared to the rest of my life. We're going through a crazy patch. Nothing is going right. As soon as one thing is sorted out something else goes wrong. Why is it that you can't rely on anyone these days?"

"Are you having more trouble with the builders?" Elsa put on her sympathetic voice.

"No, thank God, that's all over and done with. I don't think I'll ever do anything to any house, ever again. No. This time it's the caterers. Apparently they've double booked us for next Saturday. The girl rang this morning, very apologetic, which is a fat lot of use, but they simply can't do it. So there I am, dinner for eight and no help."

"Ah." Elsa looked meaningfully over her coffee cup.

"I don't suppose you know of anyone who could fit us in, do you? You and Lionel always did such lovely meals and there's nothing like a personal recommendation. You have to be careful these days about who you let into your house."

Elsa's heart skipped. "Actually I think I can," she said.

"Yes?" Ever efficient, Valerie whipped out her phone.

"We'll do it for you," Elsa said.

"You will?"

"Oh yes." Elsa tried a light little laugh. "I've just started a small venture. Nothing too large, just something to keep me amused. Lionel's abroad; James spends most of his time in London. So I thought I could do with something to fill in the time and I got together with a couple of old friends and we're going to do private dinners. Good home-cooked food, that's the idea."

"You're a life saver," Val cried. "Let me be your first client."

"That would be perfect. You tell me what sort of evening you have in mind and I'm sure we can give you a meal to remember."

THERE IS SOMETHING particularly empty about afternoons, Liz thought. *The only way to get through them is to have a list of things to do, or someone special to be with. Bed is the best place to be with a young and eager lover or, failing that, a large pile of Sunday supplements.*

The paper, however, had been read and recycled. The house had been cleaned, the garden weeded. She'd sent off yet another e-mail to Poppy, who still hadn't managed to pick up the last one.

Hope you're having a better time than me, kid. Liz looked out of the window at the bright spring sky. A small breeze shook the budding leaves on the trees. She could almost taste the sharp freshness of the air. Should she take her camera and go out on the Downs, or into the centre of the city and along the river bank to the exciting new development, or down to the Christmas Steps where the wattle and daub houses hung over the narrow street and cast strange shadows on the ancient buildings?

If she did someone might see her. Might point her out as that child abuser. Or she might be stopped and asked by a concerned friend or acquaintance why she hadn't been at work. Then what should she say? Since the Head had told her to stay at home all she could manage was a quick drive to the local supermarket, either late at night or very early in the morning, when she was sure no one she knew would see her. Crazy though it was, she could not rid herself of an overwhelming sense of shame.

Trapped indoors, Liz went from kitchen to dining

room and then to the living room. There was nothing she wanted to watch on the TV. None of her collection of DVDs appealed. There was a pile of novels she had saved for when she had time to read. But she could not concentrate. Every time she opened a book the words danced on the page. Like the beads in a child's kaleidoscope they rearranged themselves. "Abuser," they said. "Unfit teacher."

However many times she told herself she was innocent she could not banish the words that threatened her very sense of herself. How could she have let this happen? What were the signs she had missed? She was a professional, she had always done things professionally, never cut corners, always treated her staff and pupils with respect. She had done nothing to deserve this yet could not rid herself of the fear that somewhere some long-forgotten action, some throwaway line, an unintended insult, had slipped through her guard and so brought her down to the level of teachers who shouted at their classes and clipped their pupils around the ear.

If only she had some marking or preparation she could do. She could plan some courses for next year but she had no resources, and even if it were possible to go into school the very thought of walking through the gates made her whole body feel too heavy to move.

The house echoed with emptiness. She needed someone to talk to; she lifted the phone to call Jilly then, glancing at the clock, realised her deputy would be teaching.

It was still only half past two: there was another hour to go before the bell and the pupils spewed out into the streets, leaving the staff to heave a collective sigh and slink off to the staff room to repair their shattered nerves. She could see them now, the smokers congregating in their hidey-hole, the long-standing stalwarts brewing tea and complaining that someone had stolen their milk, again. She hadn't realised how much she would miss the collective whinge and black humour of her colleagues.

Someone else would have gone crazy by now. They would have run to the doctor, demanded Valium, Prozac, whatever combination of pills would keep the horror at bay. Not Liz Mckendrick. She was different. Whatever life and love threw at her she coped. That was what she had always done. That was how she survived.

Tea helped too. Liz made herself a pot of Earl Grey. Then to make sure she kept up standards she set a tray with a cup and saucer and carried it into the living room. The single cup emphasised her loneliness, the sudden pointlessness of her existence. If she didn't speak to another human being she would implode or, even worse, burst into tears. She tapped her fingers on the arm of the chair. Who would be at home at this time of day? There was Elsa, of course, but she was not in the mood for Elsa. Hoping that Bernie was not on shift she picked up the phone.

"Yes." The voice on the other end was so flat that she thought she had the wrong number.

"Bernie?"

"Yes." This time it was a sigh

"It's me, Liz. Are you okay?"

"Don't know."

"You sound awful. Are you ill?"

"No I'm not ill."

"Then come round. Come and have a cup of tea. I'm going crazy here all on my own. I need someone to help take my mind off things."

There was an uncharacteristic pause then Bernie said, "I'm not very good company at the moment."

"Never mind, we can be miserable together." There was no reply and Liz scolded herself for being so obtuse. It was a long way from Shirehampton and Bernie would have to walk to the bus stop at her end and again when she got off. “I can come and fetch you,” she offered quickly.

“Oh no.” The response was automatic. “I’ll get the bus. There’s one due in about ten minutes. If you can cope with me looking like I’ve been dragged through a hedge backwards, I’ll be with you in about half an hour.”

“I don’t give a monkey’s tit what you look like,” Liz laughed, but Bernie had already gone.

NINE

"BERNIE," LIZ CRIED as she opened the door. "Thanks for coming over."

"It's okay," Bernie mumbled. She was pale and drawn; her whole body sagged as if bones had been removed from her spine. Liz ushered her into the living room, poured tea and held out the plate of chocolate biscuits. Bernie helped herself automatically, putting the biscuit on the side of her plate while her fingers toyed with her skirt. Then as if she had finally remembered what she should be doing with it she took a sip from her cup, sighed, and stared out of the window at the last of the afternoon sun.

"Isn't the weather lovely," she said at last.

"Bernie." Liz put down her teacup. "What's wrong?"

"Nothing." Bernie's eyes skittered around the room. She perched on the edge of her seat, tense and alert, as if she were about to run away.

"Your tea's getting cold and you've completely ignored that hobnob, so stop pretending. Either you've slipped into early Alzheimer's since yesterday or there's something really getting at you. Is it one of the boys?" Liz added more gently.

"Oh God, Liz I feel so bad. I shouldn't have come. You don't need to hear about my problems. Not when you've got enough of your own."

"My thing is only work," Liz said, determined to be sensible. "I'm sure it will all be sorted. The union lawyer is confident it's just a matter of time. In a few weeks I'll be wishing I was still at home with time to chat to my friends. So come on, what is it?"

"Trev." Bernie stared down at her hands. "I think he's having a breakdown."

"Is that what the doctor says?" Liz asked carefully, her mind flooded with foreboding. She had been here before.

"Oh no. I could never get Trev to see the doctor. In any case we haven't even talked about it."

"Then what makes you think he's not well?"

Bernie's eyes filled with tears. "He's not been himself over the past few months. I never know where I am with him. One minute he's fine – the next he's flying off the handle about every little thing. He doesn't talk to me. He's always in late. I hardly ever see him in the evenings. By the time he does get in I'm dead to the world. Sometimes the only way I know he's been home is because of the dent in the pillows on his side of the bed. Oh, and the dirty laundry on the floor of course." She managed a shaky laugh.

"You're not having sex?"

"There's no time or energy. Anyway all that had tailed off a lot recently. Well actually, since Pat was born. I don't think he wanted to risk another accident."

"He's moody, angry, and there's no sex." Liz ticked off the list on her fingers. Bernie nodded. Liz gathered her courage and looked her straight in the eye; then hesitated. Would telling her friend what she really thought do more harm than good? "Do you think," she said taking the risk, "he could be having an affair?"

"Never." Bernie's response was too quick, too forceful. "He's not the sort, not Trev."

"All men are the sort," Liz said sadly.

"No, I don't believe it. I won't believe it. They're not all like that. My dad never cheated on my mum, I bet your dad didn't either."

"They're a different generation, Bernie. They had good

old Catholic guilt and a large dollop of the fear of everlasting fire to keep them on the straight and narrow. Things aren't like that anymore."

"Trev would never do that to me. I trust him," Bernie protested. Liz looked at her quizzically and the colour rose in her cheeks.

She's hiding something from herself if not from me, Liz thought.

"Look Liz, you know Trev."

Unimaginative, stolid and often boring, Liz acknowledged.

"He's not the sort, is he?" Bernie asked, her voice desperate for reassurance.

"Well..." Liz began. She would like to be able to give her friend hope but long experience told her that Bernie's fears were more than likely to be realised.

"He isn't, is he?" Bernie demanded.

"I wouldn't have thought so but you never know." *It's the quiet respectable ones that often surprise you.*

"He stood by me, remember. He didn't have to. He could have gone off and left me to have Aidan on my own. He even came with me to tell Mum and Dad. After all we've been through together he's not going to go and cheat on our marriage, is he?" Bernie sighed and gulped her tea. "It's me," she said at last. "I'm getting paranoid. It's probably the last mutterings of the menopause. You know, how it makes you insecure about your femininity and things. That's what it is. Hormones, or lack of them. That, and practically no sleep last night. I'm tired out, that's all. I couldn't have had more than a couple of hours. And you know what I get like when I'm tired."

Liz, who had never been unsure of either her femininity or her sexual attractiveness, nodded even though she believed that sometimes being tired helped her to focus, to see things more clearly.

Bernie dunked her biscuit in her tea. "I need sugar and chocolate. A bit of a moan with my friend and I'll be okay," she said. The phone rang in the hall. "Shouldn't you be getting that?" she said as Liz failed to answer it.

"I suppose I should." Liz hauled herself to her feet.

"I've got our first booking," Elsa bubbled on the end of the line. "We're in business. Aren't I brilliant? My friend Valerie wants dinner for eight next Saturday. I told her, I said no problem. Leave it in our capable hands and enjoy."

"What are we cooking?" Liz asked. There was a pause.

"Something traditional," Elsa ventured.

"You didn't ask her?" Liz held back a sigh. Sometimes dealing with Elsa was like teaching the bottom set. She tapped her pencil against the table. "Did she say what she wanted?"

"Oh no, she's left it up to us. She said she loves my dinner parties so something along those lines will be fine."

"You order your dinner parties from Waitrose."

"I know." Elsa giggled. "But I didn't tell Val. She thinks I've done it all myself."

"What is it?" Bernie appeared at the doorway.

"We're off," Liz mouthed. "Our first booking, okay," she said to Elsa. "That's fine. And as Bernie's here we can start planning straight away."

They went into the dining room and Liz fetched paper and pens. Bernie sat down opposite her and pen poised waited for instructions. A spasm of irritation shook Liz. Why was she the one who always had to take the lead? But almost as soon as the thought crossed her mind she grinned ruefully and shook her head, knowing that this was for them the natural order of things and if Bernie started telling her what to do then they would both be very uncomfortable. "I'd be a right pain," she said without thinking.

"What?" Bernie asked.

"Nothing," Liz said. "Elsa hasn't a clue about asking

the clients the right sort of questions. But she did manage to glean that Val and her friends like the same kind of dishes that she does so we'll do an Elsa type menu."

"Which is?" Bernie and Trev had never been invited to Elsa's.

"I don't know for sure but something fairly unadventurous I would suspect."

"And expensive."

"Definitely expensive."

"In that case let's go for a smoked salmon starter, then Boeuf-en-Croute and a chocolate pudding. A roulade would be good, 'cause that can be done in advance," Bernie said, her problems shelved as she turned her mind to food.

"Elsa can put together the starter. I know she thinks her role in the business is to get the clients and set the table but there's no reason on earth why she can't get her hands dirty occasionally," Liz said. "I can do the pudding and if you do the main course we've cracked it. Is that okay?" Bernie frowned.

"Oh yes. I was just wondering, where does it happen? I mean, where do we do the actual cooking?"

"I hadn't thought that far." Liz stared at her paper for a moment. "The logical thing would be to prepare as much as we can at home then finish off in their kitchen. We don't know what sort of oven and equipment they have. Knowing Elsa's friends, it will all be top of the range but if they're not into cooking, and they probably won't be, then they might not have some of the basics. Everything we've planned is easily transportable," Liz said. Bernie began to note down a list of ingredients.

"You and me can shop on the morning. If I do it from work it will be cheaper and I can be sure of the quality," Bernie said.

"I'll pick you up late afternoon or early evening and we're away," Liz said.

Bernie looked up from her list and for the first time since she'd arrived that afternoon her smile was genuine.

"Sounds good to me," she said.

TEN

THE FOYER WAS full of kids when Liz walked into school. As she came through the doors they all turned to stare at her. She nodded and said good morning.

She was greeted by blank silence until Norman Johnson burst out of his office and face purple with rage lifted a finger and shrieked: "How dare you?"

She was naked. Grabbing a poster from the notice board she tried desperately to cover herself up. The kids closed in on her.

"Pervert, abuser, lezzie!" Chanting and leering they began to circle, their teeth sharp and feral. A hand shot out and grabbed her covering. She clasped her arms over her breasts, her pubes. Her tormenters laughed and jeered pointing at her nakedness, making lewd comments about her ageing body. Somewhere in the distance came the shriek of police sirens. Liz looked desperately around for somewhere to run, somewhere to hide, as the mocking, gesturing children pressed closer and closer.

A hand stretched out to pull at her hair. She screamed and woke.

Her pillow was soaked with sweat. The cat was butting at her arm. Liz curled the duvet over her head and huddled beneath it.

"LIZ." JILLY'S VOICE on the phone was impossibly bright and cheery. "How are things?"

"Fine," Liz muttered. What else could she say? That

the days dragged, grey and pointless, that her nights were full of terrible dreams, that the only thing keeping her even vaguely sane was planning an evening of cooking for Val's dinner party.

"I've got some news," Jilly bubbled. "I know I shouldn't be telling you this but balls to them all. The system's iniquitous so why should we take any notice of it?"

Please, Liz thought, *stop wittering and tell me.*

"Remember I said I'd find out who it was. Well I didn't even have to do that much. Sam Boyd is going around telling everyone. Only today she came up to me and said did I know what Mrs Mckendrick had done to her. Of course I didn't so I nodded and waited and she just looked at me and came straight out with it." Jilly paused, expecting a reaction.

"And?" Liz managed wearily, knowing she had to say something.

"The little toe-rag claims that you hit her. I didn't think it was a good idea to say very much. I did say, 'Really Sam, I think you should be absolutely certain of your facts before you go around saying things like that,' and left it at that. I wish now that I'd probed a bit further. She's going round the school boasting that she's got you kicked out. She and that Amy Andrews and Leanne..."

"Thompson," Liz supplied.

"Yes her. The three of them should be excluded. If you're not allowed to come in to work then I don't see why they should be in school. But you know Norman, he's useless. It's the same old story, the kids are always right until they're proved wrong and even then they only get a quick tap on the wrist. While we..."

"We lose everything," Liz finished bleakly.

"Oh." Jilly was instantly contrite. "Don't let it get you down. The fact that it's Sam Boyd is bound to be in your favour. Everyone knows what a liar she is. If she told me today was Monday I'd have to check my calendar before I believed her. They'll see through her, no problem. To be honest I'm surprised it's gone on so long."

"Yes well," Liz mumbled a few anodyne comments and finished the conversation. She put down the phone, trembling with fury.

How dare she? What gives Sam Boyd the right to lie about me? To ruin my life. To put me through this hell. And all because I was trying to help her. What did it matter if Sam was not very bright, that she was being manipulated by Leanne and Amy? If she could, Liz would grind her into the dirt from which she'd come.

And that was the problem. All three girls came from a world in which drama mattered more than the truth and everyone vied to be centre stage.

It's all they've got. It's what makes them feel important. I should be sorry for them, but I can't, not yet. Not until it's over. And I'm safe.

Then she could go back to being her detached non-judgemental, tolerant self. The self she'd always prided herself on being; unless this was the real Liz and she was as driven by emotion in exactly the same way as Samantha Boyd. Liz half shut her eyes and made herself take a deep breath. If that were true then she was going to have to re-evaluate everything she'd believed herself to be.

"I USUALLY DO this with Trev." Bernie laughed nervously as Liz parked her bright yellow Citroen in the supermarket car park. "We did the family shop last night but thought it would be too complicated to do both at the same time. He wasn't very pleased. He likes to go out for a drink on Fridays."

"He's not used to you doing things on your own initiative."

"No. It's not like that." Bernie as usual sprang to her husband's defence. "I mean I got my job and he said that was all right."

You're working part time stacking shelves in a supermarket. You're still dependent on him. And you never stand up to him. No wonder he thinks it's okay to do what he wants, when he wants.

The more Liz thought about Bernie and her situation, the more convinced she was that the marriage was in trouble. Bernie would be much better off without her boring husband but Catholic conscience and an old fashioned sense of responsibility bound her to him.

"Gareth in butchery has done us the meat. He's chosen a really good joint," Bernie said as she wheeled the trolley down the aisles and Liz was struck how the staff laughed and joked with Bernie, teasing her about being the new Jamie Oliver.

"So long as I don't have to cook in the nude." Bernie laughed, referring to the celebrity's first cookbook.

Naked in the foyer. Sagging stomach and wrinkly thighs. Firm fleshed teenagers jeering and chanting; hands darting to tug at thinning hair. Nowhere to run. The main doors barred, Norman blocking the door to his office, grinning inanely as she desperately tried to cover herself.

Liz clutched at the handle of the trolley. Shelves of tins seeming to spin to the ceiling as she wrestled the demons of her dream.

"Are you all right? You've gone white. Shall I get some water?" Bernie cried

"It's nothing. I'm fine. Really I am," Liz protested.

But Bernie would not have it. She sent Darren, one of the shelf stackers, for a stool and another to fetch a glass of water. They settled Liz in a corner by the baked bean stand and watched her anxiously until the colour crept back into her face and she felt strong enough to send the staff back to their jobs and Bernie to finish the shopping.

I can't let this get to me. This is not happening.

Samantha Boyd is not going to ruin my life. Liz willed herself to be calm, to behave in a rational adult way, and by the time Bernie was back with a loaded trolley she was on her feet and ready to go.

ELEVEN

BERNIE HAD CLEARED the kitchen and scrubbed down all the surfaces. Elsa assured her that there would be no need for an inspection by Health and Safety, but the very thought of anything she produced making someone ill was enough to bring her out in a hot flush. The dog had been banished to the laundry room, the oven sparkled, and she was kitted out in a clean apron. It was early evening, count down time, and she was feeling excited and alive.

The potatoes had been peeled; the carrots scraped and sliced ready to be cooked in butter and cream. The broccoli would be steamed. Bernie hoped that Val would have a steamer but in case she didn't she would bring her own.

The next job was to prepare the stuffing for the Boeuf-en-Croute. Bernie chopped mushrooms and onions. She took the joint out of its packaging and admired it: top quality fillet. Gareth had made a good choice. Leaving the meat on the chopping board she turned to the puff pastry. She was about to roll it out when the kitchen door banged open and Pat ran in.

"Mum," he yelled, his face scarlet with fury. "Joe won't let me have the *Star Wars* DVD."

"Not now, Pat. I'm busy."

"But Mum."

"I said not now. This bit is complicated and I have to get it right. I'll deal with it in a minute."

"Where is it? What have you done with it? You've

been in my room. You've gone through my stuff!" Joe stormed into the kitchen. "You little shit. I told you you're not to go in there." He aimed a blow at his brother who ducked and ran behind his mother. Bernie, her hands floury, side-stepped.

"Pat, Joe stop it."

"But he's..." They squared up to each other. At any moment a full-scale war would be breaking out in her pristine kitchen.

"Get out now. Go on, the pair of you!" Bernie yelled.

"Mum!" Pat howled. Joe swiped at him and he ran out into the hall. Joe raced after, swearing at the top of his voice.

"Mother of God," Bernie breathed, trying to stifle the guilt at ignoring her children. She should be sorting them out but there was no time. Liz would be arriving at any moment to pick her up and she still had to assemble the dish.

Turning back to her preparation she saw a flash of brown fur. Woody had somehow escaped from the laundry and was skulking under the table.

"Out of my way you horrible dog," Bernie snarled. She reached for the dish where the beef was waiting. The dish was empty. Bernie stood and stared at it unable to believe what she was seeing, then a cold feeling swept up from her feet to the top of her head squeezing the breath out of her lungs. She stumbled against the table under which Woody was busy eating the last of the beef fillet.

The front door bell rang but mired in fear and guilt Bernie could not move. It rang again and again.

"Bernie," Liz called through the letter box. "We're going to be late."

Oh God, Bernie thought, why hadn't she shut the dog in the garage? Why had she let the boys into the kitchen? Holy Mother of God what were they going to do now? If only she could lock herself in the house and wait for Liz to go away but she couldn't do that. She had to let her in and confess the terrible truth.

"It's gone," she howled. "The meat's gone. What do we do now?"

"What? Bernie, you're not making any sense. Wasn't the beef with the rest of the shopping? I'm sure I saw you pack it. It's got to be here somewhere." Liz strode purposefully into the kitchen coming to a sudden halt when she saw the empty dish and the dog under the table.

"Right." Drawing back her shoulders she went into what Bernie thought of as her crisis management mode.

"It's half-seven already and we need to be at the house. Elsa's got the salmon so you two can get the starter going while I rush off to Waitrose and get some more meat."

"There won't be time to get it ready, let alone cook it. Oh God, the whole thing's a disaster and it's all my fault," Bernie wailed.

"We'll sort it," Liz said. "Now get everything else and pack it in the car." Bernie nodded. Feeling too clumsy and stupid to speak, she did as she was told. She sat in the passenger seat with her hands clasped tightly as Liz drove quickly and efficiently out of the estate and then turned right into the High Street. In front of them a huge lorry lumbered painfully up the hill. Bernie swallowed a sob. Now they were not only going to arrive without the main course, they were also going to be late.

"Bloody thing shouldn't be allowed. Why the hell isn't it on the motorway?" Liz edged the little Citroen around the back of the lorry. Coming straight at them was a white sports car. Bernie shut her eyes and prayed. "Shit." Liz swerved back behind the lorry.

Bernie let out her breath and murmured a quick prayer of thanks. She glanced at Liz who was hunched over the wheel, her shoulders tense.

"I'm sorry. I feel terrible about this. I should have

kept an eye on Woody. I should have."

"It's okay," Liz muttered. Then spotting a clear stretch of road she accelerated past the lorry. "Sorted," Liz breathed, leaning back in her seat.

VAL AND BOB'S house was an imposing Edwardian detached overlooking the Downs. Liz swung the car round to the back and parked near the kitchen door. Bernie clambered out. Her hands were damp, her legs heavy. If she could she would have jumped back in the Citroen and driven far, far away out of this nightmare.

Liz however remained undaunted. "There's been a bit of a blip," she told Elsa. "You and Bernie get started. I've got a detour to make."

Elsa looked doubtfully at the dishes set out on the work surface. "Is that everything?"

"Not quite," Bernie muttered, whipping foil from the roasting dish and sliding the potatoes in the oven.

"I can't see the meat." Elsa peered into a bag.

"It's on its way." Bernie's throat was dry. "Liz says, will you do the starters."

"I've already done that." Elsa smiled. "I've set the table, arranged the flowers and folded the napkins. All we are waiting for now are the guests."

"This all right?" Val's husband Bob bumbled into the kitchen holding a bottle of wine out for inspection. A round avuncular figure, he was an amiable contrast to his spiky nervy wife. "Val said it would be beef so I thought a bottle or three of Nuits St George."

"We'll need some white for the salmon, or do you think bubbles?" Elsa asked, fluttering her eyelashes in a manner that made Bernie want to slap her.

"A Chablis will fit the bill. I've some bottles in the cellar so they'll be chilled, but I'll get out the ice bucket."

"Perfect," Elsa breathed.

Bernie meanwhile had turned her attention to the vegetables. If only she knew what Liz would buy then she could decide whether to make a sauce. But what would she use? She scanned the gleaming kitchen. There were no spice racks, no cupboards bursting with basics, only a sterile blankness. *Holy Mother of God,* she prayed silently. *Let it be all right. Don't let me have ruined Elsa's first job. Please.* The doorbell rang and her knees went weak.

"We're off," Elsa exclaimed happily. "We'll let them have their drinks then I'll set out the first course."

Over the thunderous beating of her heart Bernie heard Val let in the first of their guests.

"Tony and Julia," Elsa whispered. "They're both with Grindley and Knight"

Bernie's stomach lurched. She didn't need to know that she had ruined the meal she was to have prepared for one of Bristol's most successful lawyers and his beautiful, much younger wife.

"It's really brave of you to ask us, Val," Tony boomed. "It's not many people entertain at home these days, as Julia is always telling me."

"I bet she is," Elsa giggled. "Did you see her kitchen? There was a full spread on it in the *Bristol Magazine.* Everything was top of the range."

And she probably never cooks in it. Bernie thought, and wondered how much longer Liz could possibly be.

"Ian and Moira," Elsa mouthed as more guests were welcomed in. "Isn't it time you put the beef in the oven?"

"Well, actually..." Bernie began steeling herself for confession.

She was rescued by Val who, poking her head around the kitchen door, announced, "We're just waiting on Malcolm and Erica, then it's all systems go."

Please let them be late. Liz where are you? Bernie looked at her watch. If they didn't do something about the main course soon all her timings would be out. The potatoes would be shrivelled, the carrots dried up; but if she switched down the oven temperature then her roasties wouldn't crisp.

"I think they're here," Elsa cried. "Shall I put the smoked salmon on the table or will that be too soon for the main course?"

"There is no main course," Bernie blurted. "The dog ate it." Elsa stared at her open mouthed.

"Don't be silly, of course there is. You put everything in the oven. I saw you."

"Potatoes but no meat. That's where Liz is gone. To get something else."

"I don't believe you."

"I'm sorry." Bernie screwed up her eyes to hold back the tears. If only she could crawl into some deep dark hole and howl.

"What are we going to do?" Elsa hissed.

"Start the meal. Liz will be here soon."

"What if she isn't? These are my friends. They're doing me a favour by giving me the catering job. I can't go in there and tell them there's no food. God, Bernie, how could you be so stupid?"

Bernie flushed and looked down at her feet. What could she say? Elsa was right: it was her fault. She should have kept a closer eye on the dog and the boys and the whole of her life.

"We'll be ready to go in, in a minute," Val chirruped. Elsa picked up a couple of plates of smoked salmon and sailed into the dining room. The table was covered with a damask cloth, the glasses were crystal, the dinner service Val's best Wedgwood. A bowl of cream roses was the centrepiece to what could have been a photograph in a glossy lifestyle magazine.

"We've got to slow everything down," Bernie said as she put another two servings in their places. Elsa did not reply. Her hands shook slightly as she adjusted one of the immaculately folded napkins. Bernie felt sick.

"I'll get the rest. You go back to the kitchen." Elsa's voice was strained, her colour high.

She's going to scream at me, Bernie thought, backing away. In the hall she could hear Val and Bob and their guests moving towards the dining room.

Elsa swept past her in a whirl of indignation and stood listening at the kitchen door as Bob poured the wine and people began to eat. Bernie peered anxiously through the glass door of the oven.

Elsa shook her head like a nervous horse, starting back as she heard the sound of knives and forks being laid down on empty plates. "They've finished."

"They can't have," Bernie gasped. At which point Bob launched into one of his long-winded anecdotes. More laughter followed, then an expectant pause.

"Well what do we do now?" Elsa's nostrils flared. Her lips tightened. Bernie's hands were slippery with sweat, her throat dry.

"Clear the table and..." Bernie faltered, desperate for inspiration.

"And serve up the veg," Liz said as she swept in through the back door. "Come on where's the microwave? Don't tell me this kitchen doesn't have a microwave. Bloody traffic. And nowhere to park, of course." Plonking her bags on the granite worktop, she ripped off the tops of the cartons she had bought and tipped the contents into a serving dish. Pieces of poultry stuck out over the edge. "Damn. This casserole is too small."

"Anything bigger won't fit in the microwave." Elsa waved her hands helplessly.

"Then we'll do it in two batches. Bernie go and pour the wine. Buckets of it. Red, remember. Elsa, get another dish. No, forget that. Elsa, you go and play butler. Bernie, finish off the broccoli and I'll deal with the guinea fowl."

Under Liz's command they sprang into action. The casserole was dished up, the vegetables presented, the wine kept flowing.

"What I wouldn't do for a drink." Elsa sank into a chair and looked meaningful at a bottle of red that Bob had left to breathe.

"Not yet." Liz steered her away. "The servants have to stay sober until the meal is over. And the driver can't drink at all."

From the other side of the door the sound of voices and laughter grew louder and coarser. Moira giggled weakly. Erica boomed out her opinion on the State of Art Today.

"They sound as if they're enjoying it," Bernie said hopefully. She was beginning to feel human again. Her heartbeat had steadied, her hands did not shake as she and Liz went to clear away the plates while Elsa put the finishing touches to the pudding.

"I'll make the coffee," Bernie volunteered eager to make up for the calamity she had almost caused.

"Val wants that served in the drawing room. She said she'd come and tell us when they're ready for it." Elsa yawned.

"What time is it now?" Bernie asked anxiously.

"Only half-eleven. It feels like tomorrow," Elsa groaned. "I am absolutely shattered."

"All that flower arranging certainly takes it out of you," Liz said dryly.

"Do you think it's gone okay?" Bernie fretted as she loaded the dishwasher.

"I think so." Elsa stretched her arms and rolled her neck.

"Final scene coming up," Liz warned as Val came into the kitchen.

"Thank you all, that was delicious. That casserole, was it guinea fowl? Out of this world. Bob was raving about it. And the chocolate pudding. My waistline! And Moira would like to know how you do your roast potatoes. She says she never manages to get hers so crisp." And without waiting for reply she swept out again.

"Coffee's ready." Bernie looked at Elsa who yawned loudly and shook her head, so it was Liz who carried in the coffee and Bernie who brought in a plate of beautifully presented petit fours.

In the drawing room Bob was topping up glasses with port or brandy. Moira and Val were talking quietly on the sofa. Erica pontificating about some exhibition of a rival's work to Julian.

"And not a blind bit of notice taken of the servants," Liz said as they walked back to the kitchen.

I don't mind, thought Bernie, who would rather fade into the wallpaper than be centre stage.

"In fact it was like watching a film. You can get a sense of all sorts of scenarios being played out. I wish I knew what they were talking about. It's really strange only getting odd bits of conversation," Liz mused.

"I can tell you all about that." Elsa poured herself a glass of wine. "Julia and Tony will be talking work with Bob and Ian. Malcolm will be pushing Erica and her sculpture at anyone who will listen, while she'll be putting him down and rubbishing everyone else's work. Val and Moira will be talking houses and extensions and they'll all be discussing holidays and where they are going next and where they have been and how awful it all is."

"Well that's sorted so now you can give us a hand with this."

Bernie hid a smile as Liz handed Elsa a tea towel.

"That's what the dishwasher's for," Elsa protested.

"It doesn't do crystal, as you well know. And we've got to pack up our things. Then it's time to go. I don't know about you two but I am absolutely knackered."

"Me too," Bernie sighed. "I'm glad it's Sunday and I don't have to go to work tomorrow." She looked at her watch. "I mean today. It went well though. Didn't it? In spite of what happened to the meat."

"All's well that ends well. I thought at one point we were going to blow the whole thing. I had visions of fish and chips or MacDonald's and talking them into believing it was the in thing this year." Liz laughed. "Thank God for supermarkets."

"Alleluia," Elsa chorused. "And Glory be."

"And thank You and Your Blessed Mother," Bernie added under her breath.

TWELVE

BERNIE'S EYES FELT full of grit, her mouth stale. After a night of fitful dozing she risked a glance at the bedside clock. It was six a.m. so there was no point in trying to get back to sleep. She eased herself out of the bed where Trev lay with his back to her, curled away as far as he could, and crept downstairs to make herself a cup of tea. Her feet ached, her back hurt, and her skin and hair smelled of yesterday's cooking. She'd give anything for a shower but that would wake Trev and the boys and for once she wanted to make the most of the time she had to herself in a house that was beginning to feel too full of people.

The kitchen looked as if a bomb had hit it. The pans still stood on the hob, chopping boards lay on the work-surfaces, while the packaging from the boy's supper had been strewn all over the table. There were dirty cups, plates and glasses waiting to be loaded into the dish-washer and someone had knocked a tea towel onto the floor and left it where it fell.

"No rest for the wicked," Bernie sighed. Hearing her come in, Woody woke and stretched. Head on the floor, tail and buttocks in the air, he yawned, then catching her eye slunk back into his basket.

"That's right. Feel guilty. We very nearly lost the business because of you," Bernie chided and Woody snuffled and covering his eyes with his paws pretended to sleep.

Bernie tied an apron over her dressing gown, pulled

on rubber gloves and began to clear up. This was what she got for trying to carve some time out for herself. She should have known. A mother's place was to be on call all the hours God sent. It was also, in some strange way, payment for almost having ruined everything yesterday.

When she'd finished she drank the tea she'd promised herself and watched the spring sunlight move across the garden and in through the window flooding the room with light. Her heart lifted and she rested her chin on her hand. She'd been too negative.

It's all my fault. I always look at the black side. Trev's right. I have to have something to worry about, she mused. *The truth is that he's tired and I'm shattered. What we need is a holiday. A few days away without the boys.* She pictured herself lying on white sand under a blue sky. Someone handing her a long cool drink with a paper umbrella balanced on the side. Bernie laughed softly. Now where did that come from? Liz would definitely not approve. She always said that anything sticking out of a drink was common.

Bare sweaty feet padded across the tiles. There was a musky smell of unwashed flesh and stale alcohol and a dark figure sloped across to the fridge. Joe took out a carton of orange juice and poured himself a glass. He stared at it balefully as if trying to decide whether he dared try it, then picked it up and gulped down half a glass. He was very pale. Watching his throat working as he swallowed, Bernie wondered if he was going to throw up.

"Are you all right?"

"Hmm," he growled.

"Do you want me to make you some toast?" It was her failsafe antidote for too much alcohol. Someone had once told her that if you could keep it down then toast soaked up all the toxins and made you feel better. Joe moved his head carefully in what could have been a nod. "I hope you didn't do anything stupid last night."

"No," he muttered and slumping down at the table, leaned his head on his arms and half closed his eyes. When Bernie put the toast in front of him he reached out automatically and crammed chunks of it into his mouth, letting the butter run down his chin and onto his T-shirt.

"Mum, I'm starving. What's for breakfast?" Pat bounced in crackling with energy. "I sleeped and sleeped," he announced.

"Slept," Joe corrected.

"Leave it," Bernie warned, hoping to deflect yet another battle between the brothers. "Bacon sandwich all right Pat?"

"Can I have two?

"You can have as many as you can eat." She smiled at him fondly. "And how about you, Joe?"

"Okay," he muttered.

Water gurgling through the pipes told Bernie that Trev was about to get in the shower, but she was strangely reluctant to call him to join them for breakfast.

The kitchen filled with the smell of bacon grilling. She brewed another pot of tea and in celebration of this rare moment of peace and sibling harmony ignored her spreading waistline and sat with her boys as all three of them tucked into bacon sandwiches liberally doused with brown sauce. When she'd cleared away their plates Bernie looked at her children.

"Since we've all managed to get up in time this morning you can get yourselves washed and dressed and we'll make it to the twelve o'clock Mass." There was a pause. Joe lowered his head.

"I'm not going," he muttered.

"Pardon me? You what?" Bernie wondered if she were hearing things. Never before had one of her younger ones defied her so openly.

"I said I'm not going." Joe met her eyes. "I'm never

going again. It's all shit and anyway I don't believe in God."

Bernie clutched the back of a chair. Her heart seemed to leap into her throat choking off her breath. How could this be happening? Surely she was bringing up her boys properly. She'd sent them to Catholic schools, she'd done all a good mother should to safeguard her children's faith. Aidan still went to church. Chris, her wayward second son, had long since lapsed but he was an adult and she couldn't be blamed for his decision. Joe and Pat, however, were still children. It was her responsibility to make sure they practised the Faith.

"I don't either. Believe in God," Pat added bravely.

"Stop it. That's nonsense. You're just copying your big brother. And you, Joe, you don't mean what you're saying. You can't be bothered to get washed and dressed that's all."

"No it isn't." Joe pushed back his chair. "I've never believed. Ever. I'm not going to church. You can't make me.

"Trev, tell him." Bernie whirled round to face her husband who had just come downstairs.

"Tell him what?" Trev was smiling to himself. A small secret smile holding something back from her.

"Tell him he has to go to Mass." Bernie's voice rose shrilly.

"I don't see why he should. Not if he doesn't want to."

Bernie stared at her husband in shock.

"Do you want to go to Mass, Joe?" Trev asked.

"No."

"That settles it."

"He's a child. He's not old enough to know his own mind," Bernie wailed as the abyss opened up in front of her. What about their eternal souls? She wanted to ask. What about Hell and Damnation?

"Have you made coffee?" Trev was behaving as if he

had no idea of the significance of what had just occurred.

Bernie ignored her husband. "You'll come with me." Taking Pat by the shoulders she looked deep into the blue eyes of her youngest child. "Won't you Pat?"

"No. If Joe's not going nor am I. It's not fair. I don't see why I should. Church is so boring," he said, squirming under her grip.

Bernie turned to Trev, who was calmly spooning coffee into the cafetière as if the whole of her life had not crumbled around her. "Do something," she begged.

"Leave it, Bernie. You've got to face it. They don't want to go," he said with barely suppressed irritation.

Joe grabbed a piece of cold toast and sloped out of the room. Pat hesitated then followed. Woody went after them.

"You let me down," Bernie said bitterly.

"No I didn't. All I did was let the boys make their own choice. Now they've made it, that's that."

"Aidan still goes," Bernie said.

"Saint Aiden would," Trev muttered. "Pious little git."

"Trev. This is important. It's a family thing."

"For God's sake Bernie, stop fooling yourself. When was the last time we did a family thing?"

Bernie felt as if she had been punched in the stomach. Trev was right. The last time they had done anything together was Christmas dinner, sitting through an awkward day with her elderly parents and her sister Maureen, who had temporarily split from her husband, and Maureen's two teenage daughters. "All right, all right," she said, "it's been a while but this is why it's important that they keep going to Mass. That we all do."

"The family that prays together stays together," Trev mocked.

"Stop it," Bernie hissed. "You know how much it matters to me."

"It's irrelevant."

"It's what?"

"It doesn't matter. Not in the greater scheme of things."

"I don't believe you said that."

Trev shrugged. "Bernie," he said softly, looking at her properly for the first time since he came into the kitchen. "Oh Bernie."

There was something about his gentle, yet distant concern that scared her. Why should her husband, the man she had known since he pulled her hair in the school yard at Our Lady of Fatima Primary, the man she had loved and respected almost all her life, sound as if he were sorry for her?

"Trev, are you all right?"

"I'm fine," he said flatly.

"You're depressed," Bernie blurted. She hadn't meant it to come out like that. She'd planned a quiet talk, putting the suggestion into his mind so he would be the one who decided to go to the doctor's.

"I'm tired."

"You need a holiday," she said, thankfully.

"No Bernie. I am tired of all this," he said in a low voice, his eyes focused on the garden where the sun was shining on the japonica.

And she knew. There was no more fooling herself. No more pretending that what had gone wrong between them could be put right with a course of anti-depressants. "There's someone else," she whispered.

"Yes." He wouldn't meet her eyes.

"That Amanda that was here. Is it her?" He nodded and she wanted to slap him, to bring him back to his senses. "You can't do this to us, not after all we've gone through together. Don't I mean anything to you? Don't the boys?"

"Mum!" Pat burst in with such speed that she knew he must have been listening. "Mum, Dad, you're not splitting up, are you?"

“Oh darling, no.” Bernie’s anger was washed away by the sight of her distraught child. “Grown-ups have rows sometimes, that’s all. I’m sorry you had to hear it but it’s one of those things.” She looked up but Trev had gone. “Everyone gets cross sometimes. You get cross with me, don’t you?”

“Yeah,” Pat said doubtfully and she knew he was not fooled but that it made him feel better to pretend he believed her.

“I’m going out for a bit.” Trev poked his head around the door.

We haven’t finished, Bernie wanted to yell at him but Pat was watching his face, scared. Woody, sensing something was wrong, came to stand close to him. “Can you tell me what time you’ll be back?” she said as calmly as she could manage.

“I’ll be in by two.”

“Can I go to Tom’s?” Pat said quickly. Bernie nodded. At Tom’s house there would be no warring parents. His mum and dad had split up years ago, and there would be new games and apps to blot out what her littlest one had seen.

The house emptied. Joe muttering something about a mate’s house had gone. Pat biked to Tom’s. Trev was God knew where. Even Woody had removed himself and now lay on the patio stretched out in a patch of sun.

THIRTEEN

BERNIE THOUGHT ABOUT going to church but how was she going to sit in an empty pew without any of her family? What would she say if anyone asked about Joe or Pat? Or even worse, about Trev? At the end of the Mass Father Thomas would be there outside the church waiting to shake hands and have a little chat with members of his congregation. He'd be sure to comment if she had come on her own.

It was too much. She couldn't face it. God would forgive her for missing Mass this once. He'd know how terrible she felt, how guilty and useless. She should pray for His help to get through this time of trial, and she would, but right now she simply wasn't up to it. Every part of her ached – and she was so cold.

Bernie went upstairs and ran a bath. She poured in bath oil and lay up to her neck in hot water, pushing aside the boys' flannels and sponges and the plastic bath toys that she still hadn't managed to throw out, and tried hard not to think about anything.

If she could slide under the water and stay there it would all go away. All the pain and fear would wash down the plughole.

Bernie sat up. She couldn't think like this. She mustn't. Suicide was one of the worst sins and what would her children do without her?

In a flurry of scented drops she got out and was drying herself when the phone rang. For a moment she dared hope that it was Trev ringing to tell her it was all a mistake. There was no affair with Amanda. A momentary infatuation. That was all. A fantasy. What he really wanted was not her skinny body but Bernie's infinite softness.

"I think we should meet to discuss last night." Liz was brisk.

"Sorry I can't." Somehow Bernie managed to choke back her disappointment.

"I'm calling a board meeting." Liz ignored her refusal.

"Stuff your board meeting!" Bernie slammed down the phone.

DRAWN BY HUNGER and the fact that Tom's dad had taken him out Pat came home at lunch time. Bernie made sandwiches then, unable to do anything more, sat and watched her child eat. Her own appetite had seized up. Her head was full of cotton wool. It took all her strength to keep upright.

Pat was wiping the last of the ketchup off his mouth when Trev walked in.

"She's busy then is she?" The words slipped out unbidden.

"I told you I'd be back at two and I am," her husband said wearily.

"Can we talk?" Bernie said.

Looking past her Trev said to Pat, "How about a bit of a kick about, mate?"

Mate! Kick about! Bernie could not believe what she was hearing. Trev never had time to play with his younger sons. Now, however, everything had changed and it was Bernie he had no time for.

"You'll ruin your lawn," she muttered bitterly as they went out into the garden. Pat was so excited that he'd be rushing around, throwing himself on the ground at every opportunity as he imagined himself saving goals. He'd come in filthy, needing a shower, and his clothes washing.

Suddenly, she could stand it no longer: the dirt and filth and chaos of her life. The male bonding. The sense of being on the outside of their lives. Washing, cleaning, cooking, it was all she was good for. Trev and Pat didn't want or need her. If she walked out they wouldn't even notice.

"YOU WERE RIGHT," Bernie said sadly.

"I'm so sorry." Liz went to hug her but Bernie moved away. She desperately wanted to be held but was terrified of being touched. If Liz held her she would cry and cry until there was nothing left and then what would happen to her family? "Is there any of that chocolate pudding left?"

"Funnily enough I froze the tiny portion we managed not to eat," Liz said. "I'll put it in the microwave."

Timbo jumped onto Bernie's knee. Absently she stroked his fur and he began to purr. Was she going to end up living alone with a cat, like Liz?

"Chocolate and red wine." Liz set down the tray and poured Bernie a large glass. "It's medicinal." She watched as Bernie took her first sip. "Do you want to talk?"

"What is there to say? You were right. I was wrong. There is someone else. She's younger than me and more sexy."

"I doubt it."

"No, she is. Honestly. She's slim and blonde."

"Skinny and bleached, I bet."

"No, she's gorgeous. Well not gorgeous. She's got a big nose and her eyes are a bit too close together."

"A hag in the making then," Liz said.

"I don't know. All I know is he wants to be with her and not with me."

"He does at the moment. He might still come to his senses and see how much he would lose if he went. After all, there's you and the boys and the house."

"All the things we've worked for all these years." Bernie's voice trembled. "But none of that seems to matter to him. Do you think he will leave?" Liz said nothing. "Men do, don't they?" Bernie persisted, both fearing and wanting to hear the worst.

"Mostly," Liz agreed, "but they tend to regret it afterwards."

"Afterwards is too late." Bernie pressed her lips together to stop herself from crying.

"Darlings! The side door was open so I walked straight in."

"Elsa," Liz said.

"Don't sound so surprised. You called a meeting. A board meeting." Elsa giggled. "I don't know why you had to call it that. It makes it sound so serious. Is the wine part of the celebration? You know last night was such a success. I had Val on the phone this morning. She was impressed. She said she'd be more than happy to recommend us to all her friends. Do you think we should have some cards printed?" She clapped her hands in delight. "Or even better, we should have our own website." She faltered to a halt as she was met with a blank response. "We have done well, haven't we?"

"Brilliantly! Last night's effort shows a deficit of twenty pounds," Liz said.

"But they paid us! I've got the cheque here."

"Yes but it doesn't cover our expenses or our time. Which is what I want to talk about."

"It's all my fault. Woody ate the beef. I'm useless." Bernie burst into tears. "My husband's got another woman. The boys won't go to church and I can't even control a Water Spaniel."

"Oh Bernie!" Elsa flung her arms around Bernie and held her close. Bernie breathed in a lung-full of Chanel No. 5 and sobbed and sobbed.

FOURTEEN

BERNIE SLUMPED IN the passenger seat of Liz's car and stared mutely out of the window. It was as if she was wrapped in a blanket of fog. Nothing mattered. Nothing hurt. By the time they reached Shirehampton she was sinking into a state of complete unreality. The neat little houses, the shiny cars, the empty cul-de-sac: none of it had anything to do with her.

"Do you want me to come in with you?" Liz asked.

"What good will that do? Nothing's going to make any difference. Good night Liz." Bernie slammed the car door. It was late. The boys were in bed. Through the frosted door of the lounge she could see Trev watching something on TV. His back was turned to her and she noticed for the first time how his once-thick hair had thinned over the years. There was a definite bald patch spreading from the centre of his skull.

He's getting old, she thought. *He'll be fifty-five next birthday. It's all so stupid. He should be making plans for retirement, not swanning off with a new woman.*

Woody was in his basket in the laundry. Once, the dog would have been curled up beside Trev on the sofa, jumping off guiltily when she came in. Trev sat with his shoulders bowed as he focused on the screen. Bernie surmised that perhaps Amanda didn't like dogs so Woody was banished. What if she didn't like kids? Too bad. They'd have to see their dad. Let her have them for a weekend, let her cope with Joe and his moods and Pat with his endless demands. They'd do her head in. Two days with the boys in one of their fighting moods and she'd soon be yelling and screaming and losing her cool. That would show her. You couldn't take a father away from his sons, not without paying the price.

The Water Spaniel lifted his head and looked at her mournfully as she picked the boys' shirts out of the laundry basket. They needed ironing and she'd still got to find some dinner money. She hadn't checked their school bags or asked if they needed their games kit or nagged to see if they'd done their homework. Bernie selected Pat's shirt then let it fall back on top of the other clothes. She hadn't got the energy. Maybe after a cup of tea she'd feel more like it.

Bernie sat at the kitchen table and stared blankly in front of her. The tea grew cold, and as if he knew she needed comforting the dog came and laid his head on her knee. Time ticked by. The heating had clicked off and the room grown cold. She wondered if she should make Trev a drink but it all seemed too much effort. Everything seemed so pointless. Her whole life had come to this: sitting alone in a dark kitchen unable to move.

Trev turned off the TV and checked the front door. Coming into the kitchen he flicked the switch filling the kitchen with a cruel light. Blinking against the sudden brilliance, Bernie drew in her breath.

"I'm sorry. I didn't see you there. I thought you'd be in bed," Trev said.

"I haven't got round to it yet. There's too much to do."

"Getting the boys ready for school?" He half smiled and the reference to their children melted some of her misery. He might be unhappy just now but he'd got it wrong, they were a family and all that was needed was a little effort and they could get through this.

"Trev," she began tentatively, "I know things haven't been good lately. What with the boys getting to be teenagers and Joe the way he is, all hormones and aggression. Then there's the house and us both working, especially with me doing shifts and not always being there for you all, but it doesn't have to be like this. If you like, I'll be at home more. I'll keep the boys out of your way. We can spend some time together. We can make it better. It's just a stage. It's where we are in our lives."

Trev sat down opposite her. "How it is now is not the problem."

"What then?"

He reached across and covered her hands with his. "If you want the honest truth, it's never been good. Not from the very start."

The pain ripped through her. How could he say this, after all this time? Her heart was tearing apart. "Because I trapped you?" Her voice was a whisper, she could barely force out the words.

"I didn't say that."

"But that's what you meant."

"Bernie, don't put words in my mouth."

"What else can I think? I want to understand. I want to know why after thirty-six years you can turn round and leave me."

"You don't want to hear."

"I do. I must. I've got to know."

Trev sighed. "Right from the beginning I felt, I don't know... I felt responsible."

"You were," she snapped.

"Yes. And I did what I had to."

"I can't fault you on that," she said bitterly.

"What else did you want me to do? Leave you up the duff."

"You put me there."

"You didn't say no."

"I was seventeen and I was head over heels in love. I thought you loved me too or I would never have given in." A horrible thought crossed her mind. "You did love me, didn't you?"

"I fancied the pants off you."

"Was that all?"

"I was nineteen. A good Catholic boy who'd never had it. I was raring to go."

"That was all there was to it? Sex?"

"I liked you. I thought I loved you." He shrugged. "I was a kid. I've changed. You've changed. You said so yourself. People grow apart. I guess that's what's happened to us."

Bernie gulped air like a woman drowning. "So none of this means anything to you?"

"Of course it does. The boys, they're my kids. I'd do anything for them."

"But not for me."

"That's not what it's about and you know it. I want some fun, Bernie. Before I get too old. I want to live a little."

"And you can't live with me?"

He looked at her for a long time and said simply, "No."

"But why?"

He shook his head and Bernie knew with a terrible bleak certainty that he could not explain because he did not understand, that the pattern of their relationship had been set on the day she had told him she'd missed her period. From then on he'd had to be a man, had to provide for her and his family. There had been no time to be one of the lads, to do the sort of things he had seen his older boys doing. If he'd gone to the pub he'd had to be home at a reasonable time or she would be hysterical, imagining him dead, when all he was doing was staying late. He'd had to be around at weekends, too. There was the house to do up and the boys to take out. There had been no time for living, for either of them. For her, the kids had been enough; for Trev, she realised, it had not.

"It's not working for us. It never did and it never will,"

Trev said sadly.

"Because of her?"

"I suppose with Amanda..." Bernie flinched at the name, but Trev continued as if he had not noticed. "I can be myself. I'm not a dad or a husband. I can have fun."

"You're just her bloke, conveniently forgetting that you have a wife and a couple of kids at home. Not to mention two older boys who will be devastated when they find out what you've done."

"Aidan and Chris will be all right," he said, squirming a little. "They'll understand."

"You think so? No lad in his right mind would understand how his dad could do this to his mum. Throwing her over for a woman young enough to be his daughter, how pathetic is that? Your *Amandaah...*" Bernie drew out the name mockingly, "...is young enough to be one of their slags."

"Don't talk about her like that. You don't know anything about her."

"I know what she's done. And she knows what she's trying to do. She's breaking up a family. What kind of woman does that?"

"She's not breaking anything that wasn't already broken."

"That's what you say. I know better. We've done a good job with our boys, you and me."

"That's why they'll be all right."

"But the little ones, Joe and Pat, still need you. They need their dad here at home with them." Bernie got up and put her hand on his shoulders, pressing him gently into his seat. "You saw the state Pat was in this morning when we were rowing. He hates it. He's scared we're going to break up. He said so. He doesn't want you to go."

"He'll cope." He shrugged her off.

"He's only twelve!" The pain her child would have to

bear was almost too much for her to imagine.

"Most of the kids he knows only have one parent. Face it Bernie: what's happening to us is normal. That's how it is. Marriages don't last anymore."

"They should."

"It won't be that bad. It's not as if I won't see them. I'll take them out. I'll be able to concentrate on them more, away from here." The moment had come. There was no avoiding it.

"You're leaving? You're going to her?" The pain was terrible; every word made it worse but she had to know.

Shamefaced he nodded "That's the plan at the moment."

"What will happen to us? Where will we live?"

"You'll be okay. I know you will. Look, let's talk about it in the morning. We've both had enough tonight." To her surprise his eyes were full of tears. She stretched out her hand to stroke his cheek but he moved quickly out of her reach. "I'm going to bed. Don't stay up too long."

Her heart leapt. What did that mean? Was he going to be waiting for her? Would they make love? Would he realise that there was still hope? Then she heard his footsteps along the landing as he carried his things into the spare room.

FIFTEEN

BERNIE COULDN'T FACE going to bed. The thought of the empty bed stretching away for the rest of her life was more than she could bear. Sensing her despair, Woody pushed his nose into her hand.

"He's abandoning you too," she told him. "He's the one that wanted you. He looked up Water Spaniels on the web and talked us all into how much fun it would be to have one. And who ended up having the fun? Or rather cleaning up the messes, dealing with the disasters and taking you for walks? It's even me that gets to comb the mats out of your coat. And in spite of all that you think he's the best thing since sliced bread." Her voice faltered and the tears spilled over her cheeks. "That's what I thought too." She sobbed. "He was my first and only lover. My husband, the father of my children and my best friend, and what does he do? He throws me on the rubbish heap because I'm not any fun. How could anyone be fun with four growing boys and a massive mortgage?" The sobs subsided and she slid into a half sleep.

SHE WAS AT the youth club dance, wearing a mini-skirt so short that she'd had to slip out of the house without her dad seeing her. Trev was with her, pressing her up against the wall. His kisses hot, his tongue sliding into her mouth. The whole of her body was electric with a desire she couldn't name. Her legs were weak, her knickers damp. She pressed herself against him, harder and harder.

"Bernie don't," he groaned.

She shuddered remembering the thrill of illicit love making. Then it had been fun. He wanting, she wanting, but feeling she shouldn't. Leading him on until they were both so wound up that the only thing left to do was give in. Then the hiding, the quickies in his bedroom with his mum downstairs; against the wall in the church car park; under the trees in the park, lying on his coat looking up at the stars. She could walk past and give him that look that would make him follow her and take her wherever he could. It would never be like that again.

After the wedding, going up to his old room with the second-hand double bed, the excitement had simply leaked away. She thought it was because she was pregnant but the weeks before the wedding she hadn't been able to get enough. Her body was constantly aching for his. She was always damp, her nipples hard against her bra. Now that it was all legal they were suddenly shy with each other. It was the first time she'd seen him completely naked, and she undressed quickly and slipped in between the sheets waiting, knowing they would do it but not really bothered. Kind of hoping he'd get it over with quick because she was tired and praying that she wouldn't have to go to the toilet in the middle of the night in case she made a noise and woke one of the family. The next morning Trev's mum brought her a cup of tea in bed and she hadn't known where to look, pulling the eiderdown up to her chin and muttering a quick "thank you".

It had it got no better when they moved to their own place. The run-down terrace in Shirehampton that Trev had spent his spare time doing up while she dealt with a crying, puking, colicky baby that never stopped screaming except when she stuck a nipple in his mouth. The whole of her nineteenth year she'd had a tit permanently hanging out. All she did was feed the baby, clean, and cook something to put in front of Trev when he got home from work. Then while Aidan curled his legs and screamed and puked all over her shoulder, Trev got out his tool box and sandpaper and plane and started on his next project. On Saturdays they went to his mum's for their dinner. On Sundays, after church, they went to her parents.

The years went by. There were more kids, a bigger house, but the basic pattern of their lives did not change much. She got a job, the older boys left home, and they got a dog.

"But it's a good life," she said to the darkness pressing in at the window. "There are people in the world, starving and dying of cancer. We've got the kids; we've got our health; why can't he be grateful for that? Why does he have to throw it all away?"

"The tears started again and she thrust her hands into the tangled fur on Woody's shoulder for comfort. He leaned against her leg and gradually the warmth of his body soothed her. She lay her head on her arms and shut her eyes.

She woke with terrible back ache. Her eyes were swollen and red, painful in the brightness of the kitchen light. For a moment she could not remember where she was and why, then the memory of last night twisted in her heart and she had to thrust a fist against her mouth to stop herself from screaming.

A thin grey line appeared under the blind. It was almost morning and there was still so much to do. Bernie got out the board and ironed the boys' school shirts. She found their dinner money and set out the breakfast. She let Woody out into the dawn and waited while he did his business then cleaned the yard, swilled out his bowl and gave him a double helping of his favourite food.

When Trev went into the shower she retreated into

the family bathroom and locked the door. She didn't want to speak to him. She didn't want to see him. She stood behind the door waiting until she heard the car reverse out of the drive, then let out her pent-up breath and went to wake the boys.

Pat, half asleep, held out his arms to her and she cuddled him close until ashamed of his babyish behaviour he pushed her away and scrambled out of bed. With Joe, she knocked on the door and stood there until she heard him get up. If she didn't, she knew he would turn over and go back to sleep.

"Mum, I can't find my PE shorts," Pat cried.

"Second drawer down in your chest," Bernie answered automatically. "Joe are you up yet?" A grunt issued from the bathroom. "Then clean your teeth. Think of the dentist's bills."

The boys showered, dressed, and ate. Pat was smart in white shirt, black trousers and blazer, and purple and yellow tie. His face was bright and eager, his bag over his shoulder.

"Come on Joe," he said impatiently, "we're going to be late."

"So?" His brother scowled beneath his brows. He looked dissolute, a mess. He'd cleaned his teeth but his face was pitted with spots, his eyes underscored with shadows. With his pale skin and dark hair he looked like a creature of the night.

Bernie knew she should tighten the tie, send him back to clean under his nails, check that his bag, which looked very light and which she suspected he would fling into the hall cupboard before he left the house, at least had a pen in it. There were all things a good and caring mother would do but she couldn't be bothered. They were fed; they were dressed. She could do no more.

"There's Tom." Pat, dancing with impatience, slapped a wet kiss on her cheek and was gone, slamming the front door behind him. Bernie eyed Joe.

Please Oh Holy Mother of God, today of all days let him go without a fight. She hadn't the strength to deal with any confrontation. Leaning against the wall in the hall she waited until at last he decided that he wouldn't get away with any more delay and with deliberate slowness slung his bag over his shoulder and sauntered out.

When the house was finally empty she hauled herself up the stairs, step by step, her hand on the bannister like an old woman. In the bedroom she kicked off her shoes and without taking off her clothes curled up and pulled the duvet over her head.

She didn't sleep. A grey fuzziness filled her brain; it dulled the throb at the base of her spine and soothed the grit in her eyes. From some dim distance, she heard the sounds of the day: the post, the milkman, neighbours going to work, mothers and children coming to and from school and playgroup. At some point Woody whickered then barked softly for her attention but she slid deeper under the covers until at last he stopped and the house was silent again.

SIXTEEN

ELSA STOOD IN the hall with the letter from the Official Receiver in her hand. Her head felt strange, as if she were under water and however hard she tried she couldn't get back to the surface. As if all she'd gone through in the past few weeks was not enough, the penthouse was to be sold to pay off Lionel's debts. The contents of her stomach lurched to her throat and she had to force herself not to throw up on the Persian rug.

Her phone bleeped and she grasped it like some sort of lifebelt, holding it close to her face to make out the message.

Darling Mum, Hope u r sorted now. Things gd here, so won't be bk for few months luv, J.

"Oh, darling boy," Elsa moaned softly at the text. Lionel was gone and James was on the other side of the world. But at least he wouldn't see her like this, battered on all sides by demands for money. By the time he was back winning awards, which he was sure to do given his talent, she would be solvent again. The business would be booming and she'd be featured in glossy magazines in articles on how women over fifty, no scrap that, women in mid-life, had made a success of adversity.

"I NEED TO extend the overdraft," Elsa said.

"This is the second time in the last twelve months," the bank's customer services manager replied.

"I know." Elsa shrugged prettily. "But that was due to

unfortunate circumstances."

"And how have your circumstances changed?"

"I am starting up a new business."

"Then you want a business loan?"

Elsa thought rapidly. Did she? Was that what she needed? Would it pay the bills for the next few months? She wished she had consulted Liz, who having lived on her own for so long, knew about these things.

"We can arrange that but we would need to see a business plan."

"Right," Elsa said slowly. "Actually, it's not the business that needs the money. I have some personal expenses."

"Another month then we will have to reconsider."

A month. She walked out into the June afternoon, smiling. So much could happen in a month.

After the trauma of the meeting at the bank she needed coffee and not in some café crawling with university students and mothers with babies in buggies. She needed elegance and refinement. The Grand would be perfect but that was too far to walk and given the state of her finances she really shouldn't take a taxi. Instead she opted for The Conservatory, the roof-top restaurant of the department store on the other side of the road.

As soon as she entered the light airy space she knew she had made the right decision. Sitting at one of the stainless steel tables was Margery Franks, another old St. Cecilia's girl, who had both made and married money.

"Elsa," she called. "How lovely to see you. Come and join me. I could do with some ideas. I'm looking for something for Mum's birthday. It's so difficult when she already has so much to find something really unique." Elsa nodded sympathetically. Since both her parents had died years ago she did not have this problem, but here was a potential client.

"She's eighty-four, would you believe, and still in her own home. The energy that woman has puts us all to shame. If we'd let her she'd organise her own birthday party."

"You're doing it for her?" Elsa was all attention.

"We're taking her out for a meal. Just close family. It's easier that way."

"You haven't thought of having caterers, then?"

"We considered it. It's always an option of course, but going out is so much easier. I don't know many people who do entertain at home these days. None of us have the time to cook. I'd much rather go out to a good restaurant. Everyone can eat what they like and there's no need to worry about vegetarians and food fads and special diets. To be honest it doesn't even cost that much more. You can get a very reasonable dinner for four for a few hundred, so why bother?"

Elsa sipped at the froth on her cappuccino, struck by how much her life had changed. Once she too would have thought nothing of spending that amount on an evening out with friends. Now it was a very different story.

"There is something very nice about celebrating at home," she suggested.

Margery shook her head. "Passé," she said in a tone that brooked no argument. "The whole house thing. It's too much bother. Getting Gerald to move his books and papers from the living room wouldn't be worth the effort. No. Going out is the way it is. Fashions change. It used to be the thing to have some little woman come in and do it all for you; not anymore. Must be off. Things to do. It's been lovely to see you. Must do it again some time."

More likely never, Elsa thought gloomily, staring out at a blue sky plumped with white fluffy clouds while her coffee grew as cold as the death of her brilliant idea.

SEVENTEEN

BERNIE COULD HEAR the phone ringing. Its shrill insistent tone tore through the house but she did not, she could not, move. Whoever was trying to get in touch it was bound to be more bad news. She turned her face onto the pillow and breathed in the scent of greasy hair and unwashed skin.

"JOE, IT'S THE phone." Pat stood uncertainly at the door of his brother's room.

"So?"

"We should answer it."

"Why?"

"It might be important." Pat's face was pleading. Joe scowled at his computer screen. The ringing persisted. "Should I get Mum?" Pat said.

"Nah. Don't do that." Joe pushed his chair to one side and ambled down the stairs. With any luck, whoever was on the line would have given up by the time he got there. His luck however was out.

"Bernie?" Liz asked.

"Nah," Joe mumbled.

"Joe. Is that you? Where's your mum?"

"She's sick." His voice trembled.

From the top of the stairs Pat asked, "Is it Dad? Is Dad coming home?"

"Shh." Joe put his finger to his lips. He was trying not to listen to Liz, trying to think of an excuse to put down the phone. Okay, so his mum was ill and his dad wasn't around, but they were coping all right, him and Pat, and anything was better than being at school. It wouldn't be for long. She'd be up soon. Then everything would be kind of back the way it was. Meantime he and Pat could have more holiday, especially if no one found out until after the end of term.

"Is she in bed?" Trust Liz not to give up.

Joe nodded. "Mmm," he managed.

"I'm coming over. I'll be there in about half an hour."

"Yeah well," Joe began. "Shit," he finished as she cut him off. "Now what?" he snarled as Woody scrabbled desperately at the laundry door.

"He wants to go out." Pat came slowly down the stairs.

"You take him, then."

"I can't, he pulls too hard. Please Joe, you come."

"Someone might see us."

"Not if we go down the old railway line. No one goes there, not in the middle of the day, not on a Tuesday. Please."

IN THE DISUSED cutting, narrow paths twisted through the long grass. Let off his lead, Woody raced away, his curly brown coat disappearing into the undergrowth. Joe pulled at a grass stalk; Pat watched anxiously for the dog. "Call him," he said at last.

"It's all right."

"But he might be lost."

"He isn't. He's over there." Joe waved his hand vaguely.

"But what if he doesn't come back?"

Joe heaved an exaggerated sigh, put his fingers in his mouth and whistled. Woody bounded towards them, ears flying, tail wagging frantically. "See, no problem. You're a worry guts, you are."

"I'm not." Pat launched into the familiar pattern of wrangling, but Joe didn't take the bait. Somehow fighting his little brother wasn't fun anymore. "Pooh. He stinks." Joe bent down to slip the dog's lead over his head.

"He's rolled in something yucky." Pat held his breath to stop himself from gagging

"In something dead. Long dead," Joe said

They shut the stinking Woody in the laundry and went back to Joe's room where he let Pat sit on his bed. He knew that Pat really wanted to be with their mum but when they went into her room she just lay there and didn't say anything, which was scary, so his little brother had better stay with him for a bit. Which would also stop him from phoning Dad or Aiden and telling them what was going on. Joe put on his headphones and turned up his music.

"THEY ARE IN," Liz said pressing the bell once more.

"Yes, but no one is coming. Should we go?" Elsa glanced back at the yellow Citroen.

"We will try one more time." Liz was worried. This was not like Bernie. There was something wrong and she was going to get to the bottom of it.

"Dad?" The door opened and Pat's face, bright with hope, crumpled. He rubbed his nose on his arm and snuffled back tears. A wild barking came from the laundry, followed by an ominous crashing sound. "It's Woody. We shut him in," Pat said timidly.

"Well don't you think you should go and let him out?" Elsa said. Pat nodded but made no move to do as she suggested and with a dramatic sigh she strode past him into the kitchen.

"Yeek!" she screamed as a rancid, stinking Woody flung himself joyfully at her.

"We took him for a walk and he got dirty," Pat explained. "We didn't mean to let him but he rolls in things, 'specially rotting things. Dad says it's what Spaniels do."

"Elsa will deal with it," Liz said briskly. "Is Joe upstairs?"

"He's in his room."

"Do you want to call him or can I go up?"

"No. I'll get him." Pat sounded horrified at the thought of Liz invading his brother's lair. "Joe!" he cried, as he scampered up the stairs. "You've got to come." The door opened surprisingly quickly and Joe came downstairs without any fuss. Both boys looked unwashed, dishevelled, and somehow lost.

"I'm going up to see your mum in a minute," Liz said. "Has she been ill long?"

"Day or so," Joe muttered.

"About a week," Pat amplified. "I wanted to tell Dad, but Joe said to wait. She's never been like it before so we thought..." He trailed off as his brother glowered at him.

"It's okay," Liz reassured him. "I'll see if she needs to go to the doctor. If she needs looking after then I can do that while you're at school. You can't stay off, you know, or you and your mum will be in trouble." The boys stared at the floor. "She'll write a note to say what's happened so you won't end up in court." Liz winced inwardly at her controlling tone. "At least not unless you skive off again."

"They won't put us in care, will they?" Pat's eyes were terrified.

"No, of course not. But I am going to have to tell your dad. Move," she warned, sidestepping swiftly as a grim-faced Elsa dragging a reluctant Woody made for the stairs.

"This animal is having a bath. Boys you'd better find me his shampoo. No, on second thoughts I'll have anything that's going. The more powerful the better. And I'll need towels and a hair drier."

They stared at her, this mad woman in the beige dress and coat and high-heeled boots, but they did as she told them.

Liz tapped softly on Bernie's door. Nothing. She knocked a little louder then hoping it was not locked turned the handle. The air was stale and musty but there was no sickly-sweet reek of fever. The curtains were drawn and Bernie lay huddled under the duvet.

"Bernie," Liz said softly. "It's me. Elsa and I have come to see how you are."

"Oh." Bernie's response was barely a sigh.

"Can I get you anything? A cup of tea?"

"I'm okay."

"You're not. The boys tell me you've been ill."

"Yes. Maybe. Sick. I don't know." Bernie turned her head from side to side. "I'm useless. I can't do anything right."

"That's nonsense and you know it."

"No, it's the truth. I'm an awful mother and a terrible wife. I can't even keep a job at the supermarket."

"Who needs to work stacking shelves now you're part of Elsa's new business empire?"

"Which I nearly ruined." Bernie turned over onto her side so that her back was to Liz.

"Okay, so you're hopeless. That doesn't mean you get to stay in bed all day."

"There's nothing to get up for," Bernie whispered.

"Is that so?" Liz asked, but her friend was beyond reason.

"There's nothing for me. Not anymore."

"Dog on the loose," Elsa shrieked. The door burst open and a wild, wet Water Spaniel flung himself at the bed and leapt on top of Bernie. "God, I'm sorry. I'd almost finished when he jumped out of the bath. I'm soaked. There's water everywhere. That animal!" Elsa tried to pull him away from Bernie. Woody looked up at her reproachfully, streams of water ran down his fringe into his eyes and onto his mistress's face.

"Mum!" Pat ran into the room. Woody jumped off the

bed and as Bernie turned towards her son Elsa grabbed at the dog, who shook even more water over her.

"Out," she ordered. Woody gave a final shake and slunk down the stairs.

"Right." Liz took control. "Pat, you go and put on the kettle. I'll get rid of the wet bedding and your mum is having a shower."

While Bernie stood under a stream of hot water Liz fetched clean towels and stripped the bed.

"You get dressed while I get this lot in the washer." Liz left to give Bernie some privacy but when she came back her friend was standing in front of the wardrobe unable to decide what she should put on.

"Jogging bottoms." Liz pulled out a pair. "Nice and comfortable, and this top." She handed Bernie the clothes and waited until she was ready before suggesting they went downstairs.

Bernie trod carefully, hand on the banister like an old woman who had to measure every step. Pat watched anxiously from the hall and when she reached the bottom he dived at her and clamped his arms around her waist. She stared over his head at the wall for a long moment before she managed to lift her arm and stroke his hair. His whole body convulsed and burying his face in her chest he broke into sobs. Then without warning he pushed her away and ran upstairs and slammed the door of his bedroom.

Bernie neither moved nor spoke, simply stood in the hall seemingly oblivious of her child's pain.

"I've shut that horrible creature in the garden and opened all the windows to let out the smell of boy and wet dog. And I've made tea and found some biscuits. Not Waitrose but they'll have to do," Elsa announced.

Liz sat down beside Bernie on the sofa. Elsa poured tea and offered chocolate hobnobs.

"The boys have promised to go to school tomorrow and I'll ring Trev, if you don't feel up to it," Liz said.

"No," Bernie wailed, "don't tell him. Please."

"He needs to know how you are. You're not coping too well at the moment. He has to do his bit."

Bernie's eyes filled. "If he finds out he'll take them away," she murmured, twisting her hands in her lap. "He knows I'm a bad mother. He'll have them put into care."

"Don't be so stupid," Elsa declared. "No one's going to take the boys away. You've been a bit down, that's all. It happens to us all. God knows, after a bad day who wants to get out of bed. I tell you there have been times I couldn't get myself up until well after mid-day."

"I don't think this is quite the same." Liz shot her a look, which as usual Elsa ignored.

"Anyway," Elsa continued blithely, "why don't you let their father have them for a bit. Give yourself some space."

"I don't think that would be a good idea." Liz wished she could find some way of shutting Elsa up. "Bernie's going to be fine. We all are."

"If we win the Lottery," Elsa said. "You know there must be some way of making a living and not having to get out of bed."

"There is. It's called the oldest profession."

"I didn't mean that. That would be too much effort. All that heaving and humping. And the men! They could be anybody. They could have smelly feet and bad breath. There has to be something else. I saw an article in a magazine once about phone sex. All you have to do is read from this script that they send you. It doesn't matter if you're old, or fat, or ugly." Bernie winced but Elsa was in full flow and nothing was going to stop her. "And you need a sexy voice." She lowered hers and drawled huskily: "Come and take me, darling. I'm waiting." She opened her arms to an imaginary lover and a tuft of Water Spaniel hair floated down from her sleeve and settled on the tea tray.

“Elsa, you’re moulting!” Liz couldn’t help it: she clamped her hand over her mouth and began to laugh.

“I am,” Elsa screamed and suddenly the tension of the afternoon dissolved into giggles. They laughed until their stomachs hurt and even Bernie’s lips curled into a smile.

“Remember I’m checking on you tomorrow,” Liz told Bernie. “All of you,” she added, for she had insisted the boys were there before she and Elsa left.

“And for God’s sake keep an eye on that dog,” Elsa added. “If you have to take him for a walk, make sure he doesn’t go near anything dead.”

Joe nodded and Pat promised. Bernie put her arms around their shoulders. Her friends’ concern and the warmth of the boys’ bodies thawed the great block of ice inside her. She held them close until Pat wriggled free and Joe, with an embarrassed shrug, moved away.

The bedroom smelled of lavender and fresh linen. Through the open window came the sounds and scents of a summer evening. Music playing, people talking, car doors opening and shutting. She undressed and slipped into bed. The sheets were clean and cool, the newly washed and tumble-dried duvet settled over her as light as a feather. She stretched out relishing the luxury of a freshly made bed. Then her legs grew heavy; she sank deeper into the mattress, her eyes closed, and the greyness swept over her again.

EIGHTEEN

LIZ COULDN'T SLEEP. It was still dark but worry gnawed at her insides like a stomach bug. Her teeth were clenched, her limbs stiff with tension. She looked at the clock on the bedside table and reached for a book. She tried to read but the words meant nothing. She read and re-read the same page over again then threw the book onto the discarded pile on the rug.

"Come on Timbo." Gently she eased the cat out of the dip in the mattress. He mewed crossly. It was too early to get up but his mistress was already on her way downstairs so he followed in hope of an early breakfast.

Liz watched the sun rise over the garden wall. She wandered out into the fine summer morning, her nightdress trailing in the dew, as she inspected the borders for slugs and snails. She carried a jam jar of salt and when she saw a fat bloated body on the honeysuckle, or lurking under the protective leaf of a hosta, she sprinkled it liberally and watched with grim pleasure as the slug curled up and died.

The air was fresh and cool, the sky blue. It was going to be another beautiful day but she could not shake the feeling of dread that weighed her down. She knew that there were people whose situation was far worse than hers. Elsa for one. There had been no more dinner parties and she was facing eviction. Then there was Bernie curled up in misery at losing the one man she had always loved. Both her friends, in their different ways, were sliding through the safety nets that had held their lives in place. The thought that she was not in such a precarious position should make a difference to how she felt, but it did not.

However hard she tried she could not shake the fear of what might happen. If she had no job her house would have to go, her life would be destroyed. Found guilty of abusing a child she would be ostracised by society, no one would have anything to do with her, even her friends would abandon her. Sweat broke out under her arms. Her heart banged loudly.

"Stop it," she said out loud. "They might have decided not to follow it up. It's been weeks since I heard so it's going to be all right. But not for you, you bugger." She poured a cascade of salt onto a slug and imagined it was Norman who was shrivelling and dying beneath her gaze.

The tiny moment of triumph was replaced by emptiness. If only there were someone she could turn to, someone to look after her and tell her that all she had to do was hold on and this nightmare would pass. If only Poppy was home.

"Mum," she'd say, "Mum, it's all a load of pants."

As she came back into the house the phone rang. Praying it might be her daughter, that by thinking of her she'd made the call happen, she snatched it up.

"It's bad news, I'm afraid," her solicitor came straight to the point. "The CPS have decided to prosecute."

"What?" The blood was pounding in her head.

"I've made you an appointment for two this afternoon. Is that okay?"

PARKING IN THE centre of the city was impossible. The sun shone bright and warm and Liz decided to walk. On Black Boy Hill people sat under parasols in pavement cafés drinking coffee and chatting. Everything was as it should be, except that she was caught in some sort of bubble. It muffled sound, hazed colour, so that she was only vaguely aware of the stream of traffic crawling down the hill towards the Centre. She saw, but did not quite register, the people strolling in front of her, the antique shops where she liked to browse, the restaurant with the steel iguana clinging to the railing, the wide trees casting their dappled shade over the passers-by.

She continued past the groups of students sunning themselves on the steps of the university refectory, down Park Street and along College Green. Crossing the Centre she was about to step out into the road when the lights changed.

"Not now, my lover." An old man with the strong Bristol drawl grabbed her arm. "You're to wait for the green man." A wave of buses and cars swept past. Caught under those wheels her troubles would be over.

"No. That's giving in. Don't let the buggers get you down." She was unaware that she had spoken aloud.

"That's right." The old man smiled, winked at her, and nodded.

The offices of Nichols, Partridge and Fenn were housed in a tall narrow building squeezed in between two blocks of shops. The reception area was dark and uninviting, like a seedy dentist's waiting room. There were brown plastic chairs, a side table piled with magazines, and a display of silk flowers on the desk. Liz waited as the receptionist phoned up to announce her arrival.

Jane Langdon was small and her rather square shape was emphasised by her grey suit and pale pink shirt. Her face was broad and an Alice band held back her light-brown hair. There were pearl studs in her ears and a single pearl on a gold chain around her neck. She led Liz up a narrow dark staircase, opened a door and they stepped into an airy open space where sunlight streamed in through wide widows. A spider plant stood on Jane's desk beside the computer and a photograph of a man with dark framed glasses looking serious and another of two blonde children in stripy T-shirts sitting on their bikes and grinning cheekily at the camera.

"I know this is very difficult for you, but we deal with this sort of thing all the time." Jane opened a file.

"False accusations you mean." Liz's throat was dry and she would have liked to ask for a drink of water but her usual assertiveness had drained away.

Jane nodded briskly. "We're seeing a lot more of them than ever before. It's something to do with the current climate and the general concern about any sort of child abuse. The papers have made a lot of it, of course, and it's true that too many vulnerable children have slipped through the net, so every accusation, even if there is no substance to it, has to be taken very seriously. Try not to worry. What we need to do first is to look at what we have and see the best way of proceeding. I have the details here." She glanced at the page. "Apparently Samantha Boyd says that on the eleventh of April you head-butted her."

"I did what?" Liz's helplessness was swept away on a wave of outrage.

Jane smiled. "I agree that it appears rather unlikely but believe me we've heard worse. Now is there anything that might have led her to accuse you of that?"

"I'm... I don't..." Liz spluttered. "I'm gobsmacked. That's the only way of putting it. I have never, ever in the whole of my career hit a child. As for head-butting, that's what football hooligans do. I mean this is ridiculous, outrageous." A shudder crawled up her back. "Anyone who knows me knows I would never do such a thing. So why has it come to this?"

Jane ignored her question. Perhaps she knew the answer, perhaps it was not relevant. "We'll get statements from your colleagues, which will prove your good character, etcetera. Unfortunately, Samantha has witnesses who are prepared to swear that you did in fact head-butt her."

"Don't tell me. Amy Andrews and Leanne Thompson."
"Friends of hers?"
"Blood sisters, bosom buddies, best mates."
"Would you say that you had issues with them?"
"No more than with any of the rest of 10C. They're a difficult class. There are all sorts of problems with literacy and they're not used to having to work. Up until now most of them have got away with doing very little. Well it's not like that with me. I make my pupils work."
"So there were clashes?"
"Yes. But never anything physical. Believe me I rarely even raised my voice. I always think that when I've had to shout at a class I've failed but I have to admit that I did occasionally give them the sharp end of my tongue."
"And this would set them against you?"
Liz stopped to think. "Yes. I suppose it might. It wasn't what I intended, it was meant to challenge not insult them."
"Did you say something that she would consider offensive to Samantha Boyd?"
Liz shook her head. "I gave her a few detentions but I never said anything derogatory. I wouldn't do that to a pupil who wasn't very able. Keeping her in at break or lunch time was more of a coaching session than a punishment. It was meant to help her with her coursework."
"What about the other two?"
"I confiscated Leanne Thompson's make-up on numerous occasions. Her idea of an English lesson was to sit there reapplying eye liner and touching up her lip gloss."
"Amy Andrews?"
Liz's stomach twisted as she saw Amy's sharp pinched face, her way of looking sideways from under her lashes, like a viper about to spit her venom. "She was moved from Veronica Hartington's class to mine. She was causing trouble there and she needed a firmer

hand."

"I'm assuming that she resented the move."

"Yes. She was going down a group and in my class she had less opportunity to misbehave. Look, all this is ridiculous. It's kids playing games. None of it is real. Is there no way of stopping it?"

"Not now the process has started. If we are unlucky the Crown Prosecution Service will bring it to court." Liz shut her eyes. "That is only if we are very unlucky. From what you are telling me there may well be an argument that these girls are trying to get back at you. If that's the case..."

"It is," Liz interrupted. "It's the only explanation."

"In that case the CPS will throw it out and you will be able to go back to work and resume your career without a stain on your character."

"Then why has it gone so far?"

"The Head was following procedures. Once the girl said she had been attacked there are certain things he has to do."

"Why didn't he talk to me? Why didn't he get my side of the story?"

Jane looked through her papers. She selected a sheet of A4 and scanned it briefly. "According to his report you have a history of confrontation and the Head does not give much credence to your opinions."

"He's a wanker!" The words came out before she could stop them. To her relief Jane carried on as if she had not spoken.

"In his report to the police there is some suggestion that you have a tendency to overreact," she said tactfully.

"If you saw some of the things that are going on there you'd over react," Liz said bitterly. "I have made it clear I'm in favour of better discipline. I make my point in meetings and I make suggestions about how the system might be improved. That doesn't mean I beat up my pupils."

"You're saying that there has been some previous conflict between yourself and the Head?"

"Not exactly. I would say we had professional differences of opinion. He wants to run his school in one way. I would do it another. But we're adults. We ought to be able to disagree on matters of principle. It's not as if I ever refuse to carry out any reasonable request. Oh God, this is crazy. I've done nothing and I'm going to be put on trial."

"It's hard but try not to let it get to you. It's rare on this sort of evidence that these cases come to court."

"You can't say for sure that will happen."

Jane half smiled and shook her head. "It would be very unprofessional of me to give an opinion at this stage."

NINETEEN

LIZ STUMBLED OUT of the solicitor's into the afternoon. The sun still shone, the Centre was full of people and cars. The river glittered and the traffic swept up Park Street. Everything was as she had left it. The interview had lasted only half an hour but she felt as if she had been in that office for at least a century. Her head throbbed and she needed a coffee but when she reached the cafe she could not bring herself to go through the door. She had the crazy feeling that if she went inside everyone would know where she had been and what she was accused of doing.

Don't do this. Don't give in. Don't let them drag you down. She put her hand on the glass, she pushed. She stepped inside, found a table, gave her order, and made herself drink.

How was she going to prove her innocence? It was the girls' word against hers; there were no other witnesses. If 10C were interviewed, she was sure they would all confirm Samantha's story. Except perhaps Laura Harris, but who would believe one rather sad, overweight child when Amy Andrews was shouting about pupils' rights and threatening to phone Child Line?

If that were not enough she was also battling the Head. Surely as a member of his staff he should have given her his support? Deep down she knew that Norman Johnson had never liked her and he would use this as the perfect opportunity to rid himself of a teacher who had always questioned his methods. She was old fashioned, she liked formality and discipline. In her book teachers had rights, as did the pupils, and there were some things which were not negotiable.

Earlier on in the year she had come across Gemma Charles crying in the toilets. Gemma was a newly qualified teacher, doing her probationary year. She was young and pretty but not very effective. In one of her classes she was being bullied by a gang of feral girls. She was on the way to the Staff Room for break when Barry Sutcliff, a Year 11 boy, had cornered her in the corridor, pressed her against the wall and fondled her breasts. Too shocked to scream, Gemma had tried to push him away while the rest of his gang chanted, "Give it her Barry."

Liz had sent them on their way, put her arm around Gemma and let her cry until she could cry no more and taken her to the Head. Norman had looked up from his desk obviously irritated at having to deal with two emotional women.

Gemma was incapable of speech and it was Liz who had explained what had happened and demanded that Barry and his gang were excluded immediately. At which point Norman had started fluffing and flannelling about how nothing could be proved, how the boys, and the by now totally distraught Gemma, would have to write statements before he could take action. The swift retribution that Liz had demanded turned into a written apology and a detention. Gemma went off sick and had still not returned.

I showed up his inadequacy, I tried to make him act. That's what he doesn't like about me and this is his revenge. He wants to get rid of me; he wants to ruin me. That's why he has not supported me. This business with Sam was what he was waiting for.

Norman had lied and would continue to lie about her. As the head teacher, he was more likely to be believed than a mere member of his staff. She was going to have to fight to clear her name, to get back her reputation, because without it she was nothing. Liz paid her bill and pushed back her chair.

She started up Park Street but the hill was steep and as the tension drained out of her she began to wish that she'd risked the horrors of city centre parking and had brought the car. The muscles at the back of her legs ached and she was suddenly too weary to walk the rest of the way home. A bus toiled up the slope and pulled into the stop. Liz got on. She paid her fare and sat down. It was not until the driver took the left fork at the top of the Downs that she realised that far from going home she was on her way to Bernie's.

What am I doing here? Is this some sort of displacement therapy? Is solving Bernie's problems going to take my mind off my own? she thought as she rang the doorbell. The sun beat down on her head; she was hot and sticky and longed for the coolness of her own kitchen and a glass of iced water. It didn't look as if Bernie was in. Liz rang the bell again and was about to leave when the door opened.

"I suppose you had better come in." Bernie was in her dressing gown. Her eyes were rimmed with red, her skin puffy. Her breath stale. Liz was glad to see that the boys were at school, the dog sunning himself on the patio. She followed Bernie into the conservatory where they sat among the wilting plants. Liz tried to get Bernie to talk but all her questions were answered with single words. A hot stuffy silence pressed in on them and Liz was grateful when her mobile rang.

"How's things?" Elsa's voice was bright and bubbly but there was a brittle edge to it, which Liz was too miserable to react to.

"Been better," Liz replied. "I'm at Bernie's."

"It's not that dog again?" Elsa was determined to remain cheerful.

"No," Liz said flatly. She looked across at Bernie who had sunk back into herself. "It's difficult to talk right now."

"It's that bad is it? Shall I come over?"

"Don't bother," Liz began. "I was just leaving anyway. It's been a pig of a day."

"Why? What's happened?"

"I've been to see the solicitor." Liz no longer able to hold back poured out the events of the afternoon.

"I don't believe what you're telling me," Elsa said. "You head-butting someone? It's an outrage. A slander. You should write to your MP. When this is over you should sue. Yes, that's what you do. Sue that moron Norman Johnson for mental cruelty. Screw him for every penny you can get. Then you can retire and never ever have to work again." Elsa rang off triumphantly leaving Liz feeling worse than she had before.

It had been a mistake to come. She could do nothing for her friend and her friend could do nothing for her, while Elsa's fury and outrage only served to irritate her.

When she had finally dragged herself home it was too early to go to bed and even if she did she wouldn't sleep. To pass the time she checked her e-mails. There was one from Poppy.

Dear Mum, Tour's going fine. Have sneaked into the school's IT room to send this. The mean bastards won't give us free internet access even though they charge an arm and leg to educate their little darlings. The kids actually are OK. It's some of the staff, who act as if they are God's gift to education. Personally I suspect they are out here cos no one would give them a job in the UK!! How's things with you?

Liz stared at the screen. Her daughter was thousands of miles away. She was having a great time. She typed:

Darling Poppy, Everything's fine.

What else could she say?

TWENTY

"MRS McKENDRICK? ELIZABETH Mary?" the policewoman glanced down at her clipboard.

"Yes." Liz drew in her breath. The air felt thin, her head spun.

"You are charged with assault on the person of Samantha Boyd at..."

She heard nothing more. She simply blanked the words out of her brain. She had known this was coming. The formal charge. She had been waiting for the moment, for the knock on the front door, and now it was here crazily all she could think about was whether any of the neighbours were watching.

The policewoman stopped. She waited. Liz glanced over her shoulder. Thankfully the street appeared to be empty. Even homeless Iris was somewhere else. The policewoman cleared her throat. She was still waiting. What did she want her to do to?

"Thank you," Liz said at last and shut the door.

Thank you. I said "thank you". What am I doing? I must be going mad. I've just been charged with a crime I didn't commit and all I could say was "thank you."

She sat down on the bottom step and covered her head with her arms.

THE CAR DREW up outside the house. In the stale fug of her bedroom Bernie heard the key in the lock, her eldest son's voice calling her, and forced herself out of bed. She could not face Aidan seeing her in this state.

With shaking hands she pulled on her dressing gown and went slowly down the stairs.

"Mum, are you ill?" He started towards her.

"I'm okay. I was having a lie down. I'm not sleeping very well." She stroked his cheek and kissed him quickly. She didn't want to get too close. Her skin was sticky and unclean and if he touched her she'd cry and a good mother didn't cry in front of her children.

"Come on through. I'll make us a cup of tea." Bernie moved automatically around the kitchen, her bare feet slapping on the tiled floor. Her toenails were thick and yellow, her thighs shook like jelly. She poured milk from the carton into two cups. There were brown spots on her hands. Her breasts hung loose and empty against her chest.

"No sugar," Aidan reminded her and Bernie stopped, spoon poised in mid-air. "Look Mum, I've come to say if you and the boys need anything you can rely on me. I'm doing well now and with this promotion, money's going to be okay. He has sorted something out for you hasn't he?"

"I don't know." Bernie tried to remember if money had entered her discussions with Trev. She was still drawing on the joint account so she supposed that for the time being there was no problem. But what was she going to do in the future?

"What I can't understand is why he went and did it. Another woman at his age." Aidan's face wrinkled in disgust. "You do know, Mum, don't you, that I'm never going to speak to him again."

"He's your dad," Bernie protested weakly. She should try harder to convince Aidan not to cut himself off completely from his father but she hadn't the energy or, if she was being totally honest, the will.

"Not any more he isn't and if he thinks I'll have anything to do with her, then he can forget it." Aidan slammed his mug down on the table; his face set.

Oh Trev, Bernie thought. *What have you done? You've lost the respect of your son. The one you always had a down on. The one who was too goody-goody for your taste. You thought he was a bit of a wimp and look at him now. He's the grown up, the mature one with a job and a house. He's going places; making a success of his life while you're off with your bit on the side.*

It was odd but she found herself feeling sorry for Trev, as if he were one of her boys and not her husband.

"I think you should get yourself a solicitor. Get all the legal side sorted out. Make sure you get everything you're entitled to. It's especially important at your time of life. There's Dad's pension to consider and the house. To be honest, Mum, if we can play this right you'll be fine. I've got a good guy: he did the conveyancing on the house for me. Do you want me to set up an appointment for you?"

No, Bernie screamed in her head. *I don't want you to do anything. I don't want anyone to do anything. All I want is Trev to come back and everything to be like it was before.*

"Not yet. Give me a bit of time," she said.

"That's right, Mum." Aidan smiled. He got up and kissed her on the top of her head in an unconscious echo of his father. "You'll cope. You'll be all right. You always are."

As her son's car turned out of the cul-de-sac, Bernie put her head on her arms and wept. Why did she always have to cope? How could he think she was going to be all right? Couldn't he see how she was feeling? Old, unwanted, useless, abandoned. But no, she was a mum; she would cope. She could even feel pity for the husband who had walked out on her and their kids without a backward glance. It wasn't fair. She needed someone too, someone to take care of her. She raised her head and howled, "What about me?"

Terrified, Woody slunk out into the laundry, lay down

in his basket and covered his eyes with his paws.

LIZ WAS CLEANING. She had hoovered the house and was in the kitchen polishing cupboard doors. They were solid pine; she'd had the kitchen re-fitted when she'd had a promotion and now she knelt in front of the sink and rubbed in the wax until her arms ached. Physical work concentrated her mind, stopped her thoughts from going round and round until her head ached, and she wanted to shout and scream and take a knife from the drawer and plunge it deep in the nearest object.

"I tried ringing the door bell but you weren't answering." Elsa appeared at the back door. She was wearing flat shoes and causal trousers. "I walked over," she announced proudly and waited for the praise, which Liz couldn't bring herself to give. After all, what was so impressive about walking around the corner and into the next street?

"Your phone is off." Elsa was getting cross. "You know you shouldn't do that Liz. Someone may need to get in touch with you urgently."

"Poppy e-mails me." Liz stood up. "As for everything else, I don't think I really care."

"You have to. I've got us another booking."

"I thought that was all over."

"No." Elsa sounded offended. "I had a call from Moira. Remember she was at Val's? She wants dinner for six on Saturday, so I thought Bernie could do one of her roasts." She sat down at the table and took out a pad and a pen, which she held expectantly over the paper while looking up at Liz as if to say "aren't I the efficient business woman".

"Bernie can't. I don't think she's capable of boiling an egg at the moment," Liz said.

"Oh Liz, she has to be. We can't let it all go."

"Face it Elsa." Liz wiped her hands on her skirt, leaving gobs of lavender wax polish on the fine cotton material. "It's not working. We haven't had the bookings. People don't seem to want what we're offering."

"That's only because I should have put more effort into it. I need to get out there more, see a few people, ring round a few friends," Elsa said desperately. "It's a good idea, Liz, and we're going to make a go of it. We have to. At least," she begged, "let's do this one for Moira. You never know where it might lead."

"Why not?" Liz heaved a sigh. "It will give me something to do before they haul me off to prison."

"That won't happen. It can't happen. It's too ridiculous. You're going to be all right. You have to believe it. We both have to believe it," she said trying to convince herself. There was a pause, then: "If the worst comes to the worst I'll sell my soul to the devil."

"Is it that bad?" Liz asked. Elsa nodded. It was obvious that she could not trust herself to speak.

"If you need some money I can lend you some," Liz offered.

"No." Elsa jumped back as if she had been shot.

"Why not? I'm okay at the moment. I'm still being paid."

"You must never borrow from friends. My mother always said that and she was right. Besides, I'm not sure if any of my friends would have enough to bail me out. There's the penthouse, which Lionel borrowed money on, and the credit cards. No, if you're going to jail then I'm out on the streets."

"The Gucci bag lady."

"Quite." Elsa giggled. "Do you think I can fit my duvet into the Louis Vuitton luggage? I could be like on *Desert Island Discs* when they ask what you'd take to the island. With a duvet and suitcase or two I could construct a shelter under the by-pass."

"I'll join you when they let me out of prison."

"Bernie can bring us hot soup and bacon rolls."

The image of the two of them, Liz in her floaty skirts

and velvet jackets, her beads and her earrings, and Elsa in her designer clothes and handmade shoes, sitting on the pavement together was too much. The laughter bubbled up in Liz's throat. She caught Elsa's eye and they began to laugh.

TWENTY-ONE

WHEN ELSA GOT home the bills were still waiting. She stared uncomprehendingly at the final demand. If she had not settled in seven days' time the electricity company was threatening to cut her off. She was to inform the office, or Social Security, if there was any reason why she was unable to pay.

Elsa traced the words with her finger. She ran over the shapes again and again and they still made no sense. There could not be a time when there would be no light or heat in the apartment. She wandered over to the picture windows and looked out on the lighted windows of houses, the dark expanse of the Downs, and headlights of the cars and buses moving along White Ladies Road. How would she manage? She had plenty of candles left and she could boil a kettle on the stove, which luckily was gas. If she needed a shower she could go to Liz or Bernie's. She could even volunteer to bathe the dog again and if she got wet and dirty she would be entitled to have her clothes washed and dried.

The image of herself and Liz as two wizened bag ladies squatting under the arches of the flyover came into her mind. But this time there was no laughter. Liz could not bail her out and Bernie was permanently broke, and James, she had to admit it, had little or no money.

Who else could she turn to? She had friends, plenty of friends. For years she had a very active social life. There were Val and Bob and Moira and Ian but even as she named them she knew that these were people she could never confide in. There were only Liz and Bernie. That was why she had invited them to her final tea party at The Grand.

Unless she could think of something she would have to leave the flat she had lived in for nearly thirty years. Where could she go? Even if she had the money how was she going to find somewhere to live? She had never done anything like that in her life. Marrying Lionel straight from home, she had never rented or bought property; her darling ex had looked after the practical things in life for her.

Less than six months ago she'd thought she would be in the apartment for the rest of her life. She looked around the living room. In contrast to the summer darkness the walls glowed with a warm peach colour, the carpet was white, the sofas deep and lavishly cushioned. Two antique side tables were filled with photographs. A Hockney drawing hung above the marble fireplace. Silver candlesticks stood on the mantelpiece. She owned all these expensive things and yet she could not pay her bills.

Elsa stroked the ivory netsuke clustered under the shade of the table lamp, fingered the floor length velvet curtains, silk cushions and the cashmere throw that lay over the arm of an easy chair. Over the years she had spent a fortune on this flat. There had to be a way of recouping that money.

She would sell some of the furniture. The Davenport itself was worth a thousand or so, and then there were the pictures. Lionel always said she had a good eye. She would find some reputable dealer and get a valuation but this could not happen immediately, and if the electricity bill was not paid she would be cut off.

Elsa's stomach knotted. This kind of thing happened to families on council estates, not to someone like her. Nervously she twisted the rings on her fingers. They too would have to go. Her engagement ring, which had cost so much, was made up of three large sapphires set with diamonds; surely she would get a few thousand for it. The problem was how? The thought of going to her regular jewellers filled her with horror. She was a respected customer who had been able to buy whatever she wanted without asking the price. To offer something for sale would be too humiliating. That long nosed manager would sense immediately that she was only doing it because she was desperate and needed the money. There had to be another way.

The next morning she woke early. She waited until those neighbours who had not yet amassed sufficient capital to retire had gone to work, then slipped out of the apartment and took the lift to the ground floor. Wearing flat shoes, trousers and a jacket, she put on her sun glasses and without looking round hurried to the bus stop.

When the number 34 stopped in front of her she was not quite sure what she should do but as she dithered a young woman stepped in front of her and slipped the bus fare into the machine. "Park Street," she announced, was given a ticket and made her way down the bus.

"Are you coming or what?" the bus driver shouted. Elsa scrambled on board. She glanced around fearfully in case anyone she knew might have seen her. She paid her fare and the bus lurched forwards leaving her to grab hold of a bar to steady herself. As the bus slid into the flow of traffic she stumbled to a seat and sat down with her knees pressed together clutching her handbag.

People got on and off. Elsa watched them anxiously. How did the bus stop when they wanted it to? What did they do? She peered at a couple of students as they clattered down the stairs. There seemed to be a bell attached to one of the poles. Elsa heaved a sigh of relief. She knew about ringing the bell from when she used to take the number 42 to school on the days neither parent was available to take her in the car. Her next worry was when she should ring it. Too soon and the bus would stop in the wrong place, too late and she would have to walk back. Luckily as they neared the Centre there were so many people ready to get off that all she had to do was follow the other passengers.

The ring was heavy on her finger as she made her way along the crowded pavements and slipped into a narrow street at the side of St. Nicholas' Market. Three golden balls hung above the doorway of Wendell and Black. The windows were half covered by thick wire mesh and Elsa had to squint to read the price tags on the trays of dusty looking rings and thick gold chains as she tried to work out what she might get for the ring that Lionel gave her all those years ago. He had been so pleased, so grateful when she agreed to marry him. Now she knew it had been to give him the veneer of respectability he craved; then, she had thought it was because he loved her so much, couldn't live without her.

An electric bell buzzed as Elsa stepped inside.

"How can I help you?" asked the man behind the counter. What was she supposed to say? Elsa couldn't think. More than anything she wanted to turn round and run out of the shop. Only the image of that final demand stopped her.

"I need some money," she said at last.

"What do you have as collateral?"

Elsa slipped the ring from her finger and handed it over. The man took out a jeweller's loupe and examined it.

"It's worth a lot of money," Elsa prompted. Surely he could see what a highly desirable piece it was. She searched his face anxiously but he was totally focused on the ring. How much longer was it going to take?

"The quality of the stones is good," he said finally. "It is set in platinum. White gold is more fashionable but platinum is more durable."

"Is that good?" Elsa tried. There was no reply and she concentrated all her effort into willing him to make her a good offer.

"I can advance you five hundred," was his verdict.

"Five hundred! But it's worth..."

"Five hundred," he repeated.

Elsa met his implacable gaze and realised there would be no negotiation. It would have to do. At least it would stave off the electricity company for a while.

"Thank you," Elsa breathed. The broker went on about interest and when and how she could redeem her ring but she did not listen. The ring was gone and she would never see it again because, failing one of Sister Mary Catherine's miracles, she would never have the money to get it back.

In the meantime she would still be able to boil a kettle and keep herself clean. Elsa folded the notes carefully in to her purse and hurried back to the Centre. Where was she supposed to catch her bus? She had no idea where to go or what to do. Choosing a stop at random she tried to make sense of the numbers and routes. As she screwed up her eyes and peered at the board a man in a torn overcoat lurched towards her. His eyes were glazed, his hair matted and greasy and he stank of stale booze and urine. Elsa clutched her bag, holding it against her chest as she backed away. The man leaned closer, he opened his mouth. His teeth were black, his breath rancid. He was muttering wildly.

"Help me!" Elsa gasped. No one stopped. No one heard. A group of young men, jostling each other and shouting insults, sauntered round the corner. The homeless man moved away. Elsa cowered against the side of the bus shelter. The buckle of her bag bit into her breasts as she pressed it closer. One of the lads dipped towards her. She screamed and he laughed coarsely. He was going to mug her, snatch her bag, rape her. Elsa's head spun. There was a blanket of darkness in front of her eyes. A terrible thundering in her ears.

"Stupid cow. Stupid fucking cow," he jeered, then hawked and spat a green gob of phlegm that only just missed her feet, turned and was gone loping after the others, leaving Elsa quivering with fear.

She was drenched with sweat. Her legs were so weak she could hardly stand but her money was safe. Staggering like a drunk she stepped out into the road and flagged down a taxi.

"Downs View Court," she breathed as she sunk back into the seat.

TWENTY-TWO

"YOU CAN GO. The detention's over. You've done your time."

Joe shoved his chair hard into the table behind him and sauntered out of the classroom his hands in his pockets, deliberately ignoring stupid Mr Potts who had kept him in for not doing his homework.

The corridors were empty, chairs stacked on tables, classrooms unlocked to let in the cleaners. Passing room E2 he saw the handbag on the desk. Dozy Mrs Summerville hadn't even bothered to shut it properly. Sticking out of the side pocket was a purse. He stopped. Part of him hoped that the cleaner would come while another part wondered if he could get away with it. Who was going to know? All he had to do was nip in quick, take what he wanted and go. He glanced over his shoulder. There was no one about. He slid into the room, his body light with excitement, his fingers tingling as he slipped his hand into the bag.

"Joseph Driscoll what on earth do you think you are doing?"

"Nothing," the answer was automatic.

"What do you mean, 'nothing'? You've taken money out of my bag. I saw you. How dare you rummage in my own private things?" Mrs Summerville's voice rose dangerously.

"You shouldn't have left it there." Joe did not know where the words were coming from. He was carried away by his own daring.

"You're coming with me. I'm taking you to see Mr Jones. Right now."

"Don't think so." He was going to get away with it. If he shouldered past no teacher would dare stop him.

"Anything wrong, Mrs Summerville?" The Deputy Head was standing in the doorway.

"Yes." She paused. "He had his hand in my bag. He was going to take my purse."

"Is this true?"

Joe could have lied but he didn't think he would be believed. He nodded.

"This is a very serious offence," Mr Jones said. "It merits an automatic exclusion." Joe's heart plummeted. "But since this is the first time you've done anything like this I'm going to give you another chance. Instead of exclusion you'll be in Remove for three days. I will of course be contacting your parents."

"No." Joe shook his head. Mr Jones looked at him sharply.

"Is there any reason why I shouldn't?"

"No Sir," Joe lied quickly. No one must know that his dad had left and his mum spent all her time in bed. Things might get back to normal sometime soon but if everyone knew then it might never get right again. He made his escape and hurried home.

"If you see a letter from school give it to me," he told Pat.

"What if it's for Mum?" Pat said.

"Especially if it's for Mum. She's not to see it. It'll only upset her. Make her worse. You don't want that do you?" Joe grabbed Pat's arm and leaned over into his face.

"No. Let go." Pat wriggled out of his grasp. "I won't say anything. I promise. Darren says you're in Remove."

"So what?"

"They won't let you out until Mum comes up to school."

Joe shrugged. It was true but he had three days to work out a solution to that problem.

DEAR MUM.

Liz opened her e-mails and her heart leaped.

Tour over at end of month. It's been great. I've learned a lot and had loads of fun. Group of us are staying over for the summer, found a really great beach and cheap place to stay. Could be some teaching at the school for posh kids in September. If no jobs coming up in UK think I might go for that and get a bit more sun. Hope all well with you,

Lots of love. Poppy.

"She's not coming home." Liz stroked Timbo's ears "It's going to be you and me, cat. Do you think Elsa could hide a file in your fur and bring you to visit when I'm locked up in jail?"

THE CAVENDISH GALLERY was in an exclusive cul-de-sac in Clifton Village. It was featuring an exhibition of Erica's sculptures. Solid, sensual pieces of polished marble and granite, they cried out to be touched and stroked.

"Elsa are you browsing or are you buying?" Malcolm fussed up to her. She glanced at Erica's voluptuous statues of naked women holding children.

"Looking," she said.

"Well, feel free. Both to look and to buy." Malcolm in bow tie, pink shirt and cream slacks, took off his glasses and polished them vigorously with a silk handkerchief. "This is our slack time. In July everyone's away on holiday. The place is dead, quite dead. Our social life has ground completely to a halt. I was only saying to Erica the other day, we may as well take a break ourselves. She fancies Greece. I say it's too hot, but there you are. You doing anything?"

"No. I don't think so." *Go anywhere? I wish I had*

enough money to take a taxi.

"Holiday time can't be much doing for your business either," Malcolm probed.

"No, like you said, it's a dead time." Elsa walked out of the gallery leaving a surprised Malcolm staring after her. Another connection had proved useless. No more dinner parties. Liz was right: her brilliant idea had not worked. She had to find something else to do. But how?

THE POSTMAN SHOVED the letters through the letter box and retreated. The flap shut seconds before a wild brown dog flung itself at the door.

"Woody, give." Joe raced down the stairs. He wrestled the letter from the dog's mouth. It was the one he had been waiting for.

"Joe," Bernie's voice floated down from the bedroom. "Is everything all right?"

"Yes Mum. Fine."

"Is that it?" Pat asked. Joe nodded. "What you going to do then? You'll have to tell her."

"No prob. It's sorted." Joe went into his bedroom and shut the door firmly behind him. "Aidan." Joe cupped his hand over his mobile even though no one could hear him.

"Are you all right?" his big brother asked.

"Yeah."

"How's Mum?"

"Okay. Well she's got one of her migraines."

"But she's all right?" Aidan persisted.

"Yeah no probs. Trouble is..." Joe hesitated; this was the tricky part of his plan. "I need someone to get me out of Remove. Mum can't come and Dad, well you know."

"I know," Aidan said grimly. "He's too busy with that..." his voice curdled with disgust and he left the rest unsaid.

"Will you do it? I've got the letter here. It says

tomorrow half eight. If you come then they'll let me out and I can go straight back into lessons." Which was shite and boring but not as boring as spending the time sitting in silence filling out pointless work sheets.

"I'll be there," Aidan said. "But you are going to owe me."

"Yeah," Joe mouthed, giving a thumbs up. He'd relied on big bro's sense of responsibility and caring and it had worked perfectly.

"Sorted," he told Pat who'd been waiting outside his room. The kid looked pale with great purple shadows under his eyes but there was nothing he could do about that. Pat needed his mum but Mum was barricaded behind her bedroom door and not likely to be coming out any time soon.

"I'm going out." Joe couldn't stand those worried eyes any longer. Now that he was going to be released from Remove there were things to sort with his mates.

"Me too," Pat said quickly.

"Yeah, good." Joe was relieved he wasn't going to hang around being miserable. "See you," he added, throwing a mock punch before hurrying down the stairs away from the airless aching atmosphere of home.

"HI." CHRIS'S VOICE floated through the house. "Is anyone in?"

Bernie waited for one of his brothers to reply. There was a bark from Woody, then silence.

"Mum?" Was Chris coming upstairs? She couldn't let him see her like this, wearing a grubby nightie, her hair unwashed, smelling of sweat and despair.

"Just a minute, I'm coming down." Bernie heaved herself out of bed, pulled on a pair of loose trousers, frowning as she had to tighten the drawstring, then a large all encompassing T-shirt. She slicked her hair into a scrunchie and slid her feet into a pair of sandals.

In the kitchen her second son had already opened

the fridge and helped himself to a beer. Taller and slimmer than Aidan, Chis was easily the best looking of her children. Her Irish boy: with his white skin, dark curls and sparkling blue eyes, he had the charm and magic of his Celtic ancestors.

"Mamma Mia." He swept her into his arms. "Beautiful as ever."

"Get away," she chided but her heart leapt.

"It's true. To me you will always be the most beautiful woman in the world."

"What about," Bernie hesitated unable for a moment to recall the name of the latest girlfriend.

"Laura? Laura is lovely, but she's not you."

"You've the charm of the devil."

"And who did I get it from?" She smiled, she couldn't help it. "So you're all right then," he said taking a swig from the bottle.

She nodded; she smiled. She listened as he told her about his latest project then, beer finished, a sandwich eaten, he kissed her and left. When the door closed behind him she stood in the middle of the kitchen unable to move. He had said nothing about Trev, nothing about her being left alone with his brothers. It was as if nothing had changed, nothing happened.

"What am I?" Bernie whispered to herself as she plodded up the stairs to bed. "Am I invisible? Am I mum and no one else?" In spite of the bright sunshine pouring through grimy unwashed windows she crawled under the duvet and pulled it over her head.

TWENTY-THREE

"LIZ." JILLY'S VOICE was bright and cheerful. "It's been ages. Sorry I haven't phoned before but you know how it is. First there are the SATS then the coursework to send off and then the GCSEs. We've been run off our feet in the department and the supply teachers the agency sent have been useless, totally useless." The shower of words poured over Liz's head. Like standing under a waterfall, there was a thundering thudding sound, but no meaning.

After a while she simply stopped listening. Nothing Jilly said could be of any relevance. It all belonged to a different world, a different time. No one except Jilly had bothered to phone her. Whether they were aware of it or not she had already been cast into the outer darkness by the rest of her colleagues. Thinking back over her career and how often people came and went without making any lasting impact, she was only vaguely surprised by how quickly she had ceased to matter. Was being a Head of Department all that defined her? If that was so, when she no longer had her work what was left?

IN THE NEWSAGENT'S shop Elsa bought a copy of the local newspaper because that was what people did when they needed a job. In the penthouse living room she poured a powerful gin and tonic and holding the paper at arm's length, in case it might contaminate her, she scanned the jobs vacant. She could work as a carer in an Old People's home, be a cashier in a supermarket, clean offices after hours.

Elsa took a large gulp of her gin. She would rather die than do any of these jobs. How could she face her neighbours, the lawyers and business people, all of them professionals, who lived in this block? Then she looked at the pay per hour. If this was all she got she would not be living in Downs View Court.

"I'll end up like Bernie in a miserable estate house and stacking shelves in a supermarket," she muttered. She flung the paper onto the floor and as it fell the pages floated free revealing a section she had previously missed. Elsa took a deep, deep breath. There was still hope. If she were brave enough...

She picked up the phone. Waiting for an answer she almost lost her nerve and put it down again. At last a broad Bristol voice came on the end of the line and Elsa stumbled into her prepared speech.

"Hullo. I was looking at your advert in the *Evening Post* and I was wondering if..."

"You were wondering if we needed any more girls. Well you're in luck there, my lover. We're always on the lookout for new talent. If you'd like to pop down to the office we'll get you going."

"Oh. I was hoping I could work from home."

The speaker chortled. "Once you're established we'll get you your own line but in the meantime our operatives work from here."

"I see," Elsa said doubtfully. This was not what she had envisaged.

"The hours are, as stated in our advert, open to negotiation. Flexitime is what most of our girls do so they can fit it round their kids and their husband. Some work nights." The voice laughed again. "Some do days, they do all sorts. Some of them are teachers or nurses and we have a lot of students. Anyone in fact who's got a sexy voice and needs a bit of money."

"It doesn't matter about age or what you look like or

anything." Elsa fiddled with her remaining rings.

"Goodness me, no. You can have a face like the back end of a bus – the punters won't know. All they get is the voice. And I can tell you now, girl, you've got the voice."

"And your office is where?"

"Glenmartin Street, round the back of those flats they built near where the Glen used to be. There's a small mews and we're shoved in between a couple of garages."

"That's just round the corner," Elsa exclaimed and instantly regretted what she had let slip.

"All the easier for you to get to work then, my lover. When will I be seeing you?"

"Would this afternoon suit you?"

"Anytime. Why don't you come round now? Melanie's off having a baby. She's due in the delivery ward any time now. We nearly had to have the ambulance to her here. She was in the middle of a call, breathing heavy as she does, and we thought she was working not going into labour. Luckily her bloke turned up before the waters broke. Lovely girl, Melanie; this is her fourth you know."

The thought that Melanie had produced four children and would not therefore be slim and svelte and firm fleshed gave Elsa enough impetus to get herself out of the apartment. It was odd how she had never noticed the line of garages in Glenmartin Street, but then she had never owned a car.

Elite Productions had a discreet notice by the door. Elsa pressed the buzzer, announced she had come about a job, and was let into the front office. The garage door had been boarded up, there was no window and the makeshift room was lit by a neon strip light. The only furniture was a plain wooden desk and chair and in one corner a built-in kitchen unit on which stood a kettle, microwave and a tray of mugs, while on the wall facing the entrance hung a huge poster of a curvaceous blonde wearing nothing but a thong, her legs spread out, her face turned upwards to the waterfall that streamed down a tropical cliff face.

A thin woman with very black hair, her face furrowed with deep lines, a cigarette hanging from her lips, looked up from her computer. "Pleased to meet you..." She paused enquiringly.

"Elsie," Elsa said quickly.

"I'm Dorothy. Lovely voice you've got Elsie, really turn them on, that will. Let me show you round and you can get an idea of how it all works. Then if you like you can get started right away. Rates are hourly, hours are flexible. In our line of work there is a lot of night time shifts but as I told you on the phone a lot of our girls prefer those."

"I'd rather work in the day," Elsa said.

"Whatever suits you. Husband?"

"I need my sleep." Elsa ignored the question. Dorothy laughed throatily and took a drag on her cigarette. "You don't smoke do you?" She wafted the smoke away from Elsa's face with her hand.

"No. It's not good for the skin."

"Quite right too. But it's too late for me. I've been smoking since my dad slipped me my first fag on my seventh birthday. Keeps me slim though, without it I'd be at the doughnuts and no mistake. Come on then, let me take you to your boudoir."

She led the way up the open tread staircase to the next floor and along a narrow dark corridor with a number of doors. She opened one and there was a cubby hole, rather like a polling booth, with a telephone and a typist's chair. The fabric cover was torn and there was a rather dubious stain on the seat. Beside the phone was a folder with laminated pages.

"There you are. Make yourself at home. Here's the script." Dorothy picked up the folder and handed it to Elsa. "It's just to get you started, of course. Our more experienced girls have their own patter but it's easier if you've got the words in front of you at first." She looked pointedly at the chair. "You did say you wanted to start straight away?"

"Yes of course. Sorry."

"Good. We're short staffed today. As I told you, Melanie's off for a bit. Give it a glance then. When the first call comes through I'll patch it through to you."

Elsa sat gingerly in the chair. She looked at the laminated page.

Hi big boy, what can I do for you today? My name's Ruby and I'm all yours. I'm lying here on my bed. She glanced involuntarily at the stained seat cover. *And all I've got on is a...* Elsa jumped as the phone rang. She stared at the script. The phone rang again. She picked it up. She swallowed, her throat dry. This was worse than waiting outside Reverend Mother's office to be told that once again she had broken some rule and this was not how girls from St. Cecilia's behaved.

"Hi," she breathed. "What can I do for you today?"

"Lick me." The voice was hoarse and urgent.

Lick. Elsa hastily scanned the script. There was no sign of any licking. "Where?" she managed at last.

"On me dick you stupid cunt."

"What? How dare you? How dare you speak to me like that?" Elsa flung down the phone, grabbed her bag and tore down the stairs. Without a word to Dorothy she stormed out into the sunlight.

Every pore of her skin crawled. It was as if she had been immersed in a vat of grease, drowning in other people's sweat, or worse. Her clothes and hair stank of cigarette smoke. Dragged down into dirt and depravity, her heart was beating so fast that her breath came in short sharp gasps. Her hands shook and waves of shivers passed through her body as she walked and walked and walked, out onto the Downs, where the clean air would blow away the stench that seemed to cling to every fibre of her being.

How could people do such things? How could some man ring her up in the middle of the day and want her to...? Elsa shuddered deeply. Such filth. It confirmed what she had always thought about sex. Although everyone said how wonderful it was, fundamentally it was no more than another basic function like going to the toilet or passing wind. Things which had to be done and which gave some people some sort of perverse pleasure but which were definitely not to be talked about by any civilized being.

Gradually the vision of the seedy cubby hole and the plastic covered obscenities began to recede and she could see the blue of the sky, the fresh green of the trees and the plump white clouds. A tall thin woman, her face gaunt and strained, her grey hair flying around her shoulders, strode across the grass. With her loose, flowing clothes and hunched shoulders she had a haunted air. She was heading towards the Sea Walls, the view point over the Gorge, and Elsa was struck by the sudden thought that the woman might be going there to throw herself over the edge. But what could she do? The woman was going too fast for her to catch up. She could try to call out, but what should she say? Should she ring someone? But whom? Nothing had happened yet, nothing might. Drawn by some mysterious force she hurried after her. The path curved around the edge of the cliff. The wind rose and caught her hair, the sun was in her eyes and she could no longer see the figure she had been following. A cloud passed over the sun. There was no one there. The cliff side was empty.

"Elsa." Was the voice in her head or was it the wind? She spun round and there was Liz sitting on a bench.

"Liz what are you doing here?"

"I could say the same of you."

"I needed some air. Oh Liz, it was awful." Elsa

launched into an account of her foray into the world of sex lines. "Then this woman with a fag dangling out of the corner of her mouth says, 'Let me take you to your boudoir'." She pronounced the word with a strong Bristol drawl. "Well naturally I think of pink satin and shiny sheets and she opens the door and there's this cupboard where I'm supposed to sit and do heavy breathing into this phone. Then this man on the other end of the line thinks I'm some pin-up blonde and..." Tears and giggles bubbled up in Elsa's throat, she hiccoughed and gulped, and Liz put an arm around her shoulders and they sat and looked out at the dark line of trees on the other side of the Gorge.

TWENTY-FOUR

BERNIE LAY IN bed. Somewhere beyond the curtains was a bright July day but there was no point in getting up. She had not washed for weeks. Her skin was greasy and sour, the sheets sticky with grime and sweat. Her hair was lank and she smelled of sweat and urine, like an old, old woman. A bluebottle buzzed against the window. Her lips were dry and cracked. There was a glass on her bedside table but the water was lukewarm and scummed with dust. Her body felt too heavy to get up and to refill it. She closed her eyes.

PAT WAS KICKING a football against the garage wall. Over and over and over again. When the car drew up Woody rushed to the side gate barking excitedly but Pat went on kicking the ball. Whoever had come to see them it would not be his dad. His dad would be there at the weekend. Next weekend. Pat flicked his hair out of his eyes. It was too long but there was no one to take him to have it cut. Joe was out somewhere and Tom and his mum had gone to Spain. It was the first week of the holidays and the summer stretched interminably in front of him.

"Get down you brute," Elsa murmured rubbing Woody's ears. She fussed over him as Liz came through the side gate and shut it firmly behind her. Thump. Pat lobbed another goal into his imaginary net.

"Is Mum upstairs?" Liz asked.

Pat nodded. He lined up the next ball and scored.

"BERNIE, IT STINKS in here," Elsa cried. She drew back the curtains and opened the windows as wide as they could go. Bernie's eyes burned and turning onto her side she pulled the duvet over her head.

"No you don't." Elsa leaned forward to grab the cover. Bernie drew her knees up to her chin. There was a strange whimpering sound coming from her throat, a sharp acrid smell rising from her unwashed limbs.

"Liz, what are we going to do?" Elsa's voice rose.

"Get her to the doctor," Liz said shortly. "Bernie, I'm going downstairs now to phone for an emergency appointment. Elsa is going to run the shower. You've got to get yourself up and dressed."

"I can't. Leave me alone. I want to die."

"Okay," Liz said. "That's fine but you're going to die clean. Elsa get the duvet." There was a sharp tug and it slid off the bed leaving Bernie exposed.

"Ugh." Elsa's hands flew to her face. "You're worse than that dog. And before you try to get away, remember I'm the one who gave him a bath so you'd better get yourself in that shower or I'll drag you there."

"No," Bernie wailed. Elsa clicked her tongue and went into the en-suite and ran the shower. In the garden, Pat thumped his football against the wall. Over and over and over again.

Bernie dragged herself across the bedroom towards the sound of rushing water. Elsa opened a bottle of shower gel and poured a little into the steam. The sharp clean scent of lemon filled the room.

"There's a clean towel on the radiator." Elsa stepped aside. "I'll wait for you outside."

The shower fell like a blessing on Bernie's head. Hot streams of water mingled with the tears that ran down her face. She cried silently, unstoppably. She did not know why, whether from grief or gratitude, that someone at last had shown they cared. That she had become visible again.

Dimly through the misted glass she was aware of Elsa moving around the bedroom.

She's making sure I'm safe, she thought and the tears dribbled to a halt as squiggle of warmth penetrated the dull greyness that had wrapped itself around her. Bernie wiped her nose on her arm and reached for her towel.

"I'll tell Liz you're ready," Elsa said as she came into the bedroom.

Bernie smoothed body lotion into skin dry as paper. Up her legs, along her thighs, over her belly and round her breasts, then over her shoulders and down her arms to her hands, where the gold ring on her wedding finger slid over the moistened knuckle. Underneath it the skin was a different texture, red and slightly rough as if it had shed a layer over the years. Hastily she pushed the ring back into place.

She brushed her teeth. Mint replaced the sour taste in her mouth; the rough feel of her teeth was gone. She felt lighter. The carpet was soft under her feet, the clothes slid over her skin, her underwear held her in. The soft slackness of her body was pulled into shape and she stood straighter. Walking down the stairs her feet were stiff and heavy; it was so long since she wore any shoes.

"Dr Thomas said to bring you in straight away." Liz ushered Bernie into the car, holding the door open and helping her into the front seat as if she were a fragile old lady. Elsa who always refused to be a back seat passenger gave way to her without a fuss.

Once in the surgery there was no waiting. Whatever Liz had said to the receptionist had given Bernie priority over the other patients.

"Ah, Mrs Driscoll." Dr Thomas did not even look up from his notes. "What can I do for you?"

Bernie looked at the thin balding man in front of her. She knew she had to say something. She cleared her throat. The words were there somewhere. Perhaps if she started they would come out of their own accord. "I can't get out of bed. I haven't been to work for weeks."

"Ah!" The problem solved, Dr Thomas looked up. "Depression. You are suffering a mild depressive interlude. There is nothing to concern yourself about. I see a lot of ladies like you, who have reached a certain age." His certainty, his refusal to meet her eye, infuriated Bernie.

"Yes," she shrieked. "The age our husbands leave us for slimmer younger women."

Dr Thomas did not comment; he offered no counselling; he asked no questions; he wrote out the prescription. Bernie snatched the piece of paper from his hand and walked out of the consulting room, oblivious to the curious glances of the other patients.

"He didn't even ask me what was going on. It wasn't me, Bernie Driscoll, in there. It was just some poor post-menopausal lump. He made me feel as if I didn't exist," she raged.

Burning with fury, her anger swept away the last of the greyness. After weeks of inactivity she could not keep still. She moved compulsively around Liz's living room picking up objects and books, fiddling with curtains and cushions.

"Bernie you're making me tired," Elsa complained.

"How dare he? How dare he think he knows what I am going through?"

"What are you going through?" Liz asked.

"I want to tear things and scream. I want them all to know how much I'm hurting. I didn't know how much till now. The whole of my inside feels as if it's being ripped apart. My breasts ache. I even..." She stopped.

"You even feel sexy," Liz supplied.

"That's enough. If you're going to have one of those conversations I'm making coffee." Elsa hurried out to the kitchen.

"I want him and I want to kill him," Bernie confessed.

“That’s good. You’ve got your energy back.”

“I want to him to pay for what he’s done to me and to the kids.”

“The best way to do that is to show how strong you are.”

“Oh God Liz, don’t you start. I am fed up with being told how good I am at coping. How whatever happens I will survive. Be there for the boys, prop them up. It makes me sick.”

“I didn’t mean that. I meant that you can make a life for yourself without Trev. You are your own person Bernie, not his wife, not the boys’ mum. You are you.”

“Mmm.” Bernie suddenly deflated. “That’s easy for you to say. You’ve always been like that. No one’s ever changed you. You’ve always been yourself. But me, well I’ve never even lived on my own. And Liz, it scares me.”

“You won’t be living on your own. You’ve got Joe and Pat.”

“They’ll grow up and leave.”

“There’s always the dog.” Elsa returned carrying a tray of freshly brewed coffee and chocolate biscuits. “In any case living on your own isn’t that bad. At least the toilet seat is always down and there’s none of those horrid sprinkles all around the loo.”

“Elsa!” Liz laughed, surprised by her friend’s sudden earthiness.

TWENTY-FIVE

BERNIE'S SUIT WAS too loose. The skirt hung from her hips and the jacket sagged on her shoulders. She stared at her reflection in the door of the supermarket. She had no idea she had lost so much weight.

"Hi, Bernie." Marie on magazines looked up from the till and waved. "Have you come to do your shopping?"

"No, I'm back to work."

"Did Greasy Gleeson take you back on then?"

"Not yet. I'm off to have a word." Marie frowned "There won't be a problem will there?" Bernie was suddenly afraid.

"It's the school holidays. It's all the young ones wanting temporary jobs. You'd best wait till September when they've all gone back to college."

Bernie laughed. "I can't wait that long. There's bills to pay and I could do with the staff discount."

Marie was about to say something when a woman came up to the counter brandishing a newspaper and a lottery ticket. "See you then," she called. "And good luck. You'll need it," she said to the bemused customer.

Darryl Gleeson was still plagued by spots at the age of thirty. That and his lank black hair and the outcrop of black heads on the fleshy part of his nose had earned him the nickname Greasy. His patronising manner, especially towards the female members of his staff, was another reason. He barely looked up when Bernie came into his office.

"Mrs Driscoll, you wanted to see me."

"Yes Darryl I did. I want to come back to work."

He smiled at her, an oily almost triumphant smile. "I'm afraid that won't be possible," he smirked.

Bernie went cold. "Can I ask why? Wasn't I always a good worker?"

"You had a lot of unscheduled time off. We had to let you go. I can't afford to have unreliable staff."

"I was ill. There were family problems. But that's all sorted now."

"I'm glad to hear you say so. Unfortunately these things are never simple. Especially with mental problems. They often come back. They impair productivity. Yourself being a case in point. We can't risk it."

"I was a shelf stacker, for God's sake. All I did was put stuff on shelves. I don't need an IQ of 120 to do that."

"I'm sorry," he said blandly. "There are no positions vacant at the moment."

"When one comes up will you consider me?" Bernie swallowed her pride.

"I don't think I can say at the moment."

IN THE GENTLE late August afternoon they sat in Liz's courtyard garden.

"It's discrimination," Bernie raged. "It's so unfair. I'm ready to go back to work and he won't give me a job because I'd been depressed."

"And you're old."

"Elsa."

"Sorry, but don't you remember when we first talked about what we could do? You said it Liz, you said we were too old at fifty."

"Not too old to work in a supermarket. There are loads of older people doing jobs like that," Bernie protested.

"Jobs they are totally over-qualified for," Liz said.

"Okay. I give you that but at least they are allowed to work." Bernie got to her feet. She wandered over to the border and started picking pieces from the plants. A leaf from the Hebe, the petals from a late flowering blue geranium. "We have to work. If we don't we don't seem to matter. We become invisible."

"Old crones," Elsa muttered bleakly. She stared into her wine glass.

"I don't see why work has to give you your identity," Liz said in an effort to convince herself.

"I don't see why either, but it does." Bernie shredded a stem of lavender scattering the scented spikes over the paving stones.

"You have to have work or money," Elsa said gloomily.

"What we're going to have to do is get the business back on track." Bernie joined them at the table and helped herself to more wine. "It's not doing very well is it?

"You could say that," Liz admitted.

Elsa nodded. "I don't want to talk about it."

"It was a good idea at the time," Liz said encouragingly.

"That's that then," Bernie sighed dramatically. "So what's left for a withered bunch of old crones?"

"Speak for yourself, I haven't quite run out of Clinique," Elsa said.

"There's always the last refuge of the unskilled woman," Liz said.

"Oh no. I tried that and it was horrible." Elsa shuddered at the memory.

"We're far too old and saggy to go out on the streets," Bernie added.

"Though there are some men who apparently get turned on by old women," Liz said.

"Stop it." Elsa clapped her hands over her ears. "I'd rather scrub toilets than sell myself for sex."

"You'd get more doing it, too," Liz said. "Which is the point I was trying to make. What do women with no skills do? They end up cleaning."

"Count me out." Elsa held up her exquisitely manicured hands

"You can wear rubber gloves," Liz said.

"Me! How could I possibly clean other people's houses?"

"How can you possibly afford not to?"

Elsa backed down under their combined glare. "All right," she conceded. "I can polish the silver and wash the crystal."

Bernie clapped her hand to her forehead as an idea struck. "We're not going to be bog-standard cleaners."

"You mean we'll contract out the bathroom part of the job?"

"Liz be serious. I've got an idea. Okay, it will involve cleaning but it will be more than that. Think of all the divorced and single men on their own. They don't want to come home after a day at work and do the housework. What they need is someone to do all those sorts of jobs for them."

"Surrogate wives." Elsa was listening intently

"Well, not quite that," Liz corrected.

"No of course not." Bernie rushed on, swept along by her idea. "In America they call them housekeepers. They come in during the day and do all the house things and maybe cook an evening meal then they go home. There's no reason why we couldn't do that. It would be more upper crust than ordinary cleaning" She looked meaningfully at Elsa. "We could call ourselves 'Bristol Housekeepers'. And I bet you any money there would be a lot of demand."

"Hey, you could be right. Good for you Bernie, you've found a gap in the market, a unique selling point," Liz said thoughtfully.

"It will work," Bernie said. "Of course, it will take time

to get off the ground but Elsa you can still try and find us some dinner dates and then Liz, you'll be back teaching."

"No I won't. Not after my conviction for battering Samantha Boyd."

"When are you planning to do that?" Bernie was sparkling.

"I had thought of going round later with a baseball bat. If I'm going to have to go to court I may as well do something to justify it."

"I wouldn't bother. She's not worth it. Look, it is a good idea; no, it's a great idea. Come on you two, let's at least give it a try." She looked at them, energised and glowing.

"Why not," Liz shrugged.

"Mmm." Elsa was more reluctant. "I don't cook."

"You can rustle up an omelette and a salad. Or we could prepare some dishes in advance. That way we can keep the catering side up too. Who knows: when our gentlemen taste what we do they might want us to do them a dinner party or a business lunch."

"We'll need an office," Elsa said. "We can run it from yours, Liz. I don't know how much longer I'll have a phone. BT are being simply horrid and your place will be nearer to get to the kind of clients we're going to attract than Bernie's. And," she put down her glass and looked at the other two, "we are going to need someone to co-ordinate everything and since I'm useless at cooking and not very domestic that can be my role."

"Not completely," Bernie objected. "I think we should all take turns on reception. Whoever hasn't got a job that day will answer the phone."

"Sounds fair to me," Liz agreed.

"Great, then we need to think about where we're going to advertise and how," Bernie said. They spent the rest of the afternoon working out wording and fighting over which paper they should use. Bernie wanted the

Evening Post, Elsa argued for *The Telegraph*.

Posh Mrs Mops. Liz smiled wryly at the thought.

When the other two had left and the shadows were growing chill, she took in the glasses and closed the French windows. Timbo had already settled himself in the spare chair in her office and with her cat for company she sat down and switched on her computer.

Dear Mum,

Am staying in the most fantastic place. It's called Krabi and the only way to get there is by boat. Hostel is basic but with sun, sea and great beach what more do you need? Might write a book or a screenplay or something. Just wait till I get home!

All my love,

Poppy.

"Enjoy" Liz whispered. "Enjoy your lovely summer. After all, who knows what lies in wait for any of us."

Darling Poppy,

Your old mum is about to go into the cleaning business...

She stopped. Since she hadn't told Poppy about Sam Boyd and the police prosecution this latest piece of news would take too much explaining. She pressed delete and wrote instead:

Sounds wonderful, looking forward to book/play whatever. Timbo fine. Am enjoying what might be the last few good days of summer.

Love,

Mum.

TWENTY-SIX

"MUM, YOU ARE going to have to take steps." Aidan followed his mother into the kitchen.

"Things are fine as they are," Bernie protested. Her eldest, most responsible son frowned.

"It won't, it can't stay like this. There's the house to consider, for a start. Who's paying the mortgage? Is it you or is it Dad? If he isn't can you afford it? Will you have to sell? Then you have to think about pension provision. You are not getting any younger, either of you. And what about maintenance for Joe and Pat and where's the money for their university education going to come from? This is serious, Mum."

"I know," Bernie sighed. "I just haven't got round to any of that."

"Which gives him an advantage. You've got to get legal advice and make sure he faces up to his responsibilities.

"*He* is your father," Bernie said mildly.

"Not any more. I told you when he left. I'm having nothing more to do with him. If you need anything, Mum, you come to me."

"Aidan." Bernie's eyes filled. This boy of hers, her first, the one that had changed the whole course of her life, of course she loved him but there had always been a shadow there, a resentment that he had stolen her girlhood. Did he feel, even though it wasn't true, that she didn't love him as much as the others? Was he using what had happened between her and Trev to steal her love away from his dad? If so, he'd got it all wrong. Love didn't come in parcels. A bit for you, another bit for you, and if you don't want your bit anymore I'll give it to someone else. You couldn't wipe away thirty years of loving someone or make yourself love somebody more than you did, however much you wanted to.

"Thanks love." She put her hand on his arm. He would like her to hug him; they have never hugged and she couldn't change that now. "I need some more time. I need to get my head round it all."

"You need to see my solicitor," Aidan persisted. "I'll make an appointment for you."

"No," Bernie muttered.

"You can always cancel," he said hastily. "You know it's for the best."

How could he be so sure? Bernie wondered when he had gone. She could understand the practical reasons but her heart told her that she was not ready, that she might never be ready to take that step.

On that grey autumn morning in the church, shivering in the wedding dress that had been passed down from each of her sisters to the next, she had promised to be with Trev for the rest of her life. For better or worse. Then it had seemed the worst it could be. The too-tight dress pressing so hard against her swelling breasts that she could hardly breathe. Her mum trying hard to look pleased and not quite succeeding. Her dad, grim-faced as he led her down the aisle, while Trev's mum wept openly, and Father O'Donovan, who must have recognised her voice from confession, looked down his long nose at her as he led them through their vows.

She might not go to Mass every Sunday but she still believed that marriage was a sacrament so how could she go and see some lawyer, so that the law could put asunder what God hath joined together?

Besides, she had to admit quietly to herself and no

one else, she still loved him. Seeing him, noting the weight loss, the spreading bald patch on the back of his head, she wanted to take him in her arms and give him a good cuddle. Make him feel better, look after him. If only he'd talk to her she'd listen and try to sort out his problems. She was sure that Amanda was not treating him properly. If she was he wouldn't have that terrible air of sadness about him. What he needed was mothering, someone to listen to him just as she listened to the boys.

LIZ PARKED THE Citroen on the drive and walked purposefully to the front of the house. Mock Tudor detached in Stoke Bishop, one of Bristol's most expensive suburbs. Everything of the highest quality, the floors solid oak, the furniture antique, the paintings originals. Only in the bedrooms of the two teenage children did it approach anything like normal. Liz opened windows to let out fusty air, stripped beds and shook out duvets. She swept debris from under beds and dumped it in the bin without looking too closely.

It occurred to her that if she were found guilty she probably wouldn't be allowed to do even this job.

"Stop it," she said out loud. She was sliding into negativity again. But who would have thought that after her Oxford First, her teaching certificate in London, the years of running departments in large comprehensive schools, she would end up fishing dirty socks out from under some unknown teenager's bed?

At least the business gave her something to occupy her mind. Their bookings were increasing for, as Bernie had said, they had tapped into a need and there was nothing like hard physical work to make you so tired that once you got into bed you could not help but fall asleep. Liz got out the polish and set to putting a shine on the hall floor. Maybe if she rubbed hard enough she would not wake in the early hours, bathed in sweat, heart pounding with fear.

BACK IN THE office Elsa should have been sitting at her desk. Instead she was in the bathroom doing her nails. She had given up her manicures and facials. Soon she would not even be able to afford Clinique and would be reduced to using supermarket own brands. There would be no more Marks and Spencer's food, no Waitrose deliveries. She would have to shop at Aldi, wherever that was, or beg for left overs at the fruit and veg stalls in the market at closing time.

"Damn!" The thought was so awful that she lost concentration and went over the side of her nail. She was reaching for the nail varnish remover when the phone rang. Sitting on the rim of the bath she was tempted to ignore it but the sight of her poor ruined nail spurred her into action. It could be another client and the more clients they had the more money Bristol Housekeeping was going to make, the longer she could stave off abject poverty.

"Good morning," she said, trying to sound efficient but not overwhelming.

"Hi." The voice was rich as chocolate with a faint but very attractive Trans-Atlantic twang.

"I'm Elsa, how can I help you?" Instinctively, without meaning to, she lowered her voice.

The man on the other end of the line seemed taken aback. "Am I with Bristol Housekeeping?" he asked.

"Yes, that's us."

"My name is Ed Morgan. I'm looking for a housekeeper."

Elsa's skin prickled. Liz and Bernie were out. She was the only one left and he sounded so civilized. Besides she should take her turn. It was only fair on the other two. "When would you like me to start?" she asked.

"As soon as possible."

Elsa glanced at her nails. They had to be dry by now. "I can be with you shortly."

He laughed. "It's not an emergency. Tomorrow will be fine. Can you be there as early as seven thirty so I can let you in before I have to go to my meeting?"

"Of course, seven thirty," Elsa said without a second thought. There was something about that voice which would override the horror of getting out of bed at what was virtually the middle of the night. "The address, please." As she wrote it down she realised that it was in the apartment block next to hers.

The next morning she woke before the alarm. Even so, she had scarcely enough time to get ready. It took three changes of outfit before she was convinced that she looked the part: smart, efficient, but prepared to get her hands dirty.

She was strangely nervous as she rode in the lift up to Ed Morgan's apartment. It was ironically the mirror image of her own: the penthouse suite at the top of the identical building to hers. Her mouth was a little dry as she arrived on the landing and the door opened, and a tall silver-haired man of about sixty came out.

"Elsa? I'm delighted to see you. Please come in. I'm sorry I don't have the time to show you around." He glanced at his watch and Elsa was seized by a desire to apologise for being late.

"You did say seven thirty?" she said.

"Yes and you were right on time. I'm cutting it fine though, so I will leave you to get on."

"Is there anything in particular you would like me to do?" Elsa said hoping to keep him talking.

"No. Just the usual. Cleaning, laundry, some shopping."

"Shopping?" *Oh, please don't ask me to cook.*

"Just for basics."

"Food?" Elsa tried not to let her voice tremble.

"Isn't cooking part of the package?"

"It can be." Elsa tried not to sound too definite.

"I'll pass on that. It's not often I eat at home and when I do I'm a mean hand with a steak. I will need coffee and bread for toast. The staples. I'm a little low at the moment."

"Of course."

"If that's everything then I'll be off." He handed her a key saying that she was to come and go when he was at the office, then the door closed behind him. Relieved, Elsa let out a long pent-up breath. She should get down to work but Ed Morgan's apartment intrigued her and it wouldn't take a minute or two for a quick look around.

She started in the main living area. Unremittingly bland, the walls had been painted a pale-coffee colour, the carpets were neutral; the furniture heavy and masculine. Two brown leather sofas faced each other on either side of a chimney breast. The fireplace had been removed and the wall left blank. There were one or two good pieces which she recognised as American colonial antiques, otherwise she could have been in a furniture show room.

There was nothing personal or intimate here except for the black and white photograph of a young woman which stood on a side table. She was on a beach, shading her eyes from the sun, her dark hair blowing in the wind and laughing at something out of shot. The whole picture radiated joy, a moment of unfettered happiness captured long ago.

Was she a wife? An ex-wife? Elsa ran her finger lightly over the silver frame and wondered if she would ever know. One thing was clear, however: whoever she was or had been she was important to Ed Morgan.

BERNIE GATHERED UP her equipment and was about to leave for work when she saw Laura wandering into the drive.

"Hi," her son's girlfriend called and Bernie's skin

crawled with scarcely concealed irritation.

Laura's hair was pulled back in a ponytail, her crop top and cut-off jeans revealed the stud in her belly button, her flip flops slapped on the kitchen floor. "I've got in," she announced.

"What?" Bernie was completely confused.

"College. Didn't he tell you? I'm doing a course. Chris thinks now I've stopped the mobile hairdressing I should get some qualifications."

"He's right," Bernie said through gritted teeth.

"Suppose." Laura grinned at her. "But I'm not clever like him." Bernie thought of her creative, artistic son who spent his days playing the guitar and his evenings working behind the bar, forever waiting for the moment when his talent would be recognised but doing nothing to make it happen. "Are you okay?" Laura parked her gum in the corner of her mouth.

"I'm coping," Bernie said shortly. It had taken Chris's partner long enough to find out how she was. She hadn't even bothered to phone.

"Have you seen him? Since he went," Laura asked.

"We went to Pat's parents evening together."

Laura went over to the kettle and switched it on; she opened the cupboard and took out teabags and sugar. "You know, Chris only just said. About you and Trev, I mean."

"Oh." Bernie's righteous indignation evaporated.

"Men." Laura shrugged, dismissively.

"Chris has always been sensitive. Even as a little boy, if there was something upsetting, he'd go and hide in his bedroom." Bernie sprung to her darling's defence.

"He could of said, though."

Bernie said nothing because of course Laura was right. Chris should have told his live-in girlfriend what was going on in his family.

Laura put teabags in mugs, poured on water and fetched milk from the fridge. "I came as soon as I heard." She held out a mug of steaming sweetened tea. "It's tough on you, Bernie. After all this time. 'Specially at your age. I mean it's easy if you're a bloke you can get a woman any time but for us, it's well..." She gazed down at a firm, but slightly rounded stomach. "You know, it's not the same."

That was it; the final straw. Bernie did not need to be reminded of her decaying body by a lithe young twenty year old. "Sorry love, got to go to work," she said, denying Laura the chat she had so obviously come for.

"That's okay." Laura gulped down the rest of her tea. "You know sometimes I miss it, the hairdressing I mean. There was always someone to talk to. Now I get a bit bored. So if you ever need any company give us a ring on my mobile."

She means well, Bernie thought as she hurried Laura out. *I just wish she'd think before she opens her big mouth.*

TWENTY-SEVEN

ELSA PULLED BACK the net curtains from the picture windows and stepped out onto the penthouse balcony. Ed had a wonderful view of the Downs. Much better than hers. She took in a deep breath of fresh air then shook her duster vigorously. Something had to be done about this apartment. The nets had to go for a start and tomorrow she would bring over some spare plants. With an equally critical air she surveyed the drawing room. It needed colour. A vivid throw, a few cushions, a rug or two, and she knew the very painting that would be perfect on that wall. Clapping a hand over her mouth she was struck by an idea. She'd sell it to Ed. It would make all the difference to the room and the money would be useful. In the meantime she would add flowers to her shopping list.

Later that afternoon she returned with a bunch of tiger lilies and a burnished copper vase. She put the shopping away and was preparing the coffee when Ed returned. He looked tired but smiled when he saw her.

"Hey this is a real treat. Coffee waiting when I get in."

"All part of the service," Elsa said.

"I didn't think we'd negotiated that."

"Perhaps not but it can be. I can do whatever hours suit you."

He looked at her curiously. "What about your other clients?"

"Oh, that's no problem. We've only recently started, so well—" She stopped, momentarily uncertain of what to say.

"I'm one of the first?" he prompted. She nodded gratefully. "Then would you like to join me? In a cup of coffee," he added, grinning at her confusion. "We'll have it in the drawing room and we'll toast your first day."

THE LATE AFTERNOON sun showed up the bleakness of the dockland apartment. The décor was minimalist, white and black, the only splash of colour the slashes of scarlet, orange and fierce green of the painting that hung above the ceramic pebbles of the hearth.

There is something very sterile about this place, Liz thought, *and at the same time aggressively masculine.*

In the stainless steel kitchen the casserole was in the oven, the salad waiting for the dressing she had prepared. The table was set, slate mats on a white marble table and there was a bottle of red wine uncorked and breathing. Gary James was a new client and this was her first day.

"A large one," he said as he came in and waved his hand toward the gin bottle.

You could say please. On the other hand you're so ignorant you probably don't know any better, Liz thought but smiled and did as he asked.

Handing him the glass she gave him a brief glance. In his late sixties but well preserved. Slim, not as tall as he would like, with thick dark hair and a slightly orange tan. Holding his glass, he struck a pose in front of the picture windows. Below him was the Cumberland Basin, in the distance the hills of Dundry, where the sun would set. He nodded at her graciously and grunted,

"Have one yourself."

"Thank you." Liz poured herself a gin without thinking. It had been a long day and the rush of alcohol would help to blot out the constant nagging worry that gnawed like toothache at the fringes of her thoughts. She took a sip then quickly put down her glass; this was crazy, she had to drive home.

"You're not in a hurry then." Gary moved across the room towards her.

"No. Yes. I mean I am. I want to get back before the traffic starts to build up. The dinner's in the oven and I've left this week's account on your desk."

"Account? But we haven't finished yet." Without any warning he took hold of her arm and pulled her towards him. He pressed himself against her, his lips hot and fleshy on hers. She jerked her head back. His grip tightened. "All domestic chores undertaken," he panted. "Bristol Housekeepers, we all know what that means." His knee came up hard between her legs; he was pushing her back onto the sofa. Liz let herself go limp. "Good girl," he muttered, half closing his eyes.

Judging her moment, Liz fell, rolled quickly to one side and was on the floor before he crashed down onto the sofa. Stumbling to her feet she fumbled with the door catch. Behind her Gary raised his head and was pushing himself up; in a minute he would be on her. She grabbed at the handle and pulled. To her relief the door opened and she was out in the hallway and banging on the button that summoned the lift.

"Come on, come on." She willed it to hurry. "Please," she cried but already the door of the apartment had opened.

"You bitch, you fucking bitch." Gary lumbered towards her. Liz turned and ran blindly down the stairs.

She staggered across to the parking space, her hands shaking so much she could scarcely fit the key in the lock, but at last she had the door open and was reversing the Citroen out into the road. A car blared its horn as she cut across it but she accelerated and kept going.

Her whole body shuddered as she leapt out of the car and flung open her front door. Safe inside, she leaned against the wall and breathed hard, fighting the nausea that rose in her throat. The man was revolting. How dare he? Anger battled with horror at the thought of his thick hands, his slobbering lips, his obscene lust. He should be castrated, put down, prosecuted. She should report him to the police. Charge him with rape. But how could she prove it? Who would believe her? She had a record. And if she did make a complaint she would jeopardise the whole business. It wouldn't be fair on Elsa and Bernie to ruin everything because of the vile, unspeakable Gary James.

In the shower Liz turned the dial to hot, then very hot. The water was almost scalding but it was what she needed. She felt so dirty she had to wash every trace of him off her skin. In the kitchen the washing machine rumbled into a spin. Her clothes were being washed. Her skin was turning pink. If only she could cleanse her mind.

The thoughts kept coming. Since the business with Sam Boyd she was haunted by an irrational guilt. In spite of all her logic something deep inside told her she must be to blame. Even in this situation, she kept wondering how much was her fault. What was it about her that made him think he could try it on? She was fifty-three for God's sake. She was old. Was he the kind of man that was turned on by sex with a post-menopausal woman? Or was it simply that she was a woman? A mere slot for his dick? That any woman would do?

She had to convince herself that what happened to her was as a one off. Perhaps their advert gave the wrong impression. Yes, that had to be it.

Liz leapt out of the shower, towelled herself dry, and flinging on her dressing gown riffled through stacks of paper in the office until she found it. "Bristol Housekeepers, for all your domestic chores." She had thought it pretty bland, unexciting even, but was it possible the words could be misinterpreted? Crazily she began to play with other ways they could have worded their adverts.

"Come to us for all your domestic needs, wants, desires." As she toyed with alternatives the phone rang.

It would be the police, or her lawyer, or the union. She had to answer it but she couldn't bring herself to move. Whatever it was, it would be bad news. Maybe it was Gary phoning to threaten her, to accuse her of leading him on. She waited transfixed with sudden terror. Two more rings and the answer phone would click in.

"Mum, it's me, just ringing to say I'm okay." Poppy's voice floated across time zones and continents. Liz lunged for the phone. Too late. Her daughter had gone.

TWENTY-EIGHT

"WHAT'S ON THE books today?" Bernie let herself into a hall splashed with late autumn sun.

"I don't know." Liz clutched the mug of coffee which had long since cooled.

"I'm due at Ed's later." Elsa breezed in. "I want to do the laundry and on the way I'm going to restock the fridge."

"So he's paying for a taxi to Waitrose," Bernie teased.

"It's all part of the expenses. He understands that."

"I'm not sure taxis count. What do you think Liz?"

"Umm, what did you want to know?"

"Only if Elsa's taxi fares are a justifiable expense to the client. If she can charge Ed then I should be able to do the same with Brian."

"Plumbers charge travelling time," Elsa said loftily.

"Since when did you know about plumbers?" Bernie laughed.

"I'm not completely stupid," Elsa pouted. "I have lived on my own for long enough."

"I thought you always ran to Lionel whenever anything went wrong."

"Well mostly. But sometimes he was away," Elsa conceded. "Whose turn is it to make coffee this morning?" She and Bernie looked at Liz who was still holding her half-empty cup.

"Liz what's wrong?" Bernie asked. "Is it the court case?"

"No." Liz shook her head vehemently. "I mean, I don't

know."

"Elsa," Bernie said. "Make some tea."

"But I've got to go."

"This is more important."

They sat around the kitchen table. Bernie poured tea. Elsa fussed and fidgeted but after a scathing look from Bernie put an elbow on the table, rested her chin on her hand, and waited.

"Come on Liz, tell us. We're your friends," Bernie coaxed. Liz looked from one to another. Bernie's face was full of concern. Elsa looked slightly impatient. It was hard, so hard to say anything, but she must.

"It's, it's about the business," she managed finally

"We're doing well." Bernie was puzzled. "We're getting lots of calls."

"And clients," Elsa added.

"That's just it. Some of them might not be the right sort," Liz whispered.

"They pay," Elsa said.

"Liz," Bernie looked hard at her friend. "Exactly what are you trying to say?"

Liz shrugged her shoulders in defeat. How could she put this? That Elsa's sexy voice on the phone was giving the wrong message. That the way they worded their advertising suggested that there was more on offer than cleaning and cooking. Perhaps their age was the only reason why they had not been groped before. At the thought of Gary James's thick fingers fumbling at her breasts her stomach lurched. She pressed her hands to her mouth and forced the bile back down her throat. "I'm beginning to think women going to men's houses on their own is not a good idea."

"What happened?" Bernie said.

"Nothing."

"That's not true."

"Gary-bloody-James tried it on. It was horrible."

"He tried to rape you!" Elsa's voice was shrill.

"Not exactly."

"Then what? He was trying to get sex from you without your consent. Tell me if that is rape or not."

"He was under the distinct impression that he was getting what he'd paid for," Liz said wearily. "He thought it was part of the package."

"No!" Bernie cried in horror. Liz put her head in her hands.

"That's what I've been trying to tell you. These men ring up, think that Bristol Housekeeping offers more than it says."

"It is rape." Elsa was furious. "You've got to go to the police."

"Elsa he didn't do anything. I got out of there."

"He still tried it on. In my book that's assault. You need a lawyer Liz. We'll get him. No man is going to get away with trying to..." Words failed her.

"I've got a lawyer, remember," Liz said bleakly.

"That's different. That's not this." Elsa's voice rose.

"I think we should stop."

Her friends looked at Liz blankly.

"Why?" Bernie said.

"It's not safe."

"No that's not right. You had a bad time. It was a fluke."

"How do we know? How do we know that it won't happen again to either of you?"

"Not poor sad Brian. He hasn't got it in him," Bernie said.

"If you think Ed Morgan is in the same class as Gary James then you have no idea, no idea at all," Elsa said stoutly. "He's the perfect gentleman."

"You mustn't tar everyone with the same brush. You've had a terrible experience but it's only once. How likely is it to happen again?" Bernie said. "Look, we'll be all right. We'll take precautions. Sorry." She clapped her hand over her mouth but no one laughed at the unintended pun. "We'll keep in touch on our mobiles. We'll be more specific on the adverts. We're doing well, Liz. We can't give this up now."

Liz shook her head. On one level Bernie's arguments made sense; on another she was angry that her friends were not taking the danger seriously. But then she had known they would not.

"You can do the office stuff," Elsa volunteered. "The rate we're going we'll be able to employ some more cleaners soon."

"What if they're pretty young girls? Or single mums?" Liz tried even though she knew they would not listen.

"We'll only take plain ugly Mrs Mops. If they've got more than one tooth in their heads they're out," Elsa said. "I still think you ought to sue."

"Not if you want the business to keep going. That kind of publicity is not what we need," Liz said.

The phone rang. They all looked at it, then Bernie leaned over and picked it up. "It's Brian," she told the others. "He wants to know if I'm coming over. There's his cupboards to do out and the back place to clear but to be honest I sometimes think that what he really wants is the company." Liz shot her a glance. "No, not like that. He's still grieving. And in any case, he's due back at work soon and then I can get to grips with the place. Are you going to be all right? I can put him off if you like."

"No. I'll be okay. You two go."

Left alone Liz wandered around the house unable to settle. When the phone rang she left it for the answer phone to click in.

"Bristol Housekeeping." Elsa's husky voice was full of invitation. "How can we help you?"

The obscenities poured from his mouth. It was so unexpected, such a shock and in the circumstances so ironic, that Liz, her point made, stood frozen, torn between a desire to tear the caller to pieces or to give in to a burst of hysterical laughter.

"When you lean over to get the dinner out of the oven I am going to..." The caller was lost in his own fantasy.

"Get lost," Liz screamed at him.

"Ooh, bitch." He gave a deep breath then she heard no more.

How dare he? How dare he invade her space, pollute her home with his vile needs? Liz shook with shock and fury. The anger predominated. She paced, she swore, she vowed to get a whistle to put beside the phone to deafen the next obscene caller.

She was not going to let this stop her. The whole of her life had been conspiring against her. First Samantha Boyd, then Gary James, now this. From this moment on, no one was going to treat her like dirt. She mattered, she was not invisible.

The first thing to do was to change the message on the answer phone. Then perhaps they should change their name. Did housekeeping have an unfortunate connotation? She didn't think so but maybe cleaning would be better. But what about their existing clients how would they explain this to them?

"It's all so complicated," she told Timbo, who looked up at her from the chair he had annexed as his and fixed her with a gaze from inscrutable yellow eyes. "It's different for cats. All you need is food at regular intervals, a warm bed and the occasional stroke. Come to think of it that's pretty much what I need. Plus, and here's a big plus, someone to talk to."

The phone rang. Liz looked at the clock and did a mental calculation of time differences. Could it be? Her lovely Poppy who would discuss and analyse her mum's current situation and infuse her with the courage and laughter to go on? If only.

TWENTY-NINE

LIZ SNATCHED UP the house phone. There was no one there. From the other side of the desk the office phone went on ringing, mocking her need to speak to her daughter.

"Yes," she snapped before the answer machine could click in.

"I'm sorry. I thought this was Bristol Housekeeping," the woman said. Liz forced herself to take a deep breath.

"Yes it is. I'm afraid I was..." What? She could hardly say that she was expecting a dirty phone call.

"Thank goodness." The caller appeared not to have noticed her hesitation. "I'm wondering, please, is it possible, can you help me?"

"I'll try." Liz was intrigued.

"It's a bit of an emergency really."

"If you tell me what it is then I'm sure we can do something." Her caller's panic made Liz slip into the familiar role of problem solving. This was surely something she would be able to handle.

"It's my mother-in-law. She's coming to stay. Tomorrow. For a week. I told my husband it wasn't convenient. I've just finished closing a big deal and I was hoping for a few days to myself but when his mother says she's going to do something he's powerless. He can deal with corporations, with big business, high powered lawyers, the tax man, but his mother ... forget it." She stopped, contemplating no doubt the full horror of her needs being overridden by the dominant woman in her husband's life.

Tell her to get lost, Liz thought. *Tell him.* "How can I help?" she prompted.

"I'm sorry, the house is a tip and my cleaner has just this minute phoned in sick. I'd do it myself but..." Liz imagined her gazing around making a mental list of all the things she had to do before the dreaded arrival. "I have to go into the office then I need to shop for tonight's meal. I'll get something from the frozen food compartment. There'll be looks. She's wonderful at giving meaningful looks. But what else can I do?"

"Go out for dinner?"

"I suggested that. But Ma is bringing her new man. I didn't say that did I? She wants to show him off to us and us to him, I suppose. Or she wants him to see me in the worst possible light. Who knows? Anyway all she wants is a simple homely supper." Her voice rose and broke into a half laugh, half sob. "Home cooking, would you believe."

"No problem. Home cooking is a speciality of Bristol Housekeepers."

"You cook as well as clean!"

"We do all, no, most domestic chores. We also have a catering branch but since the emphasis is on the homemade how about a casserole or lasagne or shepherd's pie?" There was a long pause during which she thought her caller had cut her off. "Hullo?"

"Shepherd's pie is my husband's favourite. If you can do that and make the bathroom taps sparkle then you deserve a medal. No not one medal, a whole fist full."

Liz wrote down her name and address. "I can be with you in about an hour."

"You're a life saver," the woman breathed.

THE HOUSE IN an expensive suburb was immaculate. As Liz unloaded the shopping in the pristine kitchen she wondered what there would be for her to do.

"I've tidied up a bit." Chrissie Wilson was a small wispy woman. She wore a designer suit but there was something untidy about her appearance. "Ma and her man," she grimaced involuntarily, "will be in the guest suite. I've put out clean towels and..."

"It's okay. I'll cope. You go to the office."

"She likes mineral water and fruit beside the bed. I usually provide biscuits as well. She never says anything but they do disappear. There's some chocolate Bath Olivers in the pantry." She was still talking as Liz steered her towards the front door. "I won't be long. I just have to deal with one or two things. I can't thank you enough for all this." She put her hand on Liz's arm.

"It's all part of the service. I'll have everything ready for when you get back. All you will need to do is switch on the oven and get your husband to pour the drinks."

Liz cleaned already clean surfaces, polished, buffed and aired. The dining room she set like a stage set for an informal family dinner, choosing a checked blue and yellow table cloth and plain navy napkins. She arranged flowers in the living room and was tempted to turn down the bed in the guest suite. It was almost like writing a play; she was setting the scene. All that was missing were the actors.

She pictured the cast, the overbearing mother-in-law with her compliant new boyfriend. Was he older or younger? A toy boy? The husband, successful in life except where his mother was concerned, and little anxious Chrissie, who surely had enough money and resources to break free from all this but chose to stay. Why? Were there children?

Opening another bedroom door Liz answered her own question. It was obviously a boy's room, but from the state of it he was not at home. He must be at boarding school. A weekly border at one of the prestige Bristol schools, she guessed. He would not be a player in tonight's drama. A car door slammed.

"Chrissie!" A man's voice. "Where the hell are you? And what's this car doing in the drive?"

Footsteps coming up the stairs. She was alone in the house with an unknown man. Liz gripped the bannister rail.

Get a hold of yourself, she thought. *This isn't Gary James, it must be...* "Mr Wilson?" she said as firmly as she could.

"Oh my God." He stared at her and it occurred to her that he'd been more afraid than she had. Liz pushed back the strands of hair that had escaped her combs and smoothed her skirt over her boots.

"I've finished for today. The invoice is on the hall table." She had to pass him to get down stairs but there was a moment of impasse as he stayed where he was. Then the front door opened.

"George, I didn't think you'd be back yet," Chrissie flustered.

"Well naturally I came home early. Mother's due at six. I'm going to have a shower." Ignoring Liz, he went into the bedroom.

Once in the car she leaned her head back and took some calming breaths. What was happening to her? It was stupid to be afraid of being alone in a house with a man. It was as if all her confidence in herself was draining away. She'd get over it. Once this Samantha Boyd business was over she'd be back to normal, but for the time being she wanted out. As soon as she was back in the office she'd tell them. From now on they would be running the business without her.

THIRTY

ELSA LAY UNDER her duck-down duvet and thought about getting up. It was so cold, more like December than October, but she had to go to work. At least at Ed's it would be warm. Her flat was freezing but she simply couldn't afford to have the heating on. There was a brown envelope from the power company with the final demand on the hall table, another one had been lurking in the post box yesterday, waiting to drag her down into the final misery. If only a letter would come from Lionel telling her that everything was all right, he had completed a wonderful deal, she could keep the apartment, and as a bonus for putting her through all this horror there would be an increase in her maintenance.

That, she had to face it, was never going to happen. Lionel would be leading a beach bum life with Adrian while she'd spend the winter in a pashmina, huddled on her sofa, sipping the last of her whisky to keep herself warm.

She stretched out her foot to glean the residual warmth from her hot-water bottle. There was a way out of this. There was something she could sell. There was the perfect spot for it in his apartment and once she'd shown him he'd be sure to agree. All she had to do was swallow her pride and summon up the courage to suggest it.

Elsa slid out of bed and hurried to the shower. The water was hot and she was tempted to stay under it for as long as she could but this was no time to linger. She had to keep going. After she'd dressed and done her make-up she went into the drawing room.

The rust, gold and burnt sienna tones of the Richard Stokes painting were exactly what Ed's drawing room needed. Elsa sighed. This picture of Bristol docks was one of her favourites but there was no help for it. It was either that or freezing to death.

She reached up and lifted it off the wall, found some brown paper and string and parcelled it up. It was awkward to carry but there was not far to go. She hurried across to the next block rehearsing her speech as she struggled against a biting wind.

In spite of the cold she was sweating as she stepped into the foyer. What would he think of her? What if he hated the picture? How was she going to explain why she wanted to sell it? This could be the most embarrassing moment of her life or it could ensure a warm and comfortable winter.

Without stopping to take off her coat she went straight into the drawing room and set down her parcel. The door behind her opened as she tore at the paper and fumbled with the string.

"Let me help you." Ed carried the picture over to the coffee table. "I'll get a knife."

"No." Elsa tugged furiously and the string slid away. "Here..." She propped up the picture. "Isn't it just perfect?"

"I like it very much." Ed sounded puzzled. "But I don't understand. What exactly is it doing here?"

"Oh," Elsa said. "Oh," she said again. Her cheeks flared and she stopped. To say what she wanted, no what she needed, would be to admit how much of a mess she was in.

"Do you want to sell it?" There was a glint of amusement in Ed's eyes. Elsa nodded quickly. "How much?" She named a price. Another pause. Ed frowned. "I would guess it's worth more than that," he said at last. "You know Elsa I think I'd like to get it valued properly. Richard Stokes has gone up in price recently and I'd hate to cheat you."

"You want it?" Elsa gasped.

"I love it." He grinned and in her delight and relief she threw her arms around him. For a moment he held her. There was a strange tingle on her skin, a slight weakness in her legs, which made her lean towards him, then very gently he let her go and she sank down onto the sofa. Ed sat down beside her.

"Was it really that hard to ask?" he said gently.

"I knew it would be perfect for this room. It's the touch of colour you need. Now that I've got you those cushions all you need is a rug from the antique market and the Richard Stokes and..."

"Did you think I was going to bite your head off?"

"No." She shook her head vehemently. "That wouldn't be you."

"Nevertheless, you were worried about asking me to buy the picture?" Elsa nodded. "I like it and everything else you've done to the apartment so far. However, I'm not going to buy the painting until you answer my question. It's part of the deal that comes with the Richard Stokes, okay?"

"Yes," was all Elsa could manage.

"I'd like to know why you need to sell and why a lady like you is working as a housekeeper."

Elsa took a deep breath and then she told him. Everything.

DARLING MA,

Deal's off. Gina, our actress has run off with Dave and since he's the one who was financing the film everything is on hold. I don't think they'll be back. She's never been happy with the way we wanted to film and now she's got what she wants. The man with the money and the connections.

Having come so far and still having a bit left over from Dad's last handout I've decided to stay out here and do the whole sand sun and sea thing for a little longer. Or at least until the money runs out. Keep in touch,

All my love,

Jamie.

PS don't envy you those cold autumn nights. When I am rich I'll take my poor old Ma away for the winter, every year.

THIRTY-ONE

BERNIE OPENED THE door to Laura. Wearing a skimpy denim jacket, her suede boots stained and down at heel, the girl shivered in the cold east wind. Bernie swallowed back a sigh of irritation and ushered her into the kitchen.

"How are things?" Laura parked herself next to the radiator.

"I'm all right," Bernie said.

Laura wriggled her bottom against the hot metal. "That's better. It's freezing out there. You know what I heard?" She rubbed her arms under her sleeves.

"No," Bernie said patiently.

"Jan says she's left him."

"Who?" Bernie's heart was in her mouth.

"Trev. That Amanda has left your ex."

"He's not my ex."

"Well you know."

Bernie was dying to ask if it was true but at the same time she did not want to sound too eager. She must not show this girl, whom she did not really like, how vulnerable she was.

"Amanda Jones is only interested in one thing and she'll do anything to get it. My sister's friend Jan was at school with her and she says she was just the same there. She's a user, Bernie, that's what she is. She takes men for all she can get then she dumps them. Now Trev's no use to her anymore she's left. She's gone off with one of them bank executives. Jan says she had her eye on him all the time. Trev was just a way of passing the time till she could get him to leave his wife."

"Poor Trev," Bernie sighed.

"What do you mean, 'poor Trev'? He deserves it. Treating you like that. You're too good, Bernie. If Chris did that to me, I'd..." Her colour drained. Face green, she rushed over to the sink and vomited noisily. "Sorry." Laura rubbed the back of her hand over her mouth. "I keep doing that. I didn't want to say anything yet. It's a bit soon but with this being sick I can't hide it." She smiled. "I'm pregnant."

"Oh," Bernie said.

"It isn't planned or anything. It just kind of happened." She put her hands over her stomach. "I'd like a boy, Chris wants a girl. We're already arguing about names. I want Josh for a boy and Beyoncé if it's a girl."

No grandchild of mine is going to be called Beyoncé, Bernie thought.

"Sorry." Laura was leaning over the sink again.

Why couldn't she manage to get to the downstairs toilet? Didn't she realise the kitchen sink was where food was prepared and dishes washed? Laura never cooked. Heating up takeaways in the microwave was the height of her culinary achievement and she wasn't over concerned about hygiene either. "Do you want a drink? A glass of water maybe? When I was pregnant I found dried toast helped, or a cracker, something plain."

"I can't face anything." Laura wiped her face on the tea towel and sat down at the kitchen table. "If I carry on like this I won't put any weight on at all."

"That's not a good thing." Bernie was ready to give advice.

"Yeah well. If you get too fat it's hard to get your figure back afterwards."

"You have to have the right nutrition for the baby."

How could this stupid girl put her figure before the health of her baby? "Oh God, I'm going to be a granny," she said suddenly.

"Yes," Laura murmured, her hands resting on the slight bulge of flesh at the top of her jeans.

"Oh Laura." Bernie's animosity dissolved with that gesture. She put her arm around the girl's shoulders and kissed her. "You're having Chris's baby." It was only such a short time ago that her lovely boy was a gorgeous cuddly baby, all plump round curves, gurgling with pleasure as she tickled his toes, and now he was going to be a dad!

"Whoops!" The moment was broken as Laura dived for the sink. Bernie had never seen herself as a grandmother. With Joe and Pat still at school her primary function was as a mother, and Chris had always seemed such a free spirit. He refused to get a mortgage or settle down to a regular job and there had been a long line of adoring girlfriends, stretching back to his first day at nursery. Now Laura had got him and they were going to be family.

If it had been any of them she would have thought that Aidan would have been the first but he showed no signs of marriage, or even a girlfriend. Sometimes she'd wondered if he were gay, like Elsa's Lionel, but if he was there had never been a boyfriend. She would welcome one, though Trev would never cope.

Did Trev know about the baby? If he didn't who was going to tell him? Should she? No. It was not her place. It was up to Chris. Unlike his older brother he seemed to be okay about his dad's affair. And if Chris didn't, then Pat or Joe would once they knew they were going to be uncles. Whoever broke the news, Trev shouldn't be kept out of the loop. In fairness he should have been one of the first to know. It was his grandchild just as much as hers and it didn't seem right that she knew and he did not.

Bernie made a move towards the phone then changed her mind. Why should Trev have the joy and pleasure, why shouldn't he be left in the outer darkness where he had been only too prepared to leave her? He could go without a backward glance, not caring that he had broken her heart. Let him stew. Let her nurse in her heart the warm feeling that thinking about being a Granny gave her. Why should he share it?

The flare of revenge lasted only for a moment. She remembered the tears in his eyes when he left, the swift kiss on her cheek the night of Pat's parents' evening. Deep down, she knew, he did still care. He'd left because he had been flattered that an attractive much younger woman had made eyes at him. It had made him feel good, sexy, and now the cold-hearted bitch had left him he must be feeling so hurt, lonely, and stupid for having trusted her. Which was probably why he hadn't been in touch. How humiliating to have to admit that after a few months of living together Amanda had found someone else. Even worse if Laura was right and he had realised that he was only the stop gap until she could have the man she really wanted.

Poor love. All he was trying to do was to recapture the youth he'd never had. The youth she'd stolen from him because she hadn't been strong enough to say no, to wait until they had enough behind them to get married. How could she blame him?

Where was he now? Was he still in that flat he'd been renting while they were sorting out the arrangements about the house? It was somewhere in Redland, and quite posh so the boys had said; but could he afford it without her salary?

Did he have anyone to talk to? His family would be useless. Her family would have nothing to do with him. What about friends? There were his mates from work, of course, but men never did talk to each other about what really mattered. Those sorts of things they kept for their girlfriends or sometimes even for their wives.

Swept by a longing to see him she wanted to hold him in her arms, to press his head against her breasts, as she did to the boys when they were small.

"It's okay," she'd say. "Don't cry. It will be better tomorrow." Only this was a hurt that wouldn't go away, that she couldn't kiss better because her kisses were not the ones he wanted. At least not yet. She would have to wait. If he realised, as everyone told her he would, what he had lost then maybe he'd be back. At least they would have something to work for together, for thanks to Chris and the feckless Laura they were going to be grandparents.

"I'M WAITING FOR him to ring me," she told Liz.

"And if he does, what will you say?"

"I don't think I'll tell him about the baby straight away. If he doesn't already know, and he might, it will be a big shock. It was for me I can tell you. I still..." Bernie couldn't help herself grinning. "I don't really believe it. If he does know then he's bound to mention it. In fact that will be the reason why he's phoning. On the other hand he may just want to talk."

"About Amanda?" Bernie nodded. "Won't that hurt or will you be glad that he's finally got what he deserves?"

"He doesn't deserve all that pain."

"Oh yes he does. Don't get soft on him, Bernie. He hurt you dreadfully and if you have any chance of getting it together again you are going to have to deal with that."

"I love him. I feel so sad for him."

"You feel sorry for him."

"I suppose I do but that's the same thing isn't it?"

"Oh no it isn't. Feeling sorry for someone puts you in a position of power and that's where you should aim to stay."

"I don't feel happy about that."

"Of course you don't. You've spent most of your life running around after Trev and the boys. You're not used to them having to do something for you."

"You think so?"

"I know so. Come on, Bernie, stand up for yourself. In the end it will be the one thing that will get the relationship back on track."

"I don't know about that."

"It's true. When you were doing what he wanted did he respect you? Did he stay? No, he went off with the glamorous, successful business woman. You've got to think what it was about her he wanted."

"Sex?"

"Bernie, can't you think of anything else?"

"It wasn't very good between us so I can see that as a reason. But I still don't see why I have to be the one that has to change."

"If you want him back you might have to. You've changed already," Liz said gently. "You're different, not the depressed quivering heap you were when he first left. You've come a long way since then, Bernie."

HER CONVERSATION WITH Liz left Bernie feeling good and powerful but when the phone rang unexpectedly one evening her first thought was of Trev.

"Hullo," she gasped.

"Bernie, it's me, Brian. Brain Wooliscroft. You know."

The excitement flooded out of her, leaving her flat and stale and it took a huge effort not to take her disappointment out on Brian.

"I was wanting," he began in his usual diffident way, "I hope you won't take this the wrong way, but I would like to ask you to have dinner with me one evening. In a restaurant," he added unnecessarily and it was this that swayed it for her. Waiting for Trev to ring she could understand only too well the fear, the eagerness, the desperate courage, it had taken for him to ask her out.

How could she refuse?

"Thank you, I'd love to Brian," she said.

THIRTY-TWO

ELSA STOOD IN the doorway of Ed's drawing room and smiled with pleasure at what she had achieved. Since she'd started working for him she'd transformed the whole apartment. The once dreary if expensively furnished living area glowed with colour. The Richard Stokes in particular looked amazing. Her latest purchase, a small bronze of a sleeping cat, completed the scheme. Humming loudly and tunelessly she dusted its sensuous stroke-able curves.

"Ouch." Ed walked in dropping his brief case on the floor.

"My singing's not that bad," Elsa protested though she had been the only one of the three of them who had been rejected for the school choir. "Shall I make us some coffee or is it time for something stronger?"

"A coffee would be fine. I was hoping I'd catch you. Something's come up I'd like to ask you about." He followed her into the kitchen. "It's about dinner."

"You don't want me to cook!" she cried in mock horror.

"Not after what you've told me about your culinary talents. There are only so many omelettes and so much salad a man can take."

"I can do smoked salmon, cream cheese and caviar."

"And I'm sure it is delicious but I'm talking about the full scale thing."

"You want a dinner party. That's easy, there'll be no trouble fitting you in. To be honest that side of the business is not going very well. If you can give me a date I'll get Liz and Bernie onto it. Now *they* can cook. Liz does puddings to die for and Bernie's roast potatoes are manna from heaven. If there was a Nobel Prize for cooking she'd get it."

Ed frowned then his eyes crinkled and he laughed. "No, I wasn't after some catering. What I wanted to ask you was if you would come with me to a business dinner next month."

"Oh." Elsa drew in her breath.

"It won't be very exciting I'm afraid. But being with someone whose company I enjoy will make it at least bearable." He looked at her, his eyes brown and warm and she flushed and trembled and lifted her hand as if to touch him, then dropped it before she did.

"Oh yes," she said.

DEAREST MA,

Met Poppy Mc. Didn't I push her in the pond when we were 3? Small world,

All my love,

Jamie.

Elsa stroked the screen of her mobile. Her boy, her darling son, sent her all his love. She would text back as soon as she had a moment. When her head had stopped reeling and her heart fluttering so wildly that she was afraid that she might have to make an appointment with the doctor. What was the matter with her? It couldn't be her hormones: she was long past that stage. Was it, could it be, the prospect of spending an evening with an attractive man?

I SHOULDN'T. LIZ glanced at the pile of papers she still had to deal with and ran her hand through her hair. Since the incident at the Wilsons she had agreed with Bernie and Elsa that she would no longer go to clients' homes but would take total charge of the admin for

Bristol Housekeepers. She'd spent the day sorting out bills, receipts and insurance and she needed, no she deserved a break. Logging onto her personal e-mail she scrolled down her in box and her heart leapt.

Dear Mum,

Sun sand and sea! Fantastic. Have found this wonderful place which you can only get to by boat, well there is a mini bus overland but it takes about a hundred years. I did a long tailed canoe, which was great, but arrived soaked and dripped my way to the hostel which luckily is incredibly cheap. It's packed with backpackers, students doing gap years and all sorts of interesting people.

Evenings are spent talking, drinking Singha beer and eating great food which costs practically nothing, which is good as I am counting the pennies or rather the Bahts. Thai money sounds vaguely rude!

Nearly everyone's got a guitar or is writing a travel book or has been to the outer reaches of Vietnam or somewhere equally exotic. Having just come off a British Council Tour I feel positively boring. It's like a non-stop party. It's so good that occasionally people from the posh hotel next door sneak through the fence to join in.

Next door is the most amazing place. A little colony of mushroom shaped houses, like Toyland for the super-rich. You don't even have to walk to the restaurant, you phone for a golf cart to ferry you the few hundred metres. The pool's outside your front door, too, so no effort required.

Their beach is beautiful with white sands and strange shaped rocks rising out of the sea. It's kind of private but why should the rich have the best? I often sneak in for a bit of sun worship. And I anoint myself with the required factor sun cream. I told you I'd be sensible, my career is too important to risk wrinkles!

Anyway, yesterday I'd done enough baking and thought I'd explore the cave where according to legend a princess was washed up after a shipwreck. The locals turned her into a goddess and leave offerings every day. I was thinking how good this would be, to be adored and remembered long after I'd shuffled off the mortal coil, so wasn't looking where I was going and managed to bang into this guy practically knocking him over. He grabbed my arm and I was just about to knee him when I realised. James. He's here making some sort of short film. Needless to say he's in a mushroom not roughing it, so I'll get an inside view of the fungus and report back.

Much love

Poppy.

PS Have a few days teaching lined up but after that will be home soon as I can get a flight.

She would be home for Christmas! Liz found herself grinning insanely. She'd been so afraid that she would have to spend their special day on her own. Every year it was the same. On Christmas morning they'd sit in Liz's big bed, their toes touching under the duvet, drinking Buck's Fizz and eating chocolate. Then they'd unpack their presents. Poppy would tease Timbo with the ribbons and he'd leap and hide in the dips in the bedding poised to attack another fearsome piece of wrapping paper.

When everything had been admired and discussed and laughed about they'd get up. Liz, still in her dressing gown, kept an eye on the dinner which they would eat when they felt hungry. The house was lit by candles. Lights were banned except those on the tree, which was real and filled the room with a rich scent of pine. After they'd eaten they'd lie about in the living room stuffing themselves with chocolates, drinking wine and watching seasonal rubbish on the television.

Picking up a pencil she began to list what she had to do to make this their best year ever.

THIRTY-THREE

BERNIE HAD BOUGHT a new dress. A classic design that skimmed her rapidly narrowing hips and waist, she had teamed it with strappy high-heeled sandals and an embroidered evening bag. It was, she told herself, for Christmas when the family came round and not for her first date with Brian.

"Mum, you look great." Aidan was going to sit with his brothers because whatever Joe and Pat might think, Bernie knew they weren't old enough to be trusted. To prove her point Joe was up in his room sulking while Pat had given her lots of hugs and kept asking when she would be back, before racing upstairs.

She peered through the frosted glass of the front door for the first sign of Brian's car. She was glad they were keeping out of the way. She didn't want him coming into the house and meeting her boys. It was too difficult to think of how she could introduce him to her sons. He wasn't a boyfriend. Was he even a friend? Or was he simply someone she worked for?

As soon as the Rover pulled up at the kerb she picked up her bag and wrap and was outside before Brian could get out of his car. She got in quickly and he leaned towards her. He wasn't going to try and kiss her was he? Bernie bent her head and fiddled with her seat belt and he straightened up.

"I chose Italian. I hope you like Italian, most people do. It's amazing how universal the pizza has become." Brian was as nervous as she was.

“I love it. It’s my favourite food,” Bernie said quickly, although it wasn’t true. She had dished up enough frozen pizzas to be heartily sick of them but his anxiety made her want to make everything right.

“I’ve booked Luigi’s. I hope you like it. It’s had very good reviews in the local paper but of course you never know these things have a habit of changing so quickly.”

“Luigi’s will be fine.” Bernie sighed inwardly hoping she was not going to spend the whole evening reassuring him.

The restaurant was a classic Italian trattoria with check tablecloths, candles and scenic ruins painted on the back wall. Bernie remembered being taken somewhere like this by Trev on their fifth wedding anniversary

“It’s very retro,” she said as the waiter led them to their table.

“Typical Italian.” Brian had failed to catch her meaning. “No,” he told the waiter. “Not this one. This is too close to the door. Drafts.” He looked meaningfully at Bernie. “Mother always said you should never risk drafts.”

“Getting cold is supposed to lower your immune system,” Bernie said.

“It was because of drafts that Mother rarely went out. She had to be careful. Sometimes I think she was too careful. Didn’t...” He glanced around as if his mother might loom up over his shoulder and scold him.

“Enjoy life to the full,” Bernie supplied.

“That’s it,” he said gratefully. They ordered. Bernie avoided pizza

“You know, I do miss her so very much. Even though towards the end of her life it wasn’t very easy.” Brian’s voice trembled. “I’ve told you this before.”

Bernie nodded then shook her head, not sure which was the answer he wanted. Brian didn’t seem to notice. He cut his pizza into small pieces, speared one and raised it delicately to his mouth. Worrying about dropping sauce on her dress Bernie was beginning to regret her choice of pasta dish. Brian chewed reflectively. Finally he said, "I'm sorry, I don't want to bore you but you are such a good listener."

Bernie smiled in what she hoped was an understanding way. Brian, in an attempt to change the subject, started to talk about the house.

"It needs redoing from top to bottom. I do realise that. But it will change its character. It has something of her in it still. It's hard moving away from the familiar..." He glanced across the table like a little mouse about to make a run for its hole. "...But change can be exciting too, don't you find?"

Bernie forked pasta marinara into her mouth, took a sip of red wine and carefully avoided meeting Brian's eyes over the rim of her glass.

"The wiring will have to be done. That's a priority and you can't do it yourself these days. Not since they changed the law. That makes sense in one way; it stops the cowboys and those people who don't know what they're doing, but it does seem ridiculous to me that I can't even put in a new plug. I wouldn't attempt a full-scale rewiring, naturally, as I don't have the necessary expertise."

"Would you like to see the desert menu?" the waiter asked as he took away their plates.

"No," Bernie said sharply. Another of Brian's monologues and she was going to scream. "I'm full. It was lovely, thank you," she added more gently.

"Coffee?" the waiter prompted.

"Not at this time of night," Brian said. "If I did I wouldn't get a wink of sleep."

"Me neither." Bernie stifled a yawn. She glanced at her watch. Was it only twenty past ten? The evening seemed to have stretched on for ever.

"It's been very nice," she said as the Rover drew up in

front of the house. To avoid any possibility of a good night kiss she opened the car door almost before they stopped moving and stepped quickly on to the pavement. Greeted by a blast of cold air Brian shrank back in his seat.

"Goodnight then," Bernie said briskly and he drove away without suggesting another date.

Aidan was waiting for her in the lounge. The TV had been turned down low and he was reading through a pile of papers.

"Did you have a good time?"

"Yes, no." Bernie finally let out the yawn that had been lurking in her throat all evening. "The food was all right but, oh God, I was so bored. Come on, love, let's put the kettle on and have a cup of tea."

"HOW'S MY LOVELY mother?" Chris swept Bernie into his arms and lifted her off her feet

"Put me down and then I'll tell you." Bernie smiled. The tallest of her sons, Chris always made her feel tiny and feminine.

"Looking forward to being a granny?" he asked as she smoothed down her skirt.

"Dear God it's wonderful. I still can't bring myself to believe it."

Her son grinned proudly. "I've already started on the baby's room. I'm doing a mural on a woodland theme. Laura wanted to wait until the baby's born but we'll be too busy then." He wandered around the kitchen, her restless son, who could never keep still. "I'm making a mobile too. Collecting bits of silver foil, shiny ribbon, anything that catches the light. My kid's going to be bright."

"Like his dad," Bernie murmured.

"It could be a girl, of course, but Laura thinks it's going to be a boy. Hey whatever, it's a whole new start. Laura's course, then this." He paused. "She's doing well at college, when she can get there. She's too sick some mornings to move." He strolled over to the sink and pulled a leaf off the spider plant on the window sill. "Actually, Mum, that's what I've come to see you about."

He's come to ask my advice. Bernie glowed. "It's quite normal to be sick. Most women are for the first few months. I know I was with Aidan."

"No it's not that. It's about when the baby is born. Will you look after it for us so Laura can carry on with her course? She's really keen and it would make a big difference to us if she could get some qualifications."

A baby. Bernie felt a tug in her breast and without thinking she cradled her stomach in her hands. She looked at Chris, her whole body softening as she remembered his silky downy head, tiny fists, fingers closing round hers; his hungry mouth latching onto her nipple and the fierce shaft of pleasure that shot through her as he began to suckle. He was the only one of her boys who had been planned and carrying him was a joy. There was no sickness, no fear. Her mother had been pleased too. In her book, once you started a family you kept going until Nature cried halt.

Chris had been born on a perfect summer morning. She woke up at the first contraction and lay in bed watching the sunlight play on the curtains in the front bedroom. Beside her Trev lay snoring. She poked him in the side.

"I've started," she said.

"God Bernie, I'll get your mum."

"It's all right. There's loads of time."

He hadn't taken any notice but had leapt out of bed and was in the car and driving hell for leather to Lawrence Weston and it was a good thing, too, because by the time he'd got back with her mum the baby was well on his way. The midwife had scarcely walked in through the door before Chris slipped into world. He was a placid happy baby who ate and slept when he should and grew into an equable toddler who would play for hours in the sandpit, happily making mud pies and splatting about with water. Perhaps that had been his problem all along, that was why he'd never achieved very much. He'd always been easy come easy go. Never prepared to put any effort into anything.

"So you will then?" Chris asked, bringing her out of her reverie.

"What about my job?"

"What job?"

Somehow Bernie was not surprised that he hadn't remembered.

"At Bristol Housekeepers," she said with some pride.

"Oh yeah, you told Laura."

"I can't give up the business. Not now your dad's not here. I need the money and the independence. I don't know how I'll be able to fit it in with looking after the baby."

"Mum." The slight whine in his voice reminded her of when he was a little boy. "Mum, you'll cope, you always do. After all, it's only cleaning."

THIRTY-FOUR

"I WANT SOMETHING a little different, a touch more glamorous," Elsa said to the girl at the hairdressers. Hayley stood back and gave her a professional assessment.

"A slightly lighter colour, more ashy I think. It will bring out the blue in your eyes and the tone of your skin. Is it for something special?"

"A business dinner."

"Black tie?"

"Yes," Elsa sighed with pleasure. It had been so long since she'd gone anywhere that required formal dressing. "I'm wearing my blue silk." The dress was not new but tried and tested. There was no money for something different although she could have charged it to the business, as she had done with the hair, which had got to count as an expense, but she suspected that Liz and Bernie would baulk at a dress and shoes and accessories.

She leaned back in the chair and gave herself up to the pleasure of being pampered. There was no worry about how she was going to pay because she had the company check book in her bag. After her hair had been packetted into foils she sat under the lamp and flicked through an up-to-date magazine. She sighed over the fashions, read the make-up and anti-aging articles attentively and skipped the cookery and problem sections.

"You look lovely," Wendy the receptionist said at the

end of the session. Elsa opened the cheque book and signed with a flourish. She was about to hand over the cheque when she realised that there were three names at the bottom of the page. The business cheques had to be countersigned. In a flash of panic she glanced towards the door. Then she took out her card. A prickle of sweat needled in the pit of her arms. She smiled, the muscles of her face tense, but she held the expression as she entered the pin.

"It's very slow today," Wendy remarked. Elsa's bladder filled. "Sorry." The receptionist frowned. "It says card not accepted." Elsa pressed her legs together.

"I don't understand," she lied.

"Probably some technical hitch." Wendy shrugged. Elsa tinkled a sharp little laugh.

"I'm in rather a hurry. I'd really rather not wait." She rummaged in her bag and made a big show of searching for what she knew she would not find. "Oh dear, I seem to have brought the wrong cheque book with me. This is the company one."

"That's okay, you're a good customer. You can pay next time you're passing."

"Thank you, thank you so much. I feel so embarrassed. I can't imagine why this has happened. It's so good of you," Elsa gushed.

The colour rose in her face and she hurried out of the salon into the cold air. Now what was she going to do? She had no money and no way of getting any. Dressed from head to toe in designer clothes she had over a hundred pounds of hair treatment; her bag and shoes together cost over five hundred pounds and she had no money. The cash machine wouldn't give her any; her overdraft was too big. She would have to go and beg the bank manager again but that meant making an appointment and she didn't have any time.

Her high heels clicked along the pavement as she headed towards the pawnbrokers. She walked straight in pulling off the diamond and sapphire eternity ring that Lionel gave her when James was born.

"Five hundred," the man behind the counter offered. Elsa did not argue even though the ring was worth far more.

"I'm so sorry about that." Head held high she waltzed into the salon and counted out the notes.

"It's okay. We knew there would be no problem," Wendy smiled. "Not from a good customer like you."

"This is for Hayley." Elsa peeled off another twenty then hurried out to where her taxi was waiting, the time clicking up on the meter.

ED WAS WAITING for her in the lobby, immaculate and devastatingly handsome in his tuxedo.

"You look beautiful."

"I scrub up well."

"I can't imagine you ever needed to scrub up."

"Even in my rubber gloves?"

"Especially in your rubber gloves. You are one of those women who are naturally elegant."

"Thank you." She smiled and reminded herself that this was a business arrangement and not a date.

"What do I count as?" she asked when they arrived at the hotel.

"How do you mean?"

"Am I a business acquaintance, a friend? What I mean is, how will you introduce me?"

"As my companion. They don't need to know the details. I only hope you won't be too bored by all this."

"I won't. I'm like Cinderella at the ball. I'll love every minute even if the conversation is all about facts and figures and deals I know nothing about."

"I'm very grateful to you for coming along." He looked at her and her stomach did an odd little flip.

"It will be fun," she replied as lightly as she could manage.

As they went up in the lift to the banquet suite Elsa glanced at the man beside her and wished this was for real. He was good looking, charming, easy to talk to. It occurred to her to wonder why there weren't dozens of women he could have invited. Then the lift doors opened and with head held high she stepped out into her element. Ed's hand was on her elbow, his fingers warm against her bare skin as he guided her through the room.

"Elsa, I want you to meet Gavin Harris."

Gavin Harris held out a large white hand, which completely covered hers and squeezed her fingers a little harder than necessary. "Delighted, I'm sure," he boomed. "This is my wife Marcie." Marcie was wearing a silver dress that shimmered and glittered over her slightly too plump hips.

"What a beautiful dress," Elsa said. Marcie named the designer and Elsa's eyes widened. Where once she would have been impressed by the design, now the first thing that came to her mind was the price of that dress would more than cover her gas and electricity bills. She took a glass of champagne, sipped slowly and chatted about clothes, taking care not to say too much while drawing Marcie out. They were still talking when dinner was announced. At the table the men talked business, each one trying to subtly outdo the others. Except Ed, Elsa noted, as she deftly accepted the compliments of the man on her right without flirting and kept a conversation about flower arranging going with his wife at the same time.

When her new acquaintance bemoaned the lack of domestic help there was a surreal moment when Elsa was tempted to mention Bristol Housekeepers but stopped herself because while men were allowed to boast about their work it would be out of place to mention hers.

By the end of the evening she was glowing, but tired.

They drove back through a cold November night with a crisp touch of frost in the air.

"Thank God that's over." Ed's sigh, as they turned off the main road, was so heartfelt that Elsa's bubble of pleasure burst.

"Was it so awful?" She hardly dared to ask.

"It was boringly predictable. Can I offer you a drink at my place to round off the evening?"

"I'd love a great big G and T."

"I notice you hardly drank."

"I was working. Oh, that sounds terrible, but I didn't want to say anything wrong." A terrible fear struck her. "I didn't did I?"

Ed said nothing and as they stood side by side in the lift Elsa wished that she hadn't accepted his invitation but had gone home and fallen into bed. Her feeling of foreboding grew ever stronger when they reached the flat. Ed showed her into the drawing room as if she had never been there before and excused himself. Feeling a little sick and very stupid Elsa looked out into the night sky where the stars hung like pinpricks of silver high above the orange glow of the city. Then the light went out and for one crazy moment she was swept by a wave of terror as she remembered what had happened to Liz. But that was with the vile Gary James, not Ed, who wasn't and could never be that sort of man.

"That's better." His voice was warm and reassuring as the side lamps went on. He was holding a bottle of champagne and there were two glasses on the coffee table. "Will this do? Or would you prefer to stick to your G and T?"

"Champagne. Definitely. Given a choice I'd always go for champagne," Elsa burbled a little hysterically. If he was offering her champagne he couldn't be about to sack her. He poured a glass and she sat down on the soft leather sofa.

"Cheers and thank you for a very successful

evening." Ed raised his glass. "You were stunning. You looked wonderful. You charmed everyone you talked to. By the end of the evening people were asking where I'd met you."

"Thank you. I thought, for a moment, I thought..."

"You thought what?" he was looking at her quizzically

"I thought you were going to sack me."

"Why on earth would I do that?"

"Well to be honest I'm not that brilliant at the housework and I wasn't sure about how this evening had gone. Especially when you didn't say anything in the taxi. I thought I'd done something wrong."

"You? Never. You were prefect. You know, Elsa, it's a long time since I met anyone whose company I've enjoyed more."

"Me too," she whispered. Her heart was fluttering madly and she couldn't bring herself to meet his eyes. What was he going to say next? Oh please don't let it be bed. She couldn't bear it. She liked this man. She wanted the relationship to stay as it was and if they had sex everything would change.

"You make me laugh. You listen and you've got guts. I like that in a woman. My wife Anne." His voice softened and his glance turned to the photograph in the silver frame. In the light of the lamp it captured for all time the laughing girl on the beach. His voice deepened and his eyes narrowed as if he were trying to hold back tears. "She was already dying when that was taken. She knew she was sick but she wasn't giving in. She didn't give in until the very end and even then she lived every minute."

"I'm so sorry." Elsa touched his hand.

"Me too," he said brusquely. "She had so much to live for, so much to give. There's never been anyone else but her, not seriously. Not until you."

"But I'm not brave, I'm not special. I'm..."

"You're Elsa and you're gorgeous."

Elsa's head reeled. In spite of herself she raised her face to his. His lips were on hers, soft and warm and loving. She shut her eyes and let herself lean towards him, breathed in the scent of him. She felt so safe, so cared for. Then his arms were around her, his kisses harder more insistent. He was holding her close, too close; she could feel his heart beating against hers and almost without realising it she backed away. Instantly he let her go. In her relief she smiled and reached up and stroked his face.

"I think you're gorgeous, too," she said as lightly as she could. "Thank you. It's been a wonderful evening and now I think I should go."

"You could stay." His eyes strayed towards the bedroom. She shook her head. It was impossible. However much she would like him to hold her, to keep her close, to look after her, he would want more.

Elsa was trembling as she got to her feet. Outside, the night was dark and lonely but she wrapped her pashmina firmly around her shoulders and clutched her bag against her chest as she waited for him to get his keys and walk her home.

THIRTY-FIVE

IN THE DARK it was invisible. In the dreary half-light of a November morning the estate agent's notice stood stark and red against the greyness. Sold. Elsa's apartment had been sold. It was like a blow to the stomach, a sudden excruciating stab which dulled to a persistent ache that slowed her steps as she walked to work.

The estate agent must have changed the sign the evening before or she had been too wrapped up in her preparations for the dinner to notice.

They could have told me, she thought bitterly. *Someone could have warned me.* Then she remembered that the apartment was not hers, it belonged to Lionel. No doubt he would eventually let her know that she had to move out. Where would she go? What would she do? She'd be homeless. She'd be like that mad Iris creature wandering the streets with all her possessions in two carrier bags. Elsa was almost crying from shock and fear as the lift took her up to Ed's apartment.

"What's wrong?" Ed came out of the kitchen and she had to resist the temptation to fling herself into his arms and weep on his shoulder. "It wasn't last night was it?"

"Oh no. Last night was wonderful."

"Then what is it? What's happened?"

"I've got nowhere to live," Elsa sobbed.

"Oh you." His arms were around her. "You can move in with me." Elsa's sobs grew more frantic. She beat against his chest with her fists. "I love you. That's what I wanted to say last night before you did your Cinderella act and ran off into the night." He loosened his hold on her, stepped back and studied her intently. Like a little girl she wiped her face with the back of her hand. "Is this too sudden for you? I warn you I make my decisions quickly. Once I make up my mind that's it."

"I..."

"You don't feel the same way?" His mouth tightened, the lines around it deepened.

"No! When I thought I might not see you again, that you might sack me, I felt horrible. I couldn't..." Her voice dropped. "I couldn't bear it. It's just that since Lionel there hasn't been anyone." Her eyes widened with sudden horror at the waste of all those loveless years. "I haven't been in love and looking back I'm not sure I have ever been in love." She looked away from those eyes that were longing for her to say what she was about to, what she had to say. "Before now that is."

He swept her up into his arms and kissed her. For a moment she did not know what to do then her body responded and she was kissing him back.

"I love you."

"I love you, too." She could scarcely believe what she was saying. His grip tightened, she felt his heart against hers and something inside her dissolved.

IN THE BEDROOM the curtains were open. Grey clouds scudded across the sky. A trail of clothes lay scattered on the carpet.

"Oh!" Elsa cried. "Ah," she gasped. Her eyes opened and she fell back on the pillows. Sweat slid between her breasts, her limbs heavy with pleasure. "I've never done that before."

"What," he said lazily

"That," Elsa murmured.

"You must have." He yawned sleepily. "You had James."

"Not sex, silly." Elsa leaned over and pulled at his hair. "I've never," she blushed, "I've never enjoyed it before."

"You've never had an orgasm, Elsa? You are a beautiful and voluptuous and sensual woman and you have never climaxed!" Ed stared at her in astonishment.

"I didn't know I could."

"Well, you did today and if I have anything to do with it you will tomorrow and tomorrow and as many tomorrows after that as we can possibly manage."

"That," Elsa purred, "will be wonderful."

"I AM SO happy. I can't believe it." Elsa beamed at Bernie and Liz.

"You really love him." Bernie sounded surprised.

"And he's rich." Liz's voice was dry.

"Liz!" Bernie rounded on her.

"Let's face it, Elsa, your problems are over. Once the flat is sold you can move in with Ed, who is going to support you in the manner to which you have been accustomed for the rest of your life. Sorted."

"Liz that's awful." Bernie jumped to Elsa's defence. "You've only got to look at her to know this is the real thing. In all the years we've known her have we ever seen Elsa like this? Not even in the early days with Lionel."

"Okay, I grant she's glowing so bright she could replace the national grid. It's probably the relief. I know I'd glow if someone told me I wasn't going to end up poor and alone."

"I am relieved," Elsa said slowly. "I've never been so relieved in all my life. I've been so scared these last few months. I thought I was going to die. And I did try to save money."

"You mean you only took the occasional taxi."

Bernie shot Liz a look. Elsa stayed silent. She was not going to confess the visits to the pawnbroker, or the humiliation at the hair dressers, or the interviews with the horrible man at the bank. These were things she was never, ever going to think about again. They would be blanked from her memory.

"I only took taxis, when I was wearing my Jimmy Choos."

"Or the Manolo Blahniks," Liz added sarcastically

"I'm not with him for his money. I wouldn't do that." Elsa suppressed an inward shudder. "I really couldn't."

"Of course you wouldn't. We know that. Don't we Liz?" Bernie said.

"I'm not going to stop working at the business, either." Elsa lifted her chin. "I'll still be on reception but I'm not doing any cleaning. Not even the penthouse. We're going to subcontract that because it wouldn't be right for either of you to do it."

"You mean that we're not good enough to clean your loos."

"Liz, whatever is the matter with you today? Whatever Elsa says or does you've got to knock her. I for one am very glad for you, Elsa, and personally speaking I'm glad the business will keep going, though whether we can employ someone to take over from you I don't know yet. We'll need to look at the books."

"Whatever, I want to stay involved. I like working with you two. These last few months have been such fun."

"SOMETIMES I WONDER if Elsa ever listens to herself," Liz said later to Bernie. "The things she says. *It's been such fun!* My life and yours are falling to pieces. I'm likely to end up, if not in prison, unable to work. As for you, God knows what Trev's playing at. Elsa was at her wits end with absolutely no money and no real way of making any and now she tells us it was all such fun!"

"Leave it, Liz. Be glad that Elsa's fallen on her feet."

"As she always does."

"There's some people in life that always get lucky.

Elsa is one of them. Remember when Lionel came out and we thought that would be the end of the lifestyle."

"Then it turned out that he was so full of guilt about keeping it from her all those years that he kept her in greater luxury than she could have dreamed of."

"That's what happens to the Elsas of this world. As for the rest of us..." Bernie sighed.

"We're probably paying off some Karmic debt from a former life," Liz said. "I only hope that what I did I really, really enjoyed it. Because this payment time is a bugger." Her dry, cynical air faltered.

"Sister Mary Catherine would tell you to put your trust in the Sacred Heart," Bernie said, only half seriously.

"I'd rather put my trust in this." Liz reached for the bottle of red wine.

THIRTY-SIX

"THERE SHOULD BE some catering now we're coming up to Christmas," Elsa said. "I'll start asking around shall I?"

"I could certainly do with the money." Bernie frowned. "The bills keep coming and I've got to get presents for the boys. The sensible thing to do is to go halves with Trev but I don't know what he wants to do."

"Haven't you asked him?" Liz said.

Bernie swallowed back her hurt. "He hasn't phoned. At least he hasn't phoned me. He keeps in touch with Joe and Pat on their mobiles. They're always texting their dad but I don't like to ask them about him. I don't want them to feel that they're stuck in the middle of our mess or that we're using them to score points."

"Kids inevitably end up in the middle but it doesn't do them too much harm. Look at Poppy, she's not been damaged by not having a dad around all the time."

"She never lived with him. She wasn't used to having a dad. It's different for my two. And there's another thing: should I ask him over for Christmas?"

"What do you want to do that for?" Elsa stared at her as if she had grown another head. Bernie flushed.

"I can't bear the idea of him being on his own."

"Hasn't he got his family to go to?"

"We are his family and whatever he's done I still love him." She blinked away her tears. "Anyway isn't that what exes do, spend Christmas together?"

LIZ LOOKED AROUND the office. Grey November clouds pressed in at the windows. A half empty mug of coffee stood by the computer. The year was moving on and still nothing had been resolved. The phone rang like a slap across the face.

"Liz, Jane Langdon here."

"Oh yes." Liz tried to keep her voice steady.

"They've set a provisional date for the hearing."

Liz's mouth went dry. "When is it?"

"February."

"That's months away. Grief, Jane, this waiting is driving me crazy."

"It will be all right, Liz." Jane's voice was calm and steadying. "We've a strong case and we're getting you Geoffrey Richardson. He's a very good and experienced barrister and he'll be representing you in court, so try not to worry."

Easy to say, not so easy to do, Liz thought. Harder still if you were facing this on your own. Bernie and Elsa were good but had their own problems. She would e-mail Poppy and tell her everything. Once her daughter knew what was going on she'd be on the next plane home. Liz moved the mouse to the internet icon.

Mum,

Great News!!!! James wants me in his film. So no more teaching for a bit.

Loads of love from your soon to be famous daughter,

Poppy.

Could this be the break Poppy was waiting for? She couldn't ask her to give it up. It was not as if there was an emergency. On one level, nothing was happening, only the same relentless grinding, terrifying waiting.

THE INSISTENT RINGING battered through Bernie's sleep. Struggling out of a dream she tried to make sense of what she was hearing. Of course. It was the doorbell. She grabbed her dressing gown and was still tying the belt as she hurried down the stairs. The hall was cold, the front door a black square blocked by two solid figures; beyond, the white shape of a police car.

A car crash, an accident. Please God no. Don't let it be Chris. He's having a baby. He's got the whole of his life in front of him. Or Aidan, dear sweet Aidan. I know I've never loved him as much as he wants, but I'll make it up to him. Dear Mother of God, I promise. I will. Her hands shook as she slipped the chain, her fingers, slippery with the sweat that she could feel pouring down her body, slid uselessly over the bolts.

"I'm sorry I can't... I'm coming as fast as I can." She could sense their impatience, see the hand reaching for the bell but they must not wake the boys. Whatever terrible thing had happened she must be the one to tell Joe and Pat. The thought stilled her hands. The bolts gave, she turned the lock and opened the door.

There were two of them. A young man and a girl. Both in uniform; they looked younger than either Chris or Aidan.

"Mrs Driscoll," the girl said. Bernie nodded, her head heavy with fear. "I am PC Warren and this is PC Jones." She held out a warrant card. "May we come in?"

Numbly Bernie stepped aside. The hall was too small for three adults and they stood too close, awkwardly filling the space until the female officer said, "Is there somewhere we can sit down?"

"The lounge." Bernie pushed at the door. She moved slowly hoping to prolong this moment forever, to stave off the inevitable. PC Warren nodded to her companion.

"A cup of tea."

"The kitchen's..." Bernie began.

"I'm all right. I'll find my way."

PC Warren sat down and indicated that Bernie should do the same. She stumbled into the sofa and perched on the edge, her hands twisting in her lap.

"Holy Mary Mother of God, help us in our hour of

need," she prayed under her breath, over and over again. She dared not ask for more. Dared not mention names in case she had picked the wrong son and the other would suffer for her neglect.

"I'm afraid I've got some bad news." Bernie's hands flew to her mouth, pressing back the scream that rose to her lips. "It's your husband, Trevor Driscoll."

"Trev?" she repeated blankly. "I don't understand. Where is he?"

"He doesn't live here?"

"No. Not since the summer. There's someone else, I mean we weren't getting on, we've separated. I haven't seen him since..." Bernie came to a halt.

"You are his next of kin. There is no one else?"

"No. He's my husband. Oh God, what's happened?"

"He's dead, I'm afraid. He was found collapsed on the pavement. A passer-by summoned an ambulance but he was dead on arrival at the hospital. I'm so sorry."

PC Jones came in with a tray of mugs. The tea he had brewed was sweet and scalding and when Bernie took a sip it ran like fire into her chest, almost dulling the pain of knowing that Trev was dead; that he had died alone in the street like a tramp.

"Was he hurt?" She had to ask.

"He'd not been attacked."

"Then why?"

"Was he on any medication? Did he have any underlying condition?"

Bernie shook her head. Then stopped. What did she know about her husband's health? She hadn't even known that he was planning to leave her, that he had never really loved her, that he had always resented having to marry her. That all those years, when she'd thought they were happy, had been nothing but a sham.

"There will have to be an inquest and a coroner's report. And in the morning." PC Warren glanced at the clock on the mantelpiece, where the hands stood at ten past three. "Later on today," she corrected herself, "there will have to be a formal identification."

He's not been identified. It's not certain. It might not be Trev. There might be some mistake. There's still hope.

"How do you know it's him? How did you find me?"

"He had his wallet on him. There were all the usual identification documents and a photo of your boys," PC Warren said gently and Bernie wondered if this was supposed to give her some comfort. "Is there anyone I can ring for you?"

"Aidan, our, my son." Bernie gave them his number. She did not mention Chris. It was her eldest son's calm and stolid strength that she needed, his reliable, unflappable shoulders to lean on. Chris she would tell later, in the morning, when she and Aidan had done what had to be done.

"Mum." Pat stood bleary eyed in his pyjamas at the lounge door. "What's happened?"

"Your dad," she began. He charged at her, banging into her breasts as he buried his head in her chest. Bernie held him clinging on to the reality of her child. The rest was craziness. They had told her that Trev was dead but she could not believe them.

"Mum?" Pat turned his face up to hers, his eyes wide. The policewoman looked at Bernie and she had to say it, even though it was only part of a nightmare.

"There's been an accident, love. They think your dad, your dad..." She stroked his hair; she felt his bones under her touch.

"He's dead, isn't he?" Bernie glanced across at the policewoman but there was no help from that quarter.

"Yes," she whispered. Pat wrestled himself free, glared at the policewoman and ran out of the room. Joe was at the top of the stairs, his face dull with sleep. Bernie turned to him but he took one look at her and went back into his bedroom.

"I'd leave him if I were you," the young policeman

said.

"I have to go to him," Bernie said. "I have to tell him." Her legs failed and she sank back onto the sofa, her body leaden, her mind still unable to fully grasp what had happened.

The main light was harsh, the room cold. After some fumbling with the controls DC Jones managed to light the gas fire, then made more tea. Bernie took a cup but did not drink. Finally Aiden arrived. She heard PC Warren talking to him in the hall but could not catch what was being said. A moment later Aidan burst into the room. "Mum," he said and there was something in his voice that unlocked her grief.

"I should have phoned him. I wanted to tell him, he never knew." Bernie wept and wrapping her arms around herself, rocked backwards and forwards. "The baby would have made us a family again. He was going to be a granddad. We were going to be together. Oh my God, why did it happen? Why did it have to happen now just when it was all getting better?" Tentatively, Aidan touched her on the shoulder. She took his hand and held it to her face, wetting it with her tears. "We never spoke. I never phoned," she repeated over and over again. Her son, her inarticulate desperate-to-be-loved son, sat down beside her and she leaned back against his shoulder. "He died alone. There was no one there for him."

"He left you, Mum. That's what he chose. If you weren't there it was his choice."

"I should have been with him."

Aiden looked at the clock. There were hours to go before morning

"You need a rest," he said and led her upstairs to the bedroom where she lay rigid under the duvet waiting until the bedside clock said seven and she could get up again.

THIRTY-SEVEN

WHEN THEY CAME back from the hospital Joe's music was pounding through the house and Pat was sitting on the bottom step his arms around Woody.

"I'll tell him to shut it." Aidan started up the stairs.

"Let him be."

"It's not right, Mum. This is a house of mourning now."

Bernie nodded wearily and Pat moved aside to let his eldest brother pass. The little boy's face was white and strained beneath the fall of his hair. Aidan knocked on Joe's door and the music died away.

"Should we draw the curtains? I'm sure that's what people do. Isn't it?" Bernie asked.

"I'll do that for you, Mum," Aidan said.

"No." Bernie's lips trembled and the tears began again. "I'll do it."

She moved slowly from room to room. The house, which in these past few months she had begun to see as hers, was redolent with memories. The lounge, where she and Trev had such an argument over the suite: she'd wanted something practical in grey and blue, he wanted, what was it he wanted? Why couldn't she remember? She crumpled the sodden hankie in her fist and stared at the sofa. She must remember, she must. Then it came to her: Trev wanted a recliner so he could sit with his feet up while he watched the football and she had objected because there wouldn't be room for her beside him. He had wanted it and she wouldn't let him have it. She had won that battle but what did it matter? She would let him have whatever he wanted if only she could have him back.

Aiden had phoned Chis and Laura. Chris rocked her in his arms, his tears falling on her hair. Laura hugged her awkwardly and whispered how sorry she was.

"The baby will never know its granddad." She patted her belly and she and Bernie wept together.

"Do you want me to stay?" Aidan asked "I can if you like. I'll take some time off work."

"No, love. You've been great. I don't know what I would have done without you." He flushed with pleasure. "We'll be fine." She could feel the tears welling up again but was determined to go it alone.

It was a relief when they had all gone and she could sit by herself in the kitchen. It felt almost normal. Woody whined for his supper and she fed him and remembered how he was Trev's dog at the beginning but he'd never had enough time for him and now he was hers. She tangled her fingers in the Water Spaniel's greasy curls and half shut her eyes.

"Mum?" Now that the house was empty Pat had come out of his room.

"Are you hungry?" Bernie asked automatically. Whatever happened she had to make sure her boys were fed.

He shook his head, his hair flopping in his eyes. She would have to take him to have it cut before the funeral. Joe too, if she could persuade him to go the barbers. "You've got to eat. I'll make us both a sandwich, shall I?"

"Tomato and salad cream."

"Like you used to have when you were little?"

Pat nodded and she made a plateful and carried some upstairs for Joe. Her knock on his door was not answered. She knocked again and he gave a few grunts which she took as permission to enter. Her son sat slumped over his keyboard staring at a computer game.

She put the plate down in front of him. He did not acknowledge her presence and she hadn't the energy to protest.

Pat nibbled the centre of one sandwich and pushed the rest away.

"Come on love, at least finish that one," Bernie coaxed.

"I don't want it."

"You're always hungry. You could eat an elephant, you could." Pat gnawed at his lip.

"A pink elephant with strawberry ice-cream?" Bernie tried the familiar childhood joke.

"I'm not a baby, Mum."

"I know."

"I said I don't want anything and I don't."

"All right. Woody can finish them off. He'll be grateful."

"Yeah well." He was sounding like his elder brother. Bernie's heart plunged. Why had she sent Aidan home? She was alone in this house with these hostile boys. "Mum," Pat burst out suddenly, "was it our fault?"

"What?"

"That Dad went away?"

"No of course not. The doctors seem to think it was a heart attack."

"I didn't mean that." His face was set and he was frowning with concentration as if it took all his will power to hold back his tears. "When he left. Was that cos of us? Cos of Joe and me?"

"Oh Pat!" Bernie's heart melted. "No. Of course it wasn't. It was nothing to do with you. If anything it was between me and your dad."

"He didn't love you anymore?"

"Maybe." She forced herself not to cry. "He said he needed some time to decide what he did feel."

"Okay." Pat picked up a sandwich and crammed it into his mouth. "Joe said it was cos of me," he announced as he left the room.

How could he? How could Joe be so thoughtless, so like his father lashing out without thinking of the pain he would cause? She could kill him for what he'd done to her little one, her baby. But Joe wouldn't have done it if Trev hadn't left them, hadn't torn their family to pieces.

"You stupid, stupid man, you sod." She banged her fist on the table sending the dog scurrying for the safety of his basket. "Look what you've done to your kids, to me, just because you fancied that cold-hearted bitch. You got what you deserved, you..." Her invective failed and she put her head on her arms and sobbed. Not even the ringing of the doorbell, the tap on the kitchen window, could stem the flow.

"Aiden rang. We came right round." Liz and Elsa walked in through the back door. They hugged, all three of them, then Liz made toast and hot strong coffee.

Over the next few days they were there whenever Bernie needed them.

"You'll be all right. You're well rid of him," Elsa told her.

"Elsa!" Liz protested.

Elsa shrugged. "Men are like that. If they've done it once they'll do it again. Leopards don't change their spots."

"As if you'd know from your large experience."

"You can mock, Liz, but I'd have been proved right."

"You sound like Aidan. He keeps saying good riddance." Bernie's eyes filled. "He's still so bitter about his dad. Even now. He says Trev's death doesn't make any difference and he's still a shit."

"He's right. When people die we go all sentimental about them. It doesn't change what they were. I hate all this pretending that goes on," Liz said.

"Chris won't have a word said against him. He talks about Trev being fragile and he's got a point. There were so many problems I didn't see. I feel so guilty. I should have known how he felt. How could I have missed it? But I was so wrapped up with the boys and with my own life that I never saw how unhappy he was."

"Balls," Liz cried. Bernie collapsed onto the sofa. "I mean it. Look. He did the dirty on you. Were you happy all those thirty odd years? I know *you* weren't. You had some hard times but did you go off and find yourself someone else, Bernie? *You* didn't. You stayed faithful and loyal and you spent your time worrying about your family and their happiness. You can beat yourself up as much as you like but I remember how it was and the sort of things you were saying."

"Oh Liz." Bernie threw herself into her friend's arms. She was crying and Liz's eyes were full of tears as they hugged fiercely.

"There will be the insurance and the house will be paid for. You'll be made," Elsa said. Liz let go of Bernie.

"Elsa, is that all you ever think of, money?"

"It's important. We all know how much. I'm not saying Bernie isn't upset. Of course she is but if you look at it practically." Liz snorted in contempt. Elsa ignored her. "She's going to be better off without him than she was with him. Or rather when he was with the cold-hearted bitch from hell."

"Okay, I grant you that. But money isn't everything."

"It helps. It's no good pretending it doesn't. Look at us. I was that close..." Elsa held up perfectly manicured fingers. "...To losing my home. I could have ended up a bag lady in cardboard city. Don't look at me like that. I could have and you know it."

The frightening thing was that Elsa was right. The line between a comfortable easy life and destitution was such a fine one. The safety net was full of holes.

"What about you? You did it right, degree, job, house, kid, everything we're supposed to do and now one stupid girl tells a lie and..." Elsa stopped but Liz nodded. She had looked into the pit and she feared that she would slip over the edge and there would be nothing to hold her back.

THIRTY-EIGHT

DARLING POPPY,

Some sad news. Trev, Bernie's husband, died last week. He had a heart attack but what was really bad was that he was found in the street in the early hours of the morning. He was living alone and no one had missed him. Bernie is busy beating herself up about it and Elsa and I are trying to point out that it is not her fault if her husband was mad enough to leave her. It's the funeral today so must go and search out my widow's weeds. All my love and hope the filming is going well,

Mum.

"I look like a Goth." Liz surveyed herself in the long mirror. She was wearing a black silk skirt, long lace up boots and a black velvet jacket. Her hair, which had far more silver in it than it did a few months ago, was tucked under a velvet hat with a feather.

"Make that an elderly Goth. Oh my God, Timbo, I'm going to have to go to church. It's been so long I'm not sure I'll know how to behave."

A COLD WIND gusted round corners of buildings blowing the last of the leaves along the pavement. A soiled paper bag skittered into the gutter. Liz held her jacket around her as she hurried towards the church. She had not expected so many people. The streets around St. Thomas Aquinas were packed with cars so that she'd had to park some distance away. Elsa and Ed were waiting for her in the porch. Elsa kissed her and

Ed shook her hand; he had a firm warm grip and he had managed to curb Elsa's inveterate lateness.

"Shall we go in?" he asked. Elsa took his arm and Liz prepared to follow them but he stood back and waited for her to go first.

She entered reluctantly. The building closed around her. Her boots echoed on the stone floor. It was Advent and the statues of the saints and Stations of the Cross had been covered with purple cloth. Without thinking she dipped her hand in the holy water stoup and made the sign of the cross. The coffin stood before the altar, a candle at each corner. There was the scent of incense on the air. The front pews were full of Bernie's family on one side, Trev's on the other. Liz slipped into a seat with easy egress to a side aisle and sat staring defiantly at the blank faced Madonna in the Lady Chapel. Elsa genuflected then sank down on her knees and murmured a prayer. Liz refused to pray. She would not be sucked in by something she had long discarded as superstition.

The organist began to play and the congregation rose to their feet as Bernie entered. Her face hidden behind a black veil, she clung onto Aidan's arm. Chris and a blonde girl in a short black skirt followed, then Joe and Pat. Both the younger boys had new suits. All Trev's sons were wearing black ties but Chris had teamed his with jeans and a leather jacket.

When the chief mourners were in place the priest came out of the vestry. Robed in purple he stood in front of the congregation. "In the name of the Father and the Son and the Holy Ghost," he intoned and the Requiem Mass began.

The familiar words washed over Liz. Elsa, she noted, murmured the responses; their years at St. Cecilia's had made this an automatic reaction. In spite of the heating the church was cold. The stained glass windows glowed in the dimness and above the sanctuary there was a small square of daylight. Liz wished she was out there in the grey December afternoon. What did it all mean? She did not believe in God or an afterlife. She wished she did. She was sure that Bernie with her simple faith would be comforted by the thought that Trev still existed somewhere, even if all she wanted to do was to apologise to him.

The congregation went up for communion and Liz left alone in her pew caught a glimpse of a blonde woman sitting at the back of the church, her face pale, her body poised for flight. When the last blessing was given and the pall bearers prepared to carry Trev out on his last journey the woman was already hurrying out of the church. Liz, blessing her position next to the side aisle, followed.

"What the hell do you think you are doing coming here? Don't you know this is a private family affair?" she demanded.

"I had to come."

"After all you've done, wrecking a thirty year-old marriage and almost destroying my best friend."

"It wasn't like that."

"That's what it looks like from where I'm standing."

"The marriage was over."

"That's what they always say. Believe me, you are talking to an expert here."

"It was." Amanda's eyes were sad. "You didn't know him like I did. He didn't want to do it but he had nowhere else to turn. Do you know what he said to me when we first started talking? He didn't come on to me. No, he simply told me how lonely he was."

Liz couldn't find the words. It was easy to see how the frantic pace of Trev and Bernie's life, work, the boys, the house, the dog, all these things, would come between them, leave them no time to be together.

"We talked. At first that's all we did."

"He could have done that with a counsellor." Liz was

not going to show any sympathy.

"How many men do you know who go to counselling?" Amanda flashed.

"You didn't have to move in with him."

"He was desperate. He was sad and desperate and..."

"Don't tell me you loved him. You chucked him out soon enough."

"It wasn't like that."

"That's not what I heard."

"He wasn't happy. Even though he was with me and we were planning our future." Her voice broke. "He wasn't happy. He missed her, can you believe it? He missed her. The boys I can understand but..." She shook her head in disbelief. "His wife!"

Liz looked at her pityingly. "You don't understand. You can't understand. Long-standing marriages don't end like that. People don't stop caring for each other."

"I know." Amanda glanced around, eager to escape. Then she stopped to say one more thing. "I didn't leave him. He needed me to go. I went to stay with a friend. An old friend."

"Your boss. Yes, I heard about that too. A good career move I would have thought."

"He's gay. He offered me space while I tried to work out what to do."

"And you didn't go back?"

"I was thinking I would."

"Then Trev died," Liz said, deliberately brutal. "The stress of it all, being pulled between you and Bernie and his boys probably brought on that heart attack."

The words said she turned away. She did not want to see the expression of pain on Amanda's face. Even though it made her feel good to have struck a blow for Bernie, part of her was aware that she should not have said what she did. After all, how much did she really know about Trev and Bernie's marriage? How much did anyone know about another person's relationship?

The sound of the final hymn floated out into the frosty air. Trevor's coffin was carried out to the triumphant notes of "I know that my Redeemer Liveth." Liz wrinkled her face in distaste. It was all such a lie. How could anyone know what was in store for them? Trev, who could have expected to live until he was in his seventies, had died of a heart attack before he'd even reached his sixth decade.

The wind sharpened promising snow but she was glad to be out in the cold. Now there was only the ordeal of the crematorium then back to Bernie's for the wake.

THIRTY-NINE

AT BERNIE'S, THE table groaned with food. Liz and Elsa had offered their services but the catering had been done by Trev's family. All morning, sisters, aunts and cousins had been arriving with plates of sandwiches and bowls of trifle and fruit salad. The house was hot, the rooms crowded. There were flowers everywhere, filling the air with the cloying scent of hot-house blooms. The table had been pushed against a wall in the dining room and was set with what Liz recognised as Bernie's best dinner service, or was it Bernie's only dinner service? Liz didn't know. She had eaten impromptu lunches at the kitchen table, consumed vast number of chocolate biscuits and slabs of cake, but had never been invited to a proper meal in this house.

There was no alcohol, only tea, strong with sugar. Liz, helping herself to a salmon sandwich, longed for a glass of cold white wine. Elsa nibbled celery and chatted to everyone. Ed looked on admiringly, completely at ease in what must be a totally alien environment. She wanted to go home. She couldn't even get close to Bernie, who was hemmed in by a protective ring of female relations.

Joe sloped off to his room and the ceiling reverberated to his music. Following his brother's example, Pat slipped away. One moment he was the centre of attention, the angelic little boy, his eyes shadowed, his newly cut hair shining; then he was gone. He took off his suit and went out into the darkening garden, where Liz saw him and a bunch of young cousins kicking a football over Trev's once carefully tended lawn.

In the lounge the mourners talked in soft voices. Some dabbed their eyes, other wrung their hands.

"Such a shame, such a pity," a female cousin mourned.

"Poor Bernie and after so many years," someone else added.

"You never know when you may be taken. It's a lesson for us all."

"He was such a good husband and father."

"Such a lovely man."

"Oh no he wasn't," Liz wanted to shout. "He was a shit to his wife and he left his boys." To stop herself blurting out the truth she moved away towards another group.

"It's a nice house she has," she heard an aunt say comfortably and to her shame Liz was struck by a sudden envy. It was true that Bernie had suffered, was suffering, but finally, when her grief diminished, she would be able to get on with the rest of her life and like Elsa she would never have to worry about money again. Her financial future was secure.

The evening drew in, the lamps were lit, and people began to leave. It was time for her to go.

"Bernie," Liz began but Bernie merely nodded and moved away. Ignoring her friends, she had spent the whole time circulating between her family and Trev's, a few words here, some more there. She appeared oddly serene. Her simple black dress suited her; she looked lovely, but distant.

Liz went into the hall and was searching for her coat when a furry body pressed against her legs and Woody thrust his nose into her hand.

"Woody, you shouldn't be in here. Come on." Liz pushed the dog back through the kitchen and into the laundry. A large bouquet of flowers, still in the plastic wrapper, lay on the draining board. Curious, Liz read the card:

To Bernie, with deepest sympathy. Believe me I know only too well what it is to lose a loved one. My thoughts are with you today and always, Brian.

"There you are, Liz." Elsa sailed in followed by Ed. "We're leaving. I need a very big G and T. How can you have a wake without drink? I thought Bernie's family was Irish."

"I expect they'll all be down the pub later."

"Except poor Bernie and the boys."

"There always used to be some gin in that cupboard but I don't think it's our place to look."

"Certainly not, ladies. If you are desperate I can offer you this." Ed pulled out a hip flask. "Whisky anyone?"

"I'm driving," Liz said reluctantly.

"Yes please." Elsa took a swig. "It's awful, all the things they are saying about him. Making out as if he was some sort of saint. If I stay much longer I'm going to say something I regret."

"Which is why I'm taking you home." Ed steered her towards the hall.

Car doors slammed, people hugged and kissed and murmured sympathy and condolences. Sickened by their hypocrisy Liz hovered between hall and kitchen waiting until she could leave without running into any relations.

Someone called the footballers and in they trooped with a rush of clean, cold air which dispelled the fug of too many people crammed into over-heated rooms. Liz went to the back door and looked out over the December garden. It seemed very fitting for a funeral, the leafless, shrubs, the bare earth, the stark square of the patio.

She sighed, stepped back inside. The door to the lounge was open and she could see Trev's mum being helped out of her chair.

"God bless and keep you always." With a trembling hand she made the sign of the cross on Bernie's forehead. "Now let me see my darling grandsons before I leave." Chris was dispatched upstairs to get his younger brothers. They came reluctantly, Joe slouching as usual, Pat frowning and biting his lower lip. "You will be good boys for your mother now in her time of trouble?"

"Yes Gran," they chorused dutifully, itching to get away. As soon as the door closed they raced back upstairs.

"Mum, oh Mum." Chris buried his face in Bernie's hair. "Are you sure you don't want us to stay?"

"I'm all right." There was an edge of steel to Bernie's voice that Liz had not heard before. "You get yourself home. It's been a long day for all of us and Laura needs her rest."

The room emptied and Bernie wandered into the kitchen. Liz was about to offer her help but seeing that Aidan had followed his mum she stepped out of the way into the laundry. Aidan set down a tray of dirty plates.

"I'll do these for you, Mum."

"No." Bernie was firm. "They'll go in the dishwasher."

"Shall I make us a cup of tea then?"

"No thank you, love. You've been wonderful today. I don't know how I'd have managed without you but I need some time on my own. You do understand don't you?"

"Of course." He sounded a little hurt but he kissed his mother and held her close for a long moment. "You will ring if you need anything?"

"I will. Don't worry. I know I can rely on you."

"Oh Mum." His eyes filled and she reached up and stroked his cheek

"Off with you now. We'll speak tomorrow." Bernie went with him into the hall and as the front door shut behind him, Liz stepped out of the laundry.

"I suppose I ought to be going too."

Bernie spun round, startled

"There's no need."

"I thought you needed space."

"I need space. I need some space or I will explode. And I don't want to do that. Not today, not in front of all those kind people." Bernie's eyes glittered, her face flushed. "I am so, so angry. Liz, I can't begin to tell you."

"What's happened?" Liz asked warily. Had Bernie caught sight of Amanda slipping out of the church? Was she angry that her husband's mistress had come to his funeral?

Bernie's voice was low and furious as she said, "He spent it. He cancelled the life insurance. He has left us with nothing. Me and the boys. It shows how much he cared. What I want to know is, what he did with it. Where did all those bonuses, all the extra money he got with each promotion go? We never had the benefit of any of it. He must have been salting it away for years. Was it for his women? Were there always women? Was that why he used to work so late? And what about the trips he was always going on? He said he was going to conferences but he could have been off to some posh hotel with his latest bit of fluff."

"Bernie, stop this. It's over. He's gone. There's no point in torturing yourself now."

"No there isn't. Except it's not over. It's only just beginning. Now we'll see what he's done to us." She waved her hands wildly. "How am I going to keep all this going, the house, the boys, the dog? I have no money coming in. What the hell am I going to do?"

FORTY

ELSA WANDERED INTO the drawing room, warm and sated. Beyond the huge windows the trees stood black against the winter sky. The thermostat was turned up high; she was going to enjoy her cup of coffee and latest copy of *Vogue*. Ed had already left for a business meeting; she would make her way to Liz's later.

She settled herself on the sofa and began to read. The entry phone buzzed. Elsa flicked over a page and tried to pretend she had not heard it.

"Ed, it's Oona." The voice floated eerily up from the ground floor. "Can I come up?" Elsa considered ignoring the request. It was good to have the apartment to herself and she was enjoying her moment of privacy. The sale of her penthouse was imminent and she would have to move in full time. Then moments like these would be even more precious. On the other hand maybe this Oona was an old friend of Ed's. In which case she ought to let her in. Sighing, she got to her feet and keyed in the front door.

"And you are?" Oona was a small woman with hair like liquorice plastered against her skull.

"Elsa," Elsa said shortly not knowing what to add.

"His partner, then." Oona, it appeared, had already made up her mind. Without waiting to be asked she strode across the hall and into the drawing room. "My," she gasped, "what have you done to this place? The last time I was here it looked like something in a store window. Now it's something else. It's gone from bleak to sumptuous. I'm back in Bristol and I've just bought myself a new apartment which could do with the same treatment."

"It's a very exclusive service." Elsa was thinking fast. Oona shrugged.

"That's what I like. Then I get something no one else has."

"If you give me your number I'll send you the details." She needed time to think what she would charge per hour, what conditions she would impose; already she was ticking the list off in her head. There would have to be money up front for buying and a reliable team to do the practical stuff. A good painter and decorator; a small firm, or maybe a woman, to make the curtains and soft furnishings – there could be a good mark up on those, while she herself provided the inspiration.

"Great." Oona prowled round the room. "Ed's not in I take it. Well that's no surprise. You'll tell him I called and get him to call me on this number." She scribbled swiftly on the cover of the magazine Elsa handed her. "I'm his niece, by the way, in case you wondered. His sister Alice's daughter. And you, I guess, are the live-in lover."

Elsa flushed. Only rigorous childhood training stopped her from asking this woman to leave. Then as Oona continued to circle she realised that what her visitor had said was true. She was, or was soon going to be, Ed's live-in lover and she was not sure she liked that title.

"You're nothing like her, which is kind of odd." Oona picked up the photograph of Anne and studied it carefully. "You know, he's never really gotten over her. I guess that's why he never married again." She replaced the photograph and looked at Elsa. "I'm sorry. I'm well known for rushing in and sticking both my feet in my mouth."

"That's all right." Elsa smiled stiffly.

"No it's not. You're angry and I don't blame you. Look, if you want to throw me out go ahead." She moved towards the door but Elsa stopped her. Oona was a member of Ed's family and a potential client for the interior design consultancy she had just started up.

DEAR MUM,

Sorry about this but won't be able to get back for Christmas. Met this incredible American on the beach, when James was lining up some shots. He made a comment about how photogenic I am and I thought he was trying to chat me up. He was in line for a groin kick, when James comes over and practically swoons on the sand. Seems that Cy is a up and coming film director! How was I to know? Still if he thinks I'm good, all compliments gratefully accepted and put in the cheer-up bag in the "when you think you're useless" compartment.

Don't know if he'll be any use but contacts are vital in this business, so I'll keep him sweet, which is no problem cos he's good fun. We've already spent an evening drinking and talking about Life, the Universe and Everything.

Am thinking that I might stay on for a bit longer in the New Year. Money's OK as have been doing a bit of bar work and one or two sessions at a school for snotty kids. Honestly Mum how do you do it? An hour with that lot and I want to commit murder!

Love you lots,

Poppy.

A cold, grey rain slid down the window as Liz logged off and steeled herself for a lonely, miserable Christmas. The first one without her daughter.

AFTER NIGHTS OF dreaming about being put out into the street Bernie plucked up courage and rang the Building Society for an appointment. Aidan, simmering with rage, drove her there. His hands clamped tight on the steering wheel, he could not bring himself to speak about the situation his father had left them in.

"Mum, let me come in with you."

"No." Bernie was determined to do this alone. She smiled grimly. "I need to know exactly where I stand. And," she added more gently, "I can't keep relying on you."

"You can," he insisted.

"Aidan, you're my son. You've a life of your own." *And so have I and I'm about to see how much of a disaster it's turned out to be.*

"MRS DRISCOLL, WHAT can I do for you?" The young man in the suit showed her into a small side room, barely big enough for a desk and two chairs. Bernie sat down, her heels together, knees pressed close, as the nuns had taught them. She held her handbag on her lap pressing it against her churning stomach.

"I want to delay my mortgage payments for a few months until I have sorted out my finances."

The young man flicked through her file. He frowned. Bernie's stomach plummeted. It was the worst news. The house was going to be repossessed and she and Joe and Pat would have to go and live with Aidan, in his perfect, pristine, minimalist and above all tiny house. There were only three bedrooms. How on earth would they all fit it? Where would they put Woody? Even Aidan's garage was immaculate and the garden shed looked as if it had come straight out of the shop. Her eldest son's lifestyle had no space for a dog and two teenage boys.

"I don't understand. There must be some mistake. Do you have the correspondence with you?" Bernie shook her head. "Have you not had a letter from us?"

"No." *Dear God, what has Trev neglected to do now?*

"Ah." He let out his breath. "There must have been an oversight. You should have had formal notification that the mortgage has been paid off. The insurance policy you took out when you first borrowed the capital has paid for that. I am sorry to hear of your husband's death but I'm pleased to be able to tell you that the house is yours, now. There is no more money owing." He stood up and held out his hand. She took it, her head spinning. "Mrs Driscoll, are you all right?"

"I am all right. It's a bit of shock. I didn't know."

"Naturally. It's a very difficult time." Murmuring platitudes, he ushered her into the main office.

"Well?" Aiden's voice was harsh as she got into the passenger seat.

"It's all right love. It's okay." Bernie was on the verge of tears.

"Mum." He banged his fist on the wheel. "I could kill him. I could. For what he's done to you."

"No." She put her hand on his arm. "The house is mine. As far as I understand it he couldn't do anything about the mortgage protection policy." She smiled a watery smile. "You don't have to worry, we won't be troubling you in the near future."

He didn't say "thank God" but she sensed his relief. He'd have done anything to help her but upsetting his calm orderly life would have driven them all mad.

FORTY-ONE

BERNIE OPENED THE front door and stepped into the hall. The floor could do with a clean, the stair carpet was scuffed, the paint work past its best, but it was hers. She owned it. Beneath the grief and the anger a small feeling of pleasure bubbled up to the surface. She had a house, which was good. She also had a part share in a business, though that unfortunately did not provide enough money to live on so to support herself and the younger two boys, she needed another job. She didn't want to go back to the supermarket. Although she enjoyed the friends she'd made there, the gossip and the jokes, the pay was low and to her surprise she realised that there was no way she was going to take orders from the likes of Greasy Gary again. She had already proved that she could do better than that. Maybe she should be like Laura and try for a college course. With some qualifications behind her she would be able to make something of her life. Whatever she decided, this time she was going to put herself and what she wanted first. She was filling the kettle when Chris walked in.

"Are you homeless then? Will it be the cardboard box under the by-pass or Aidan's spare room?" he teased.

"Don't mock. Your brother was prepared to sacrifice a lot for us."

"Mum!" Chris threw out his arms in a tragic gesture. "We haven't got the space, not with the baby coming."

"I know." The thought of being in Chris and Laura's tiny rented terrace house made Bernie shudder. Laura never cleaned. Chris was chronically untidy. The place was crammed with his half-finished projects: the motorbike he had dismantled in the front room was still waiting for a part he could not source; the illustrations he was working on for the cover of a friend's CD; the shelves that were going up in the kitchen, when he had the time. Then there were the piles of magazines, and Laura's clothes and shoes spilled out from the single cupboard in the bedroom. Adding to this chaos was Jasper, a huge black and white cat who left his hair over everything. His litter tray stood un-emptied in the kitchen where the floor was sticky with dirt and the sink full of dishes.

Bernie turned to her own sink because with her back to her son she felt braver about what she was going to do. "There's something I want to ask you."

"If I can do it, I will," Chris promised grandly.

"It's not so much what you can do, it's what I can't do." He raised an eyebrow and she braced herself. She had to say this but she was dreading his reaction. What if he was angry, so angry that he wouldn't speak to her anymore? "Chris," she said quickly. "You'll have to tell Laura I can't look after the baby when it comes. I will baby sit for you whenever you need me but I have to get a job to keep us, Joe and Pat and me. Your dad didn't leave us any money." With shaking hands she poured two mugs of tea. Turning round slowly she handed him one.

"Hey Mum, so you're not doing the nanny bit. That's okay."

"You don't mind?" Oceans of relief washed over her.

"Oh God, no. To be honest Laura's been thinking about giving up. College is not her sort of thing. I think she only did it because I thought it was a good idea."

"What about her exams?"

Chris shrugged. "She'll have the baby."

Bernie was seized by a mad desire to pick up the

phone and tell Laura not to give up, that she had to have some sort of qualification behind her; that relationships didn't last; that men left their women and children; and in the end the women were left to cope on their own – and it was so much better if they had a good job. But Laura wouldn't listen. She believed that Chris, handsome, loving and completely unreliable Chris, would be there for her and that she would never have to face what Bernie had. Or if she did it was so far in the future that she could not even begin to imagine it.

On the other hand it might never come to that. Bernie had only to look at Elsa and Ed to see that the only predictable thing about life was that you could never predict what was going to happen next. Maybe, just maybe, Laura and her baby would be blessed with Elsa's good luck.

"That's settled then," she said. "Do you want a biscuit with your tea?"

"I DID IT," she said in wonder when Chris had gone. "I said no." *And the world didn't fall to pieces and he still loves me. Why the hell didn't I do this years ago?*

Woody padded into the kitchen and nudged gently at her legs. It was his way of telling her he needed a walk. Bernie glanced out at the gathering darkness and sighed.

"It's horrid out there. And it's raining but I suppose I have to. We'll have a quick trot around the block if nothing else." Woody gave a low growl. "If that's all the thanks I get then perhaps I won't even bother with that."

The Water Spaniel went into the hall and growled again. There was a tentative knock at the door and as Bernie went to answer it Woody bounded in front of her and barked loudly.

"Sit," she said and he did.

"I hope I'm not intruding." Brian was on the doorstep, half-hidden behind a huge bunch of flowers. Rain dripped from his head and down his nose. In his beige raincoat he looked like the stereotypical dirty old man. Bernie, who had hoped for a quiet evening, felt her heart sink.

"Not at all." She forced a smile. "Do come in."

"Mum, who is it?" Pat was at the top of the stairs.

"It's no one," Bernie called up to him and he retreated into the safety of his bedroom. "I'm sorry, I didn't mean it like that. He's been very anxious and clingy since Trev went. I just wanted to say it was no one he had to worry about. He's got very protective of me. It's normal, I suppose, after all that's happened but—" She stopped, hoping she wouldn't have to say any more, that Brian would understand how a boy suddenly deprived of his father might feel. But Brian was busy wiping his feet on the mat.

When he had finished he thrust the flowers into her arms. The cellophane rustled loudly, exciting the dog's curiosity. Woody got up and sniffed at this stranger's legs. Brian stepped back hastily bumping into the front door as he tried to get away. He was white with fear, his teeth clenched as he held out his arms in an effort to keep the animal at bay.

"Don't worry, he's very friendly." Woody made a low threatening sound at the back of his throat. "He's only checking up on you." Woody's nose had reached the level of Brian's groin. His thin whip like tail swung from side to side. "Woody, leave." The dog backed off. Brian managed a watery smile.

"Nice boy," he quavered. Woody showed his contempt by butting him fiercely in the knees. Bernie tucked her flowers under her arm and tried to shove the dog in the direction of the kitchen.

"Basket." The dog planted his wide feet firmly on the floor. "Joe, Pat, come here and deal with Woody," Bernie yelled but there was no response from either of her sons.

She put the flowers down on the hall table, grabbed Woody's collar and hauled him into the kitchen. He resisted all the way but finally she managed to push him into the laundry and shut the door. She was turning back to Brian when he came in.

"You forgot these." He held out the bouquet

"Thank you." She dumped it in the sink which luckily was empty of dishes.

"Go on through to the lounge while I make us a drink. Do you want tea, coffee, or something stronger?"

Brian bit his lip anxiously as if she had asked the most difficult question in the world and Bernie itched to put her hand on the small of his back and give him a shove him in the right direction.

"Shall I make us some tea, then?" she said brightly to break the silence.

"That would be very nice, thank you." He watched as she put on the kettle. The intensity of his gaze rattled her and her hands shook as she put their cups and saucers on a tray. Still he said nothing and she led the way into the living room.

"Would you like to take off your coat?" she asked as he was about to lower himself into a chair.

"Thank you. I've come straight from work." He took off his raincoat and folded it carefully so that the plaid lining was on the outside, then placed it across the arm of his chair before sitting down. Bernie's skin prickled with irritation. He was wearing a suit and tie but somehow still managed to look shabby. There were flecks of dandruff on his shoulders and he sat with his hands on his knees leaning slightly forward. There was an eager yet anxious look in his eyes. His forehead corrugated with frown lines and the tip of his nose was shiny with cold. A vein throbbed in his temple. He was so ill at ease that she was becoming increasingly nervous. The teapot wobbled as she lifted it to pour the beverage and she splashed hot liquid into the saucer.

"I'll get you a clean one." She started up from her seat but he was clearing his throat.

"Please don't worry about it. It will be fine. I have to admit..." He attempted a smile and his Adam's Apple bobbed furiously in his thin neck. "Mother always used to tip it back in the cup. She could never bear the waste." He gulped then continued, "She only did it when there were the two of us. She was a stickler for manners otherwise."

"Yes," Bernie said. There was another pause. She handed him his cup but he didn't take it. His fingers drummed a frantic tattoo on his thighs.

"I know this is rather sudden." His voice rose, he coughed, then started again. "It's rather soon but as you know, I understand only too well what it is like to lose someone dear to you."

With a horrible suspicion about where this might be leading Bernie said quickly, "I haven't thanked you for the flowers, at the funeral I mean, and the card."

Brian took no notice. "It's very hard being on one's own after so many years. Not that you are on your own exactly, you have the two boys. Bringing up two lads for a woman without a masculine presence is not easy. I know that, too."

Bernie began to get up. "I'll get some biscuits."

"No thank you, not for me. I'm sure there's a wonderful supper you've cooked for me waiting in my freezer."

"Beef stew and carrots. I did it when I came in on Monday." Bernie edged away as Brian's eyes took on a frantic look.

"Let me look after you ... and the boys of course. We wouldn't get married straight away but in a few months. Once they have got used to the idea."

Bernie fought to hold back the tide of hysterical laughter rising in her chest. She tried a deep breath but her shoulders were shaking.

“Are you all right?” Brian leapt to his feet. “Shall I call someone?” Desperately, she shook her head then doubled over with the effort not to laugh out loud. She staggered out of the room and falling into the cloakroom exploded into peels of hysteria

FORTY-TWO

"WHAT DID YOU do then?" Liz asked.

"I didn't say yes." Bernie giggled. "I stayed in the toilet for as long as I dared. He was getting worried by this time and I could hear him coming into the hall. The last thing I wanted was him banging on the door and asking me if I was all right. I think I would have weed myself if he did."

"You were in the right place for it."

"I flushed the toilet, washed my hands, and came out with a straight face."

"And?"

"I said I was very grateful for his kind offer – and thanks but no thanks."

"How did he take that?"

"I was terrified he was going to burst into tears and I would have to comfort him." She shivered. "The very thought of it makes my skin creep. You should have seen him, his eyes were all watery and his nose was dripping. But he didn't break down. In fact he backed away with a bit of dignity and said he was sorry but he understood."

"All the usual stuff." Liz nodded sagely.

"He put on his coat and looked around with that funny little jerk of his head. His mouse-look I call it. For a moment I thought he was going to take his flowers back but it was more like he was storing it all up in his brain because he knew he was never going to be in my house again."

"Then he left?"

"Before he did you will never guess what he said." Bernie almost choked on the laughter bubbling up inside her.

"That you were the love of his life and he would never ever forget you?"

Bernie made a rude noise.

"No. He asked me if I would be in as usual on Monday because it is so hard to find a good cleaner."

"Oh Bernie, what a joke."

Bernie nodded but what she did not tell Liz was how sorry she felt for him as she watched Brian's pathetic figure walking down the drive. His shoulders stooped and he looked an old, old man.

"You wouldn't believe he's only a few years older than us," she whispered.

"Don't go feeling sorry for him." Liz pulled a face. "Men can't be trusted. It's one of the problems with the job. Either they grope you or they want to marry you so they can keep your services to themselves."

"What you mean is that no one could possibly want me for myself." Bernie was hurt.

"No, of course not. It's just not very likely to happen, is it?"

"There's Ed. He wants Elsa."

"He's one in a million

"A million, million," Bernie added.

The phone rang. They looked at each other. Bernie reached out across the desk but it was not the office line. Liz went out into the hallway. She came back five minutes later, glowing.

"Good news?"

"The best, Bernie. I am so relieved. That was Jane Langdon, my solicitor. It looks as if it's all over."

"They've dropped the case? Oh Liz, that is brilliant."

"Well not exactly. No one has made a final decision. Jane's been talking to a new girl at the Crown

Prosecution Service. She's really unhappy with the whole thing and thinks there simply isn't a case to answer. She's got to talk to her boss, who's away for Christmas, but she's pretty sure he'll agree with her and they'll drop the case. I won't have to go to court! I won't lose my job! Oh Bernie, I've been so scared, so very, very scared."

WITH ONLY TWO weeks to go before Christmas Liz threw herself into a frenzy of shopping. She bought presents for everyone she could think of. A silver photograph frame for Elsa, whisky for Ed, a silk scarf for Bernie, aftershave for Aidan, wine for Chris, special mother-to-be bath essence for Laura, vouchers for Joe and Pat, then because those were too impersonal, a bottle of beer and a book of terrible jokes. She even got a packet of dog chews for Woody.

She decorated the house, bringing in the small fir tree that had been growing in its pot outside the front door since the previous Christmas. She rummaged in the cupboard under the stairs for the red and gold baubles and plucked long strands of ivy from the garden wall to weave around the banisters.

Everything was looking as it should when the doorbell rang.

"Liz!" Jilly was at the door, her nose pink with cold. Liz took her into the living room where a fire burned in the grate, bringing out the resinous scent of the Christmas tree.

"This is so lovely. You have been busy." Jilly plumped herself down in a chair. "Lucky you, such a lovely house and you've missed a horrendous term. Things are going from bad to worse. The kids are out of control. It's always bad the last weeks before Christmas, but this year!" She raised her eyes to the ceiling. "You would not believe what is going on. Senior management have lost the plot. A parent even assaulted the Head the other day. He'd finally given in and agreed to have Wayne Beckford excluded. You remember him, don't you?"

"No I don't," Liz began but Jilly was in full flow and could not be stopped.

"Anyway, Wayne's dad came to school and demanded to see the Head. Norman was skulking in his office as usual but Mr Beckford wouldn't take no for an answer and barged straight in and thumped him on the nose. There was blood everywhere. The police were called and we're all waiting to see if Mr Johnson will bring charges. What's the betting he won't? Too scared of bad publicity for the school and the implications it has on his handling of discipline." She paused. Liz made appropriate noises, reminding herself that all this was relevant, that in a few weeks' time she might be back at work.

"We did the mock GCSEs last week and I've told the department that we will collate the marks the second week of term. Maths are doing it as soon as they get back but I don't think that's fair. We all need a break. Especially at this time of year." She looked at Liz who nodded her approval. "There's been so much to do. It's been such a long term." Jilly sighed. "Though I say so myself, there have been no disasters."

"You've done well. The department obviously runs perfectly well without me. Taking time off makes you realise how quickly you become redundant."

"Oh Liz, I didn't mean that. We'll be really glad when you're back. Me in particular. It will be so good to have a few weekends when I don't have to work all the time."

"It's okay." Liz wondered how soon her visitor was going to leave and whether she could drop a hint or two about how much she still had to do to hurry her on her way.

"CAN I SPEAK to my girl?" Dermot asked on the other end of the phone. Liz clicked her tongue. What was the matter with the man? Didn't he know, couldn't he remember? Or maybe, and the thought made her smile, Poppy had not been in touch with her father.

"Your girl is still in Thailand," she said more mildly than she first intended.

"Will she back in time for Christmas?"

"No."

"You'll be spending it on your own, then. Like me."

Liz could not imagine her ex ever having to spend a holiday on his own. There were so many friends, contacts, acquaintances. Whenever he split up with a woman he invariably found someone to take him in.

"Actually, I'm going to Bernie's."

"Bernie? Good God, you'll be bored stupid. All those hulking great boys and that dull husband of hers. Why don't you give it a miss and come away with me? I've got a couple of days booked in a fantastic Cornish hide-away. There will be log fires, loads of booze and long wind-swept walks on the beach."

"Sorry, no can do. I told you, I'm already committed."

"No strings attached, I promise. It seems such a shame to waste the cottage."

Liz had a sudden image of Dermot, old and alone. "You'll find someone else." It was the story of his life. "Or you could try spending some time on your own."

"Liz," he wailed. "I need someone to talk to. Jenni and I..." His voice trembled appealingly. "It wasn't working. She didn't understand."

"Was it, by any chance, because she was too young?"

"She didn't have any experience of life. She couldn't look at things from anything but her own perspective."

"Being able to see things from someone else's point of view is a sign of maturity," Liz heard herself say. She was falling into the familiar trap of listening to then analysing Dermot's problems and trying to find a solution. This was not the role of an ex-wife or at least not one who had no intention of ever rekindling a long defunct relationship. All she was doing was encouraging his self-absorption. He needed slapping down, putting in his place, or she would be on the phone for hours.

"Well that's all very sad, but I'm going to Bernie's."

"Then I hope you enjoy it." Dermot sighed heavily.

"I will," she replied with a confidence she didn't feel.

FORTY-THREE

CHRISTMAS MORNING WAS damp and grey. Liz drove through streets empty of traffic, where all the cars were parked outside houses bright with Christmas lights. Through the windows she could see tinsel and baubles, flickering television screens and laden trees. She thought of the families getting together with sons and daughters and grandparents and looked quickly away because being on your own at this time of year marked you out as a complete failure in the relationship stakes, made you the kind of person that got invited to Christmas dinner because they had nowhere else to go.

"Stop it," she told herself fiercely as she pulled up outside Bernie's house. "Things could be a lot worse. There are people starving and you're feeling sorry for yourself." She leaned over to the back seat, picked up the presents she had bought, and head held high walked up the drive.

"Hi." Joe opened the front door and scowled at her from under his hair in that Neanderthal way that reminded her of some of her least-favourite pupils. The rich scent of roasting turkey wafted out of the kitchen merging with the fug of an over-heated house and an oily doggy smell as Woody bounded up to greet her, his bald tail beating at her legs.

"Joe, get the dog." Bernie hurried to the rescue, wiping floury hands on her apron. She kissed Liz quickly on the cheek, her attention obviously on what was happening in the kitchen and waved her towards the lounge.

"Aidan, get Liz a drink. A strong one," she said and went back to her cooking.

"Happy Christmas." Aidan looked at her palely and Liz knew that he resented her presence on what should be a family only occasion. "Let me take your coat." He hung it on the banister and she followed him into the living room with her bag of carefully chosen gifts.

Although it was only mid-morning they were all slumped in front of the TV. Chris sprawled on the sofa with Laura leaning back against him, both of them clutching bottles of beer. Pat sat on the floor playing with an electronic game. Joe subsided into a chair. Chris handed him a beer, from the row of bottles on the floor beside him. Joe raised it to his lips and the drink dribbled down his chin, soaking the top of his black T-shirt.

"Would you like a sherry, Liz?" Aidan asked.

"I'd rather have a vodka."

He looked offended and went into the kitchen to fetch some ice. Liz followed. Bernie was boiling water for the sprouts.

"Anything I can do to help?" Liz asked hopefully.

"It's all under control." Bernie picked up her glass and took a huge swig. "Go and sit down. I won't be a minute then I'll come and join you."

In the lounge fairy lights twinkled on a silver Christmas tree.

"Yeah!" Pat yelled.

"Oh my head," Laura moaned.

"Rough night last night." Chris grinned. "You were rat-arsed." His hand curled around her breast and she wriggled against him.

"When I was pregnant with Poppy I went off alcohol completely," Liz said. Laura groaned.

"I know I shouldn't." She took another gulp and Liz had to look away. Didn't the stupid girl know that drinking could harm her baby?

"When do we do presents?" she said to distract herself.

"How about now?" Bernie came in flushed from the heat of the kitchen.

Liz plunged her hand into her bag and began to deal out gifts. No one was particularly interested in what she had bought. Pat and Aidan thanked her politely, Bernie exclaimed with almost too much enthusiasm, Chris and Laura barely glanced at their presents. Joe grunted unintelligibly.

"Say thank you properly," his mother snapped and Liz wished she'd stayed at home. Even a Cornish cottage with a self-pitying Dermot would have been better than this.

She had just opened her body lotion from Bernie when the timer went off. Bernie and Aidan disappeared into the kitchen and she was left staring at some mindless rubbish on the TV. She sat bolt upright clutching the blue plastic bottle of lotion and trying desperately not to think of Poppy on a warm sunlit beach.

"Okay folks, we're ready." Bernie opened the door and a delicious smell flooded in from the dining room.

They squeezed into the long narrow room. Aidan sat at the head of the table, his mother beside him conveniently close to the door. Liz was placed at the furthest end, trapped between Chris on one side and Joe on the other. Once seated she would have to disturb everyone if she wanted to escape. Laura sat beside Chris with Pat opposite her.

"I don't think I can eat anything," she whispered loudly.

"A toast first." Aidan passed round a bottle of wine. "Not you, Pat." But he was too late. Pat's glass overflowed, red wine dripping onto the table. "I told you," Aidan scolded.

"It's Christmas. Mum, tell him I can at Christmas," Pat whined. Bernie nodded and smiled. Her eldest son glared at his brother. Then in an obvious effort to lighten the mood he raised his glass.

"I want to say how good it is to see you all here." His words rang hollow to Liz, his warmth forced. Nevertheless she joined them in the toast.

"To all of us." They drank and then Laura pushed back her chair and rushed out to the toilet.

"She's being sick again," Pat announced.

"Shall I go?" Bernie asked.

"Leave her," Chris said. "She's used to it by now."

"It makes the toilet stink," Pat said.

"That's enough. I'm going to get the turkey, Chris come and help with the vegetables and Aidan you can carve."

Bernie piled their plates high; the boys slurped gravy over their food and ate in silence. Pat cast frequent glances at his mum while Joe hunkered over his plate and shovelled the contents into his mouth as fast as he could. Chris and Laura toyed with their food and Aidan ate extra slowly as if to make the point that he alone appreciated his mother's cooking. Bernie said little and kept refilling her glass. After a few false starts Liz gave up on the idea of making conversation and concentrated on her dinner, eating so much that the waistband of her skirt was getting decidedly too tight. At last the main course was finished and the dishes cleared away.

"Pudding?" Bernie asked with that forced air of jollity that grated on Liz's nerves.

"She's in the pudding club." Pat glared at Laura.

"Give it a rest," Chris said.

"Leave him, Chris, it's okay." Laura tried to make peace.

"No it's not. You don't want to be picked on by Pat."

"Chris." Aidan put his hand on his brother's arm. Chris flinched visibly.

"Get off me."

"I'm only trying to stop you two from arguing and spoiling the whole day."

"Oh yeah. And who gives you the right to interfere? You're not Dad, remember. So back off."

Aidan swallowed and went white. There was a sheen of sweat on his forehead and a muscle in his jaw twitched uncontrollably.

"No I'm not Dad, but at least I'm taking some responsibility, which is more than you've ever done."

Chris got to his feet.

"Fight," Joe breathed.

"Yeah." Pat punched his fist into the air. The two older brothers squared up to each other.

"Stop it." Bernie shrieked but her sons ignored her. Aidan was white with fury, Chris's face was flushed, his eyes glittered.

"Don't you fucking dare speak to me like that," Chris snarled.

"It's about time someone did. All your life you've been the golden boy. You've got away with everything because of your big mouth. Always knowing what to say. Making everyone like you. But guess what, it doesn't work with me." Aidan grabbed him by his T-shirt.

Chris jerked away. The material ripped. He stepped back, lowered his head and charged at his brother.

"No!" Laura shouted. The sound was so unexpected they stopped to look at her. "Chris, I want to go home. I want to go now."

"You're right. There's no point in staying where we're not wanted."

"Chris," Bernie cried.

"I'm okay Mum."

Aidan's eyes were wet; he took out his handkerchief and wiped his nose. Liz felt a pang of pity. In spite of everything, Bernie had still put Chris first.

"Get out," Aiden growled.

Chris took Laura's arm. He looked at Bernie. "I'll call you," he said and there was a stunned silence as the front door clunked shut behind them.

"Aidan?" Bernie said at last.

"I'm not sorry. He deserved it," he muttered.

"But at Christmas." Bernie sighed.

"It needed to be said." He paused, waiting for her to say more but Bernie was silent. "I'd better go, too."

"You'll say sorry to Chris?"

Lips pressed in a thin line he shook his head, took his jacket and left. The two younger boys slunk out of the room.

"God!" Bernie cried weakly. She sank into a chair and Liz poured them both a large glass of wine. "I'm sorry, Liz. I should never have asked you. I thought, God help me, you might be feeling a little lonely without Poppy, so what do I do? I invite you to the Driscoll family Christmas from Hell."

"Don't worry about it. You're all still coming to terms with losing Trev. The boys are trying to find their place in the new order, that's all." Liz touched Bernie's hand. "It wasn't all that bad, you know." They looked at the plates piled high with bones and left-over vegetables and smeared with gravy. "Woody will have a field day."

"So long as we don't feed him the bones. Two funerals in one month would be too much."

"Would you have a service for a Water Spaniel?"

"A High Mass" Bernie held her nose in allusion to the breed's distinctive smell and they collapsed into giggles.

"We're doing all right, aren't we – you, me and Elsa?" Bernie picked up an empty bottle of wine, tipped it upside down and opened another.

"We've come a long way." Liz poured a large glassful. "Shall I tell you something Bernie?" She leaned across the table, her words slurred. "I think this year is going to be a good one for all of us."

"About bloody time too," Bernie replied and rested

her head on her arms.

ELSA AND ED dined outside on the terrace. The patio heater glowed with warmth and Elsa was wrapped in furs. The night was clear and cold; the stars sharp in the sky. They ate smoked salmon and lightly cooked steak. Ed raised his glass and the bubbles sparkled in the candlelight.

"To us."

Elsa echoed his toast then she slid off her coat and naked led him into the warmth of the bedroom.

FORTY-FOUR

"HAPPY NEW YEAR Darling."

"And to you too." Elsa sipped her champagne. "This is going to be a great year, I know it." She leaned back on the sofa cushions and glanced at Ed from under her lashes.

"So when are you going to let me make an honest woman of you?"

"Are you asking me to marry you?" Elsa sat up. To give herself time she took another sip of her drink. The bubbles slid down her throat and fizzed in her veins, slightly blurring the moment.

"Elsa." Ed put down his glass and looked at her. "You're not changing your mind are you?"

"Of course not. I mean..." She was thinking as she spoke. "I mean, I love you but..."

"But what? You must tell me if you want to call it off. I'll understand." His eyes were dark with pain. "Was it too sudden? Is that it? It was for me. A bolt from the blue. One look at you that day and I was smitten. Believe me Elsa, you are looking at the world's most faithful guy. Look at my track record. How many years since Anne has it taken for me to fall in love again?"

"It's not that."

"Then what?"

Elsa shrugged uneasily. She wanted to say yes but on the other hand: "I like it like it is. I don't want it to change. I even..." She hesitated. "I even like having my own place." Ed looked at her in astonishment. She flushed but summoned up her courage and went on: "I love you and I adore making love to you and I think it..."

"You think it would be better if we kept two different apartments?"

"Yes." He understood, this wonderful amazing man understood what she wanted, to be with him yet to have her own space, too. To have somewhere she could put on her make-up or pull the odd straggling hair out from her chin without locking herself in the bathroom. To keep the mystery and passion between them. "I'll go on being your mistress and your lover for as long as you want me."

"Which will be totally, utterly and forever," he murmured.

LIZ SAT IN Jane Langdon's office. It was seven o'clock on a raw January evening.

"We have a date for the court hearing. I'm sorry Liz. I really did think that it would not come to this." The solicitor's face was impassive.

"I don't understand. You said there was no case to answer."

"That's what I thought. My unofficial contact, the girl in the CPS office was so sure, but then her boss came back. He must have refused to throw it out."

"That's crazy." Liz felt the sweat start on her back.

"I agree. It does not make sense. Either there is a case to answer or there isn't. My best guess is that he's playing safe. Because of the potential child abuse he feels he can't take any risks. If he gets it wrong the media will have a feeding frenzy."

"I didn't do anything," Liz said flatly. *I didn't, I didn't. How many times do I have to say this? Why won't they believe me?* Under the table she clenched her fists.

"And that is what will come out of the hearing. In the meantime we are dealing with someone who doesn't want to take the responsibility for making a decision so he'll let the case go to court for the judge to decide."

"There's nothing I can do?" A feeling of irretrievable doom swept over Liz as she looked at the folder which would determine her future. "I never thought Samantha Boyd hated me so much."

"I doubt she does. She probably has no perception of what she has done to you."

"Then someone should tell her." Liz thought bitterly of the Head.

"That's not our concern. Our concern is to get the case thrown out of court. The statements from your colleagues are all glowing. They're queuing up to testify on your behalf."

"They want the day off school," Liz said cynically.

"Geoffrey Richardson, your barrister, is one of the best."

Liz's eyes were filling with horrid shameful tears. She wanted to be angry but she felt weak and helpless, tossed about on a storm of other people's opinions and lies.

"It's my life," she whispered. "That's what this is all about."

"We'll talk about that later. After the court case."

"*If* I'm proved innocent."

"*When* you're proved innocent. There are things we can do. We can sue for damages for instance."

"You make me sound like a victim."

"Are you?"

"No." Liz's fire had returned. "I know I'm not. I know I've done nothing wrong but I still feel like shit."

"It's very, very hard, but we'll get you through." Jane shut the folder. "That's all we need to do today." She took her jacket from the back of her chair and stood up. Through the door of her office Liz could see there were still people working, most of them women.

"Are you going home now?" Liz got to her feet.

"I should be so lucky. No it's the supermarket first, to

get something so I can cook for the family when I get in." Jane smiled wryly. "What I need is a good old-fashioned wife. The sort that used to stay at home and do all the domestic stuff."

"Don't we all?" Somewhat tremulously Liz returned her smile.

She stepped out of the warmth of the office into the chill air and Bernie's hug.

"Ed's got the car over there. Come on, he and Elsa are waiting." Linking arms, Bernie led her to the Mercedes.

"I didn't expect this," Liz said as she slid into the luxurious warmth of the car.

"We couldn't leave you to go home on the bus!" Elsa cried as if she were about to be abandoned in the middle of the North Pole. "Not when it's this cold. Not at this time of night!"

"I'll drop you ladies off at Liz's then I'll be back for Elsa and Bernie later. I've some things to do," Ed said as he drove up Park Street.

Liz looked at his silver grey hair and distinguished profile. He was handsome and kind and there was an honesty and straightforwardness about him that she found infinitely touching. Elsa was so lucky. And so was she to have such good friends. The tears came to her eyes again and Bernie squeezed her hand.

"It will be all right."

"If I had a pound for every time someone said that I would be so rich I wouldn't have to worry about Samantha Boyd."

"We'll all be there for you," Elsa said as they drew up outside the house.

"You can count on that," Ed added. "I'll be in that court with Elsa." And once again Liz was warmed by his kindness.

"He's a good man," she told her friend as they went inside.

"I know." Elsa grinned. "You wouldn't believe what he has done for me."

"You've certainly got a glow." Bernie winked at Liz. "I think we might guess."

Elsa blushed then giggled. "I might tell you but not today. Today we've got to sort out Liz."

Liz shook her head. "I'm sorted out already. I'm so sorted I feel as if I've been shaken to pieces. In three weeks' time I'm going to face the worst day of my life."

"That's what I mean."

"Elsa you're not making sense," Bernie sighed.

"It's facing it. You know, in court. She's got to look right." Bernie and Liz exchanged glances. "No," Elsa insisted. "It's important. You've got to give the right impression. None of those flowing hippy skirts and things you wear. They make you look all liberal and..." She searched for the right word.

"Hysterical," Bernie supplied. "You're right, Elsa. If she goes into court looking like that then the judge will think that she's the sort of woman of a certain age who would lose her cool if some adolescent proves a bit difficult." Bernie frowned. "What should she wear?"

"A suit," Elsa said promptly.

"With a hat and a veil."

"Don't be silly, Liz. You've got to look sensible and respectable and reliable."

"You mean I'm not?"

"Of course you are. You've always been, but you've got to look it as well. Come on let's see what you've got but to be honest I think we'll have to take you shopping." Elsa led the way upstairs and started rummaging through Liz's wardrobe. After much tutting and head shaking she found a skirt and jacket and decided they might just do.

"I've had that for years," Liz protested. "It's dowdy."

"It's respectable." Elsa wagged her finger. "A new shirt underneath, something plain but not too severe."

"I don't suppose you want me looking like a dominatrix," Liz muttered mutinously.

Bernie giggled, but Elsa said sharply, "I'm only trying to help."

"Of course you are." Liz was instantly contrite. They were all doing their best to help her and an acute understanding of social conventions was what Elsa did so well. "Thank you. Thank you both." She held out her arms. Bernie stepped into her embrace and even before they looked round for Elsa she was there hugging them both, enfolding them with her perfume and her softness and a physicality that she had never possessed before.

FORTY-FIVE

THE FOLLOWING AFTERNOON Jilly arrived with flowers and chocolates.

"Visiting the sick is a cardinal work of virtue," Liz remarked as she took the bouquet.

"You're not sick. Are you?" Jilly shrugged off her coat and followed her into the living room.

"No, I made a point of not going off on ill health. The Head wanted me to but I refused. If he's going to let this happen then I won't let him pretend that it's some sort of breakdown. I got pretty close to it at times. But now I'm up and fighting."

"Good for you and we're all behind you. Most people know what's happened. Well, if they don't know the exact details they know that you're not on extended sick leave."

Liz wanted to ask if Samantha Boyd and her cronies had been doing any more boasting but she could not bring herself to say the girl's name.

"It's all died down rather. People do ask how you are and we're all going to be in court. To be honest, I can't wait to see her put well and truly in her place. She's a pathetic, stupid, fat blob. God knows what she thinks she's going to get out of all this. Some attention, I suppose," Jilly said.

In spite of her efforts to keep calm, Liz's stomach contracted and she gripped her hands into fists. "I'd like to give her some attention. I'd like to do something to her. Head-butting wouldn't be hard enough. I can't help it. I know she's a sad case but I find myself overwhelmed by these violent feelings towards her. It's one of the things I hate about being in this situation: it brings you down to their level. Or at least it strips you of any veneer of tolerance and understanding."

"Don't worry about it. I think we'd all react the same way if it happened to us."

Liz sighed. "I ought to be able to see her as the pathetic piece of humanity that she is, but I can't."

"Why should you? She's horrible. So many of them are horrible and vile. I only wish I could earn my living doing something else."

"Don't tell me you regret going into teaching?"

"Regret it?" Jilly considered. "Of course I do. There are good days. Sometimes. But then there's all this shit. It's a crazy way to spend your life. Working your guts out to get some sort of knowledge into kids who don't want to learn and who only abuse and insult you for trying to teach them. On which note, guess what?" She got up.

"You've got marking to do."

As Jilly left she leaned towards Liz and kissed her quickly on the cheek. "Keep going," she said and Liz was warmed by this unfamiliar gesture of affection from her second in department.

"MUM, IT'S ME."

"Poppy!" Liz held the phone as if it was made of gold.

"I'm ringing to say Happy New Year. The film is great. It's really, really good Mum. I think it will go places."

"And when..." *When are you coming home?* Liz was about to ask when the connection was broken. She stared at the phone in bewilderment. How could this have happened? She shook it as if, like the patterns in a kaleidoscope, the pieces would come together and she'd hear her daughter's voice again. Then she realised that nothing could happen while she was holding the line open. She put it down hastily and waited and waited for it to ring.

IN A BAR IN Bangkok Poppy turned to James.

"Do you think Mum's all right? Only she sounded a bit distant."

"That's because she is."

"Stupid. You know what I mean, she wasn't quite herself."

"Don't worry." He lifted his glass to his mouth. "Mums are always all right. That's what they do."

"SHE PHONED," LIZ informed the cat. "Okay it was only brief but she probably ran out of credit. God, Timbo, it was so good to hear her voice." She hugged herself. "She'll be home soon. Won't she? When all this is over and life will be back to normal?" She heard the question in her voice and answered it. "Of course it will. How can it fail to be? I've got you and Elsa and Bernie and Jilly and all the department, who are going to swear on their mothers' souls how wonderful I am. All these friends!" Her heart soared. She got out a CD and blasted out *Sisters Are Doing It* at top volume. "And I don't care if the whole street can hear," she yelled and thrust her fist into the air.

FORTY-SIX

THREE O'CLOCK IN the morning and Liz was sitting up in bed, her stomach tight, her teeth clenched. Sweat soaked her nightshirt. She drew her knees up to her chest, wrapped arms around them and lowered her head. The cat stared with yellow eyes. Liz wanted to reach out and stroke him, to feel the comfort of his warm body, but she could not move. Haunted by dreams of the thin grey-faced woman in the ragged coat, her possessions bundled into a carrier bag, she saw herself stripped of everything she owned, the house repossessed, living in a bedsit. The room was dirty, the windows smeared, the carpet torn and stained. A burnt saucepan balanced on a grease-encrusted gas ring. A draft howled beneath the door. The stairs creaked. She had not paid the rent for so long that she was about to be evicted.

"Stop it," she breathed. "This is not going to happen. They can't find me guilty of something I haven't done."

But what of all the involuntary things? The careless sweep of an arm that might have made contact, the sarcastic comment intended to put a kid on track but interpreted as an insult, a put down. Perhaps her class knew she didn't like them, that she despised their values, their looks, their scarcely veiled hostility to anything they didn't understand. Maybe there was some truth in what she had been accused of doing? Not the actual physical action but the desire to hurt, to lash out. Once she had cared, had wanted to bring out the best in her pupils, to become the best they could be, to discover the talents they did not know existed within them. Now she never wanted to step inside a school again.

Timbo raised himself on his front legs and stretched. His tail curved over his back like a question mark. When finished he nudged at her arm until her fingers uncurled and stroked his fur.

Sleep was impossible so she put on a dressing gown and went downstairs. The house was cold, the heating not yet clicked in, and the kitchen tiles were icy beneath her feet. The cat twisted around her legs and meowed loudly.

"Not yet. It's not morning. You can't have breakfast. It's too early." He stared at her in disbelief and continued the assault on her calves. "Okay." Liz gave in. She pulled open a packet and squeezed out the meat, keeping her head turned away. The smell made her feel sick. Her mouth tasted of rotting food.

The kettle boiled and she brewed a pot of tea. Should she go back to bed or should she sit it out? There were still hours to go before Ed came to fetch her. Liz stared at the milk floating on the top of her cup. Was it slightly rancid? Had she forgotten to buy fresh? Her stomach lurched, she ran for the loo and knelt by the toilet retching. She'd not eaten for days and all that she could bring up was bile. Her throat ached and her mouth burned. She hauled herself to her feet and, glass of water in hand, went back to bed.

Huddling under the duvet she took a sip of the lukewarm water then put it down. She did not want to risk being sick again. Timbo, purring with satisfaction, jumped up beside her and nuzzled her cheek. Nauseated by the smell of cat food on his whiskers she pushed him to the end of the bed. Liz stretched out and tried to relax limb by limb, tensing and loosening each muscle group, but her body refused to obey. Her calves went into spasm and she leapt up, caught in the grip of cramp.

Going into the shower she caught a glimpse of herself in the bathroom mirror, her eyes huge, underlined by the purple shadows that cast a ghastly pallor over her skin. Her face had sunk, her cheekbones stood out, her lips pressed together as if to keep back the pain. She looked old.

Her hands shook so badly she could not fasten her bra. Her back ached as she stepped into her underwear and she could not bend over to pull on her tights. Because she had lost more weight in the past week the suit Elsa had chosen for her was too loose. The skirt slipped down onto her hips and had to be fastened with a safety pin. The blue blouse she had bought for the occasion had a strangely chemical smell.

The front gate creaked. The doorbell rang. Liz stood frozen with fear until, through the half open bedroom door, she caught a glimpse of a framed photograph of Poppy as a plump five year old sitting on her bike, grinning. Moments before the picture had been taken she had pedalled down the garden path, bumped over a stone and tumbled over the handlebars. She had got up, kicked the bike and wrenching the handlebars in the right direction, ridden straight at the camera. The bell rang again.

"Here we go," Liz said and walked down the stairs.

There had been a hard frost, the air was keen and the pavement sparkled with ice. Ed took her arm and led her to the waiting Mercedes.

"You look very good," Elsa whispered. Or did she? Liz was not sure. Sound was muffled, the interior of the car was warm, but she was shivering and there was sweat trickling down her face and between her breasts. Her hands were damp. "You're going to be all right," Elsa said and Liz stretched her lips over her teeth in an attempt at a smile.

Bernie and Jane Langdon were waiting in the foyer of the Magistrate's Court. Bernie hugged her and murmured reassurance. Liz nodded. She could hear nothing but the beat of blood in her ears. Jane smiled and nodded and introduced her to a tall man with a balding head and long neck who looked a little like a vulture. It was the famed Geoffrey Richardson, the barrister whose skill was going to save her. Liz's head went up and down like a stuffed dog in the back window of a car.

"Pleased to meet you," she said inanely. He spoke to her. She could see his lips moving but the words meant nothing.

"Are you all right?" Jane asked. Again the insane movement of the head, then the usher was there to take them into the court.

The ground beneath Liz's feet was unstable. It wavered and flowed like the sea and it was hard to know where to step. The unfamiliar shoes were clumpy, her legs not willing to obey her. Her head seemed to have become detached from the rest of her body or it would if she did not hold it very steady. It was vital not to look from side to side and she must not, under any circumstances, look at Bernie or Elsa or she would do the one thing she had been told she must not. She would raise her voice and cry out to the heavens that no one should be put through this, that it was unfair, unjust; that she was not the criminal. The girls who had lied and lied about her out of malice, or boredom, or cunning, they were the guilty ones. Then she would sob and wail until all her tears were spent.

"Answer the questions. That's all you have to do," Jane said.

"Holy Mary Mother of God," Bernie mouthed the words, her finger moving over non-existent Rosary beads.

"There's a girl," Ed smiled encouragingly. Jilly and two other colleagues from school smiled.

“I’ve written it all in my statement. Everything they need to know and more about the poisonous Boyd,” Jilly said.

“We’re with you.” Emma gave her the thumbs up. Grey haired Rose looked worried.

“It will be…”

“All right,” Liz finished automatically.

FORTY-SEVEN

LIZ STOOD IN the dock. She swore to tell the truth. She answered her barrister's questions. They didn't seem to be too hard and she thought she was giving the right answers. She did not dare look at the public seating. The only way to survive this ordeal was to imagine it wasn't happening to her. That she was an actress playing a role in some dark drama.

The district judge was a man. He had a thin face, dark hair and wore glasses, which he raised to look at the papers in front of him. When he had finished reading he nodded to the court usher who adjusted the screen for the video evidence.

Liz stared at the almost unrecognisable girl in front of her. Samantha Boyd had washed her hair. It shone and hung prettily around her face. Her school uniform was clean and newly pressed, her tie the right length. She sat with her hands in her lap, facing an unseen camera.

"We was..." She hesitated. "...We were doing our English coursework. It was *Romeo and Juliet*. I didn't understand it. I told Miss I didn't, but she didn't take no notice of me." Her voice rose to its usual whine. "I couldn't do me homework."

"And," the prosecuting lawyer prompted.

"She said I'd got to or she'd give me a break detention. I said it wasn't my fault and that I'd asked her and asked her and she wouldn't give me no help." She stopped. "She got cross she came over and she head -butted me. All the class saw it."

"Then what happened?"

"Then it was break and I ran out."

Liz felt as if she was watching a film, a piece of fiction. She could see 10C sitting in their seats. They were talking, chewing, some were scribbling in their books, a few were listening to music. No one was working. She was leaning over Samantha, trying to show her how to start her essay. Her head was getting closer and closer to the fat girl's face. It was impossible to stop. Liz couldn't help herself. Jerking back her neck she rammed straight into the wide white forehead. The sharp rap of bone on bone reverberated through her brain, the pain echoed through her skull as their heads made contact. It was all so plausible. Only it didn't happen. Nothing happened.

The next witness was Amy Andrews. Her sharp little face was eager for the kill. She held her chin high and her eyes glittered.

"We was doing English. Miss made Sam stay behind cos she said she hadn't done her homework. She give her a detention. Sam said she wasn't going to stay cos it wasn't her fault. She's got problems at home." Amy smiled confidentially at the camera. "I stayed with her. Miss picked up her book and she shouted at her that it was crap, I mean rubbish, and she went right up to her and then, well, she just lost it and head-butted her. Sam was crying and screaming and I took her to the office."

Liz put her hand up to her face. Her fingers felt strange on her skin, the bones on her head hard and unfamiliar, as she searched for the bruise that had never been there. Then she remembered that she must not react. Her hand dropped to her side and she stared at the final witness.

Leanne's face was a mask. Make-up covered any flaws, her eyeliner was perfectly applied, her lips luscious with gloss. Her hair recently highlighted, she cocked her head to one side as she spoke.

"Sam was upset. She was crying."

"Why was that?"

"She couldn't do her work. None of us could. It's too hard." Leanne shrugged. "But she don't care."

"Samantha was crying and what did Mrs Mckendrick do then?"

"She went mad. She shouted and screamed. She picked up Sam's book and threw it at her. Then she went over and head-butted her."

"Where were you when this happened?"

"I was sitting next to her. Like I always do, me and Amy and Sam. We always sit together. When she lets us." There was an undercurrent of venom in her voice. The screen went blank and it was Liz's turn.

"Mrs Mckendrick, would it be true to say that 10C is a class you find difficult?"

"Yes."

"And that Samantha is a pupil you find particularly hard to deal with?" Liz clamped down the words that rose to her lips.

She's a cow, a lying manipulative cow. Just look at her, she never dresses like that, she's always late, she never does a stroke of work and when I try to explain something to her, she sits there chewing her pen, or starts chatting to Leanne.

"You have a reputation as a competent teacher. Coming across a pupil with whom you have no rapport is something you are unfamiliar with. This would make you feel frustrated and out of that frustration would come anger," the lawyer continued.

There was no answer to this for how could she say no? How could she deny that she would like to smash her fist into Samantha Boyd's fat face?

"Mrs Mckendrick?"

Liz nodded. She sensed rather than heard the indrawn breath from the body of the court.

"I'm sorry," she wanted to say, "in spite of all your hard work, all your belief in me, I've blown it."

Geoffrey Richardson rose to his feet. "Sir." He nodded briefly in the direction of the bench. "There appears to be some misconceptions about the nature of a teacher's frustration here. Mrs Mckendrick, you have been teaching for how many years?"

"Thirty."

"Can you tell the court why you went into the teaching profession?"

"I wanted to make a difference," Liz said softly.

"Could you explain that to us?"

"I wanted to help children, students, my pupils to achieve what I knew they could."

"You have what I can class as an unshakeable belief in the students you are teaching."

"Yes. So often they have been labelled slow or inadequate or with learning disabilities. I know that kids do have problems but like all of us, given help to build our self-confidence, I believe they can fly."

"Your results over your thirty years have shown the success of your system. Would you say that at your present school it was harder or easier?"

"Harder. The kids start out with little belief in themselves. Most of them are convinced, by the time they get to us, that they can't learn."

"Which you would find frustrating?"

"Yes. Because it prevents them achieving what they could in life."

"Therefore it could be said that it is the attitude of your pupils towards leaning and not the behaviour of any one individual that is the cause of your frustration."

There was a rustle of movement. Liz raised her head and met Bernie's eyes. Bernie smiled encouragingly. Had she proved she was a dedicated and concerned teacher? The tight band of control relaxed a fraction. Then came the moment she had been dreading, Geoffrey

Richardson was going to question Sam on the video link.

"Samantha." His voice was soft and gentle. "You told us that Mrs Mckendrick came over to you when you were sitting in your place and head-butted you? Is that right?"

"Yeah." Sam smiled and nodded. "Because she wouldn't help me. I told you."

"Of course you did. Now who else was in the room at the time?"

"I dunno. The class I suppose."

"This was before break?"

"Yeah I told you. I didn't do no detention I ran out."

"Thank you." Sam was dismissed. Geoffrey Richardson asked Amy the same question.

"You told us, Amy, that Mrs Mckendrick kept Sam in at break-time, did you not?"

"Yeah."

"And who was with you?"

"Me and Sam."

"And where were the rest of the class?"

"They'd gone to break of course." Her voice was full of contempt.

"Thank you."

Then it was Leanne's turn.

"Leanne, could you clear up a couple of points for me?"

She smiled a practised smile and licked her tongue over her lips in a gesture intended to be provocative. "Sure."

Liz's barrister repeated his question about who had been present when the alleged incident took place. Even before he had finished the judge was tapping his fingers impatiently.

"Thank you Mr Richardson."

He's not going to listen, Liz despaired. *It's all over, bar the sentencing.* She clasped her hands together and gripped them hard to stop herself from screaming.

The judge continued, “It is quite obvious from what we have heard this morning that there can only be one verdict.” Liz willed herself to keep breathing. “Mrs Mckendrick has no case to answer. Case dismissed.” He leaned over towards Liz. “I want it on record that this exemplary teacher walks out of this court without a stain on her reputation. She has been grossly maligned and all I can say, my dear, is how very sorry I am that you have been put through this ordeal.” Liz looked at him almost unable to believe what she had heard. “You can go.”

She had to tell her legs to move before she could step down into an explosion of shouts and screams and thanks. Bernie and Elsa hugged her. Jane Langdon beamed.

Geoffrey Richardson held out his hand. “The right result,” he said briefly. “Terrible waste of the court’s time,” he said to Jane, who looked meaningfully at the prosecuting lawyer.

Liz’s head was spinning, her chest and throat tight.

“It’s okay. It’s all over.” Ed took her arm. Her face was too rigid to smile, her throat had closed up and she could not speak. He steered her into the car. They drove and suddenly they were in a pub and someone had put a large gin and tonic in front of her.

“Congratulations, Liz.” Jane raised her glass.

“Bloody kids couldn’t even get their stories right!” Jilly cried jubilantly. “Condemned out of their own mouths. Stupid cows. That Samantha Boyd wouldn’t know what day of the week it is if Amy or Leanne didn’t tell her.”

The gin slid down cool and smooth. It warmed her and gradually Liz’s senses returned to normal and she could follow the conversation; the pulsing in her ears subsided to a distant throb. Another gin and she wouldn’t hear it at all.

“When do you think you’ll be coming back to work?”

Jilly asked.

"If I were you, I would take some time off. Go sick for real," Jane said before Liz could reply.

"Maybe. I don't know. To be honest I don't ever want to go back. I can't work with Norman again, not after what he's done to me."

"Fucking Head. It's his fault. He could have stopped them," Jilly said. "Someone should do something about him."

"He wanted to get rid of you," Emma said.

"It's true. He never liked you. You are too good for the place. You scared him and this was his opportunity," Rose added.

Liz knew they were right. That she had been shamefully treated by the man who should have protected her by searching for the truth. Swept by an overriding wave of anger she said, "He's not getting away with this."

"Way to go. Anything you want to do we'll support you." Ed beamed.

"He should be sacked, defrocked, hung from the Suspension Bridge by his you-know-whats," Elsa cried.

"Balls, Elsa." Liz was laughing.

"Another drink?" Ed asked. Her stomach growled.

"I'm starving."

"It's about time you ate something. I fancy some chips; anyone else?" Bernie bustled about taking orders. Ed brought more drinks.

"Not for me thanks. It's been lovely." Jane got up and kissed Liz on the cheek. "I've got to get back and get dinner started. A working woman's life, eh." All the women murmured agreement; some looked at their watches and began to gather coats and handbags.

LIZ SAT IN front of a huge basket of chips, gold and crinkly and delicious. She dipped in, took one then stopped with a chip half way to her mouth.

"I've got it. Bernie, Elsa, listen to this. I know what we've got to do. Wives for working women. That's us. Forget Bristol Housekeepers, forget men and all the problems they cause." She glanced at Ed. "With one or two notable exceptions. What we're going to set up is a woman-only service. We'll provide the working woman with everything she needs. Cleaning, cooking, shopping and when she comes home fed-up and exhausted, we'll be there to hand her a G and T and listen."

"Listen to her problems and not tell her what she has to do to put them right." Bernie's eyes sparkled. "It's what every woman wants."

"Sounds a great idea to me," Ed said. "If you want to discuss business plans or finance I'd only be too happy to help. But that's for tomorrow. Today we're celebrating and I'm getting in the champagne."

"Mum!" Poppy was threading her way through the crowd. She flung her arms around Liz and hugged her hard.

"How did you know I was here?" Liz gasped back tears

"His mobile." Poppy jerked her head back at James. "He texted Elsa when we got to Bristol. Mum, I've got so much to tell you."

EPILOGUE

"MUM, ELSA, BERNIE!" Heads turned in the Palm Court as Poppy Mckendrick waltzed in. There was a discreet babble of noise as she wove her way through the tables.

"I know her from somewhere."

"She's the one on the television. You know that sit-com."

"It said in the paper, she's really going places."

"I heard her on *Woman's Hour*, with her mum. They were talking about some agency for women only. When you're out at work they do all the things a wife used to."

"Sounds like a bloody good idea to me."

"You've certainly got them talking." Poppy hugged her mother.

"It could be my celebrity daughter."

"It could but I can't take all the credit. You've made the national press again this week." Poppy pointed to the newspaper Elsa had laid ostentatiously on the table in front of her.

"It wasn't a bad article. I didn't look too good in my photo though." Elsa shrugged.

"Elsa, you looked wonderful as usual. Having the shoot in your flat was a brilliant idea. A great advert for the interior design business," Poppy said.

"It's been a good year for all of us," Bernie said softly. "Yes I mean that. The new baby is gorgeous and all in one piece in spite of his mother's smoking and drinking. The business is doing really well."

"You've finally broken free of the Hell pit." Poppy

smiled across at her mother.

"You've got that series on TV."

"It's only a little part."

"It's the start, you know it is."

"All thanks to James and his film. He's doing well too."

Liz looked at them proudly. "Think where we've come from in eighteen months."

"Bankrupt, abandoned, about to go court," Bernie said.

"And look where we are now."

"Back in the Palm Court but this time we can afford the champagne. And we did it ourselves," Liz said. Elsa looked pained. "Okay, Ed helped with the loan but mostly it was us. The three old hags."

"Never say that." Elsa was outraged. "We're in the middle years. We're successful business women in our middle years. It says so in *The Telegraph.*"

"Which is never wrong," Liz said dryly.

"Stop arguing." Poppy raised her glass. "You're magic, all three of you."

AFTERWORD

THE CHECKOUT QUEUE in a supermarket: a single man muttering furiously under his breath as he packs his week's shopping into carrier bags.

"What I need is a wife," he growls.

"Me too," the woman behind him agrees, and so the seed of *Picking Up the Pieces* began to germinate.

Misha M. Herwin, 2016

ALSO FROM THE PENKHULL PRESS

House of Shadows – Misha M. Herwin

Picking Up the Pieces – Misha M. Herwin

It Never Was Worthwhile – Jem Shaw and Malcolm Havard

Larks – Jem Shaw

Sussex Tales – Jan Edwards

Tangerine Monday Blues – Jan Edwards *

Winter Downs – Jan Edwards *

Penkhull Slims:

Fables and Fabrications – Jan Edwards

It's the End of the World – Nic Hale *

* coming soon

Made in the USA
Charleston, SC
13 July 2016